Don't Tell Me You Love Me

Holly Kerr

Three Birds Press

www.threebirdspress.ca

www.hollykerr.ca

Don't Tell Me You Love Me

Chapter One

Shae

EVERYONE WHO READS LITTLE Women knows Beth is going to die. It's the worst-kept secret in literature. The fact that I'm going to die isn't as well known.

Lightning flashes in the sky above Patong Bay as though the weather is part of the light show and the audience goes wild. A teenage girl beside me screams shrilly, clutching her friends. As Denzel Duke—he of the dark curls and soulful voice, not to mention abs to die for, as seen in the latest Calvin Klein ad—starts in the chorus of *My Day*, I open Instagram and start to record, trying to keep my arm steady as I focus the camera on my face.

"It's the last night of Denzel Duke's tour," I say, not having to fake my excitement. "And it's a little wild here!"

Hearts and smiley emojis flutter up the screen, along with comments:

"So jealous!"

"Love him! Love that song!"

"Love you Shae!"

I like a few of the comments before flipping the camera to pan the crowd.

I zoom in on a girl by the stage as she bursts into a flood of tears when Denzel smiles at her.

They love him. Part Shawn Mendes, part Justin Bieber. I give Denzel six months before he's in the fight for pop god supremacy.

Lovin' you will never be the same

Lovin' you will always make my day

The audience sways to the music, like waves lapping at the shore. The stage is set up at the edge of one of the smaller beaches in Patong, right where the white sand meets the scraggly grass, long trampled by a thousand pairs of flip-flops.

Beside me, Natasha is wrapped around Dawson, her curvy figure poured into black shorts swaying to the music. I don't have to look to tell Neely is scowling at the sight of them.

Onstage, Denzel sings with a lovesick expression on his sweet face that has every female, and possibly quite a few of the men, convinced he's singing just to them.

I flip the camera to myself again. "Almost time for my song, so I'm going to pass you over to Dawson now," I say, shoving a hunk of pink hair behind my ears with a big grin. Neely might like the love songs best, but I'll take a stadium-shaking anthem-like *Daredevil* any day.

My followers love Dawson. They love Neely too, but he gets the most comments, maybe because he's the only guy.

I pass the phone to Dawson, who tries to detangle himself from Natasha. We're streaming a good part of the concert because it's the last night of the tour, taking turns with the phone.

Freed of the phone, I shake out my arms, readying myself for the opening chords of my favourite song. Instead, Denzel reaches for his guitar.

"Ah'd like to share a little diddy I've been workin' on while I've been over here in your neck of the woods," he says, the Alabama accent kissing his words. The crowd roars and Denzel smiles bashfully as he drops his head.

A bolt of excitement races through me at the same time as another flash lights up the sky. I check on Dawson to make sure he's recording because this is going to go viral and we're going to be the ones who post it.

A sudden guitar riff from one of the roadies has the crowd rushing to the stage, almost knocking me off my feet. When I look up, Dawson is gone. I jump up and down as Denzel strums a few chords, trying to see over the heads of the group of girls that have moved in front of me. We can't lose this footage.

A hand on my shoulder stops me. It's one of the roadies we've gotten friendly with, the one I nicknamed The Rock.

"Need a hand?" He towers over me like some tree hidden in an old-time forest. My face must show my confusion because he touches his shoulder. "C'mon, get up here so you can see."

He kneels and I clamour onto his linebacker shoulders, which gives me an excellent view of the stage. This is more like it because I can see Dawson right up at the front.

"You okay up there, Shae?" Neely calls up to me with a concerned smile.

I grin widely in response. "Perfect." Then I turn my attention to Denzel, who starts to sing.

Pink hair, dark eyes
I watch you watching me
Big smile, wide eyes
I love you loving me

Is he...? Is this...? My jaw drops as excitement turns into a tingling feeling of wonderment.

Pink hair, dark eyes
I like you following me
Big smile, wide eyes
I want you in my life

Neely turns with an expression of disbelief. "Is this song about you?" she shouts over the noise.

Denzel Duke wrote a *song* about me? About *me*?

"He wrote a song about you!" Neely cries, for once excitement breaking past her usual cool composure. A few feet away, Dawson comes to the same conclusion and turns the phone to me sitting on the guy's shoulders and being serenaded by one of pop music's fastest rising stars.

If there was any doubt in anyone's mind who Denzel is singing to, the fact that he catches my eyes with a big smile, and actually stops playing to hold out his hand confirms it.

"Oh my God!" Neely is now jumping up and down.

Still with me perched on his shoulders, the security guard pushes his way through the crowd to the edge of the stage. The crowd parts with a collective mutinous expression when the females realize I am Pink Hair of the song. I can't stop my grin even if I wanted to, my heart bouncing faster than the music.

Denzel Duke puts down his guitar as I awkwardly transfer from shoulders to stage.

I'm onstage with Denzel Duke!

He meets me in the middle of the stage and takes my hand, giving me a twirl before leading me into a slow dance in front of a thousand screaming fans, all singing to me.

Sometimes I really love my life.

And then it's all over.

One minute, the four of us arrived in Singapore, racing through the Crazy Rich Asians tour, filming the markets, the beaches, and the culture of Malaysia and Indonesia. And then it was on to Denzel's tour in Thailand and now I'm being handed onto the stage and dancing with Denzel himself and my head is spinning at the awesomeness of my life.

I was fourteen when the doctors diagnosed me with a bunch of big words that basically mean my life has an expiry date. It wasn't too long after that, that Dawson, Neely and I started a bucket list.

And then we grew up and that bucket list morphed into a travel vlog, which grew into a social media sensation.

Most people don't get to check things off their bucket lists, but I've got a job that pays me to do it all. And better yet, it lets me bring as many people along for the ride as care to follow me. Somewhere out there, among all those likes and heart emojis, there's a girl just like me. Someone who's been told she only has a few years to live and is desperate to cram as much into the life she's got left as she can.

I'm doing it for her.

I'm doing it for me.

Lucky me.

Emmett

"**A**RE YOU READY FOR this?"

Pulling at the sleeves of my tuxedo, I meet Ellie's reflection in the mirror with a rueful smile. "Shouldn't I be asking you? You're the one getting married."

We're in Ellie's bedroom. In two days, it will stop being my little sister's and become simply an empty room in the house on the family farm. A breeze blows through the open window, warm for May. The room is so neat and tidy that it's unnatural because Ellie has always been a slob. At least the sight of the unmade bed, sheets tangled in the middle, reassure me that my sister's not gone yet. A few of her stuffed animals are on the dresser; the only personal things left, other than a few pictures.

Ellie has been packing non-stop for the last week, and each time I carry another box to the car, my heart is pulled in two directions. I want her to be happy—I know she'll be happy with James—but I'll miss her.

"It's a big day for you." Ellie brushes the shoulders of the suit, circling me for a last look.

"Yeah, but again—*you're* the one getting married in two days."

Ellie gives the jacket hem a final tug before turning away. "At least you look good. Nice hair cut, too. It's about time because the man-bun was not working."

I rub the back of my head. The last time I cut my hair was the day Alex died. It's been three years, the number fifty-six etched in the back of my head long since grown in.

Telling Ellie the real reason I hesitated in getting my hair cut would only make her worry, and she's had enough of me to deal with. She's also got a lot on her plate with planning a wedding. Dad is great, but he's not a mother, and I know Ellie must be hurting thinking about that.

Not that she'd admit it. Us Pike children aren't ones for talking about our feelings.

I ignored Ellie's orders to have a haircut and shave my beard in time for the wedding as long as I could. "It was time," I admit with a half-smile.

Ellie grins and ruffles my hair. "Yeah. I got tired of you stealing my elastics. But I think I'm just as excited about you joining the world again."

"I've been in public. I see people."

Ellie raises an eyebrow at my defensive tone. "You see people on the farm. Once in a while Dad has you do the deliveries. You go into town maybe once a week, and usually only for Rufus's baseball games. You've practically become a hermit."

"I like my own company. There's nothing wrong with that."

"You shouldn't like it that much," Ellie says in a soft voice. "It's been three years, Emmett. People forget."

But I don't.

Suddenly the jacket feels tight, too snug around the biceps and across my back. I roll my shoulder, suddenly imagining if I were to throw a ball.

It's difficult to swallow. "Am I done here?" Without waiting for Ellie's answer, I slip out of the jacket.

Even though everyone says there's no way I could have caused the brain tumor, I blame myself for Alex being here at the farm when it happened, rather than across the country with her family like she should've been.

After...after she was gone, I'd rejoined the team back in Missouri, the guys I'd played with for years didn't know what to do with me. I didn't know what to do with me either.

Trying to drown every emotion seemed like a good idea until drinking after the game became drinking before the game, which led to one false step into the path of a ninety-seven-mile fastball.

Thus ending my baseball career.

"I think the hair is a metaphor for your life," Ellie says, putting the jacket on the hanger. "It's a new look for you, symbolizing a new start in life."

"I think that's a little too deep. The hair was hot, and the beard was itchy." I rub my smooth cheeks and grin at my reflection. "It was time for it to go."

Ellie comes behind me and tucks her arm around my waist. We might have the same dirty blond hair and blue-gray eyes, with Dad's straight nose, but there is no way that I'm as cute as my little sister. Or ever learned to pout quite so well.

"You look so much better when it's short," Ellie says. "And without the beard. I know it's a thing right now, but I miss seeing your face." She taps my cheek with the back of her hand for emphasis.

"It's nice to have one brother standing up at the front of the church with me and I want people to recognize you."

"You sure about that? I'm prettier than you now."

She smacks my arm, "You are not."

"Am too."

It's not like I'm being particularly funny, but for a long time, I couldn't bring myself to tease or joke, or even smile. I was like the tangle of blackberry canes I pruned today; overgrown and wooden and covered with annoying prickles. They still give berries, but they're dry with none of the juicy sweetness.

For three years, I've been dry and prickly and definitely not sweet. But slowly, I felt like I've come back to life. The weight of grief I've been carrying has grown lighter, like a contestant on one of those dieting shows. The world is interesting again, and it's time to use my mouth for something other than monosyllabic responses.

I still remember the day I laughed at something Rufus had said. It wasn't my normal laugh, more like a creaking bark like a rheumatic dog, but it brought tears to my sister's eyes.

The playfulness between us now, which might have ended with me sporting a bruise since Ellie's got a good punch on her, ends when Rufus wanders into the room, attention still fixed on the phone in his hand.

My nephew looks exactly like my brother did at that age. Ethan had shot up and slimmed down at eleven, gangly arms and legs replacing the last vestiges of baby fat. Rufus even has the same mess of blond hair that will soon turn darker in a few years.

"And here is the prettiest of us all," Ellie says. "Jump into the tux so I can see how it looks on you."

"I've already tried it on last week, Aunt Ellie," Rufus protests, not looking up from the screen. "Don't make me do it again."

"And you're growing like a weed, so I want to make sure everything is perfect for the wedding."

"I had to try mine on too, so do you," I say reaching for the phone in his hand. I swear, sometimes I think the phone is permanently attached to him. When I think of my youth, it was the fields of our farm, riding bikes through town with my best friend Grayson Grant, and baseball.

These days, I'm able to think about baseball without the gut-wrenching stab of pain.

The same way that thinking about Alex hurts less and less every day. Does that mean I'm forgetting her? Am I supposed to?

"What are you looking at anyway?" Ellie asks, holding out Rufus's pint-sized tuxedo jacket. She's so good at checking in with him, without making it look like she's checking in. She's nailed the cool Aunt Ellie role and I know she'll make a terrific mother someday.

I don't remember the last time anyone would call us a regular family. Before Rufus was born? Before my mother left? Before Alex—my girlfriend, who became my wife only to die two days later in my arms?

Rufus snatches back his phone to show to Ellie. "Last night's Denzel Duke concert," he says with surprising enthusiasm for an eleven-year-old. "He wrote a song about this girl and pulled her out of the audience."

"Really?" Ellie peers at the screen. "That's romantic."

"Who's he when he's home?"

Rufus glances up from the screen with disgust. "Seriously, Uncle Emmett?"

"Denzel Duke?" Ellie has a matching expression. "He's only the next Shawn Mendes."

"And he is..."

She shakes her head. "Someone you would know if you listened to music from this century."

"There's some good stuff from the 70s and 80s," I protest. "And the 90s was classic."

Ellie sniffs as she takes Rufus's phone out of his hand and tosses it on the bed. "There's nothing classic about that decade. C'mon, let's get this tried on." She helps him on with his jacket before turning away so he can change into the pants.

"What does it matter what we look like?" Rufus says when he's dressed, giving me an elbow so he can have more room in front of the mirror. "You're the bride. You're the one everybody will be looking at."

"Are you kidding? With you standing at the front of the church wearing this, *no one* will be looking at me." She playfully ruffles his hair.

"There'll be girls at the wedding," I tell him. "Do you like girls yet?"

"Do I like girls?" Rufus scoffs. Then he gives me a nervous sideways glance. "Yeah."

"Bridesmaids," I add. "You've got some single girls coming that need a partner to dance with, don't you, El? Rufus can show off his fancy footwork."

"Sorry, you'll have to look elsewhere." Ellie laughs. "Emmett, you're paired up with James's sister, but I don't know her that well because she travels a lot. And Rufus, you'll have the flower girls. My friend Amber is single and I don't think she's bringing a date. But she's pretty pregnant so I'm not sure exactly how much dancing she'll be doing."

"Pregnant?" Rufus exclaims like Ellie said the bridesmaid was sporting a second head. "What's she pregnant for?"

Ellie glances at me. "I'm not doing the birds and the bees speech now."

"I know *how* she got pregnant." Rufus rolls his eyes. "Probably."

"You *probably* know how she got pregnant?" I echo with a nervous look at my sister. "But you're not sure."

"Well, there's different positions and stuff..."

"Oh, wow," I say. "It's a good thing you'll be with your father this weekend. You tell him how to use these doctor skills and explain things to you. I'll be too busy with the single ladies at the wedding."

The fact that I'm open, if not looking forward to meeting someone new, brings a happy smile to Ellie's face. She leans her head on my shoulder. "I never thought I'd be so happy to know that my big brother is going to try and pick up one of my bridesmaids," she sighs. "But I really am. It's time for you to get off the bench and get back into the game, Em."

"Thank you so much for the baseball analogy," I say with a rueful smile. "I'll do my best to make you proud, coach."

"And I'm going to help!" Rufus says, his eyes dancing with excitement. "At least, you can help me. Because this is it—this is the night I become a man."

"No, it's not," Ellie and I say in unison.

Chapter Two

Shae

THANKS TO THE HEAVY snoring in seat 14B, I got almost no sleep during the twenty-one-hour flight and follow Dawson zombie-like through Pearson International Airport. It's been a long twenty-nine hours since I was serenaded by Denzel Duke. My suitcase bounces behind me as one of the wheels catches on a bump, and I tug it free. I'm too tired to even think about taking a picture of the Welcome to Toronto sign.

Twelve hours of adrenaline is hard to come down from and a long flight doesn't help.

After the concert, after staying up all night talking to Denzel Duke, it was straight onto our next adventure—zip-lining through the jungle. We keep a list of places we've been to on the vlog, like Costa Rica, Australia, and British Columbia, but Thailand has to be my favourite. Flying through the cool morning air as the sun crept over the horizon, the calls and cries of the animals in the jungle below were almost magical.

I say almost because flying through the air was a little different this time.

Dawson looks sideways as we pass a group of girls giggling over their phones. "I can't believe the internet saw me naked," Dawson grumbles for the tenth time as we weave our way through the crowd.

Seeing Dawson naked is most likely the reason the idea got such a good response. He's got quite the group of lovesick followers. The geeky look—tall and lanky, with black-rimmed glasses and dark hair that is constantly messy—really works for him.

"I checked and you can't see anything," I say, also for the tenth time.

The ad for the adventure company said something about finding enlightenment soaring through the Thai jungle at dawn, but I'm not sure how being naked through the whole thing enlightened me. While I'm not opposed to being naked, being strapped into a harness without clothes was a bit icky.

But I do my best to keep my followers happy, even if it means flying through the air sans clothes.

"It'll pull in some good numbers," Neely, ever the business manager, reminds us. "They said the place was already booked solid for next week, and that was only from you announcing it. You got it posted?" she asks Dawson, our unofficial IT guy.

"As soon as we landed."

"What are the numbers for the concert last night?" I ask as we head for the exit. "Or the night before that? What day is it anyway?" Friday, I decide. It's Friday afternoon.

"Huge." Neely sighs. "Like I knew they would be. I've already got an email about the possibility of joining another tour, but I said we're home for a few weeks first."

"You've got to get through the wedding this weekend." A yawn splits my face and I stumble, too sluggish to comprehend how I feel about being home. "We got back just in time for you to play bridesmaid. And then you can take a break."

"There's still so much to do," she frets. During the trip, Neely has been doing her best to stay in the loop with her family so she can put in her two cents on her brother's upcoming wedding, but I know it hasn't been easy for her to take such a back seat.

Neely needs to be in the middle of things.

"And you don't have to worry about it," I say. "I'm sure James and *whatshername* are perfectly capable of planning their wedding, especially if Mama S. is helping. You can go and have fun with me as your plus one."

"Her name is Ellie, and I'm embarrassed to admit I've only met her twice because we've been away so much," Neely frets. "I should know the woman my brother is marrying."

"You'll have lots of time to get to know her. Wedding first; make friends with your new sister-in-law after that," I tell her.

"You won't make it unless you get some sleep first. You forgot to take your vitamins again, too," Neely reminds me. "Make sure you take them when you get home."

"I think a Reuben latte will help more than my vitamins." I close my eyes, thinking about the foam on my favourite vanilla latte. I'm not a big coffee drinker but there's something about the lattes that Reuben makes at Pain au Chocolate that makes them addicting. "Do you think Adam brought us one?"

"Probably not, but he spoils you so much that I'm sure he'll stop for you if you ask nicely."

"He doesn't spoil me, he loves me," I correct, catching her arm and hugging it. "Just like you do."

"The *world* loves you, Shae," Natasha throws over her shoulder in a spiteful voice.

I don't even have to look to know Neely is ready to retaliate. "It's not worth it," I tell her before I catch the toe of my flip flops on the corner of Dawson's suitcase.

Natasha is like your favourite frenemy from high school. She's fine when you're stuck together one-on-one, like in detention—or in our case, living out of suitcases for ten weeks, in some of the sketchiest hostels I've ever set foot in—but when you get back to real life, the claws start to come out.

Dawson has brought girls along in the past, but this is the longest we've travelled with an outsider—Neely's word, not mine. Natasha is nice enough but it's clear to all except Dawson that she's along for her fifteen minutes of fame. I have a feeling Natasha won't last long now that we're back without an online audience to preen for.

Dawson is so preoccupied with tech stuff and the math equations that explode in his head on regular intervals that he only notices the way Natasha looks in her shorts. Geeks may rule the world but they're still easy targets for women like Natasha.

The automatic doors open for us. No matter how much I love the travel, it feels good to be home. When we're flying, I always make sure I look out the window to catch the first glimpse of the sprawling city and the highways leading to it. From a distance, the four-leaf clover of roads makes me forget the frustration of traffic, and the cars racing along look like tiny ants rather than angry commuters.

When we left, it was March and snow was still on the ground and falling. The day we left, our flight was delayed three hours because of a storm. Arriving in the warmth of Bangkok, it took exactly fifteen minutes for me to start stripping off my layers in the street on the way to the hotel.

A horn blasts into my reverie, wiping the smile off my face as I see the finger gestures of the drivers who just missed a fender bender.

Since we've been gone, the seasons have changed from winter into May, bringing blue skies and a blast of summer-like warm air, but obviously not a better mood to my fellow Canadians.

"Oh my God—it's *Shae!*" As soon as I step onto the sidewalk, a pair of twentysomethings rush over to me like punctuation for Natasha's snide comment. Neely drifts into the background as phones are pulled out, selfies taken, and voices are raised in excitement. I give them a few minutes before backing away apologetically.

"What did I tell you?" Natasha sneers after we move away. "Must be nice to be dying."

"Yeah, lucky me," I snap.

Fear and hopelessness roll over me like a weighted blanket, along with the ever-present rage. It's easy to be angry at the world because I'm dying; I know because I've done it.

I'm dying.

And I'm mad about it. Very, very angry. And right now, I'm all for giving Natasha a few choice words that will make her regret ever getting on a plane with me. Neely watches me expectantly, ready to back me up like always.

But instead of sinking into the rage like quicksand, I take a deep breath. Always look at the positives. There's always a silver lining. It's better to catch flies with honey than vinegar. I've got all the mantras memorized, and they usually work.

Anger is not my friend.

I don't know what Dawson's told Natasha about my condition. Probably the basics—that I was diagnosed with Batten disease, a rare form of neuronal ceroid lipofuscinosis. To me, all it means is that I will develop fatty tissue around the cells of my brain, nervous system, and—to make it worse—my eyes. I have seizures to look forward to, blindness, and decreased motor skills.

The doctors gave me seven to ten years, but I made it to lucky thirteen. I do feel lucky to have lasted this long. Incredibly lucky. But it doesn't change the fact that I am going to die. Someday. Possibly soon.

Thanks to the deep, calming breaths suggested by my many therapists, the frustration passes over me like a brisk breeze rather than a hurricane. With all the anger and fear about my diagnosis, the worst is knowing that the world will go on without me.

FOMO is a real thing, and it's not fun.

But now's not the time for that. I tamp all those emotions down like I'm smothering a fire. "She's not worth it," I murmur.

Neely reaches for my hand and squeezes it. "She'll never learn."

I never understand why Natasha isn't focused on making the best life for herself, especially since she has seventy or even eighty years ahead of her? I don't know if I have six years or even six weeks and I'm still having fun.

At least I'm trying.

I hear Adam's whoop before I see him. The crowds on the sidewalk part for Neely's youngest brother as he rushes towards us.

Like a cat being raised by a family of raccoons, I grew up thinking Neely's three brothers were mine as much as hers. When it's my turn for a hug hello, Adam picks me up and swings me around. "Where is he?" he demands when he sets me down.

"Who?"

"The rock star of course. *Denzel Duke!* I figured he'd be trotting after you like a cute little puppy."

"No one is trotting after me." I grimace at the thought as Adam grabs the handle of Neely's suitcase and wheels it to the car. "Nothing happened."

"He pulled you *onstage*! How amazing was that? And then the pictures of you and him in the noodle shop. I thought for sure it was true love. He's *such* a cutie."

I duck my chin to hide a smile, thinking of the look of amazement on Denzel's face when we snuck out of the after-concert party, commandeered the *tuk-tuk* and I told the driver to take us to Old Phuket. "It was only noodles," I say.

"That took all night?" Neely asks. "Are you forgetting to mention that you spent the rest of the night with him?"

"It wasn't like that, and you know it." We'd escaped from a group of over-zealous fans and spent the night in his hotel room talking. Literally. Denzel fell asleep about fifteen minutes before I had to leave in the morning and that was fine with me. "No one would have known anything if it hadn't been for the paparazzi. They really love him over there."

"And you?" Adam cocks his head. "Is it true love this time?"

"Not this time." And not ever, if I have anything to do with it.

Adam gives me a sideways glance as he heads to the driver's side. "Well, one night can be fun too. I'm just saying, he's a cute one."

"You're cute too, and I'm not in love with you."

"You only wish!"

After being with Neely and Dawson day and night for the past ten weeks, Adam is like a breath of fresh air. I might not want that air blowing on me for weeks on end, but small doses of Adam are a good thing.

Back in the early years after I got my diagnosis, there had been months when I couldn't stand to be around myself. Neely and Dawson stuck with me and waited it out. A few weeks before my eighteenth birthday, I had been going through a particularly hard time, my bad funk chasing off friends. I'd been at Neely's, lounging on the couch, as her mother did her best to feed me.

"I don't know why you're so bitter," Adam stormed after I'd made some snarky remark to Neely. "So you're dying—so's everyone! But you're young and cute and you can do anything you want now *because* you're dying. Stop being so pissy about it and live a little."

Because of Adam, I pulled up my britches, put on a smiley face and the Expiry Date bucket list was born.

"You could still meet up with Denzel," Neely points out after we're crammed into the car and crawling through midday traffic on the highway back to the city. "After the wedding. You could fly out and meet him wherever. It's totally something you would do."

It is. I have. I live for unplanned, impulsive, spur-of-the-moment gestures. Plans fly out the window, directions are never followed, and my motto is to travel the path less travelled.

"Yes, but I have another spontaneous plan."

A chorus of groans replies and I rest my head on Dawson's shoulder. "I know, you need a break from me. But you'll like this idea."

"I'm scared," Dawson whimpers, which makes me laugh.

"It's not bad! You know what would make me really happy?" I ask in a wheedling voice. "If Adam would be so kind to stop off at Pain au Chocolate so we can get one of Reuben's most excellent lattes. It'll help me stay awake."

"Anything for you, Shae-girl," Adam says. "But only because it's on the way home."

"It is nice that everyone loves me so much," I muse with a sideways glance at Natasha. And then I take a quick pic of the back of Adam's head and the road before us and post it with *#gladtobehome*.

♥

Emmett

"THANK YOU SO MUCH for dropping it here." The tiny woman at the back door of Pain au Chocolate bakery gives me a big smile as she accepts the box of vegetables. It's the last delivery of the day, and the hours I've spent in the truck today following the directions of the GPS has given me a headache. I've never liked driving in the city.

"Clay's out of town and we weren't sure when we could pick up the box this weekend, so this is perfect!"

Joining the cooperative of community-supported farms ten years ago was one of Dad's best ideas, but dropping off the bi-weekly boxes of produce, honey, eggs, and fresh bread has never been my favourite thing to do, especially the ones in nearby Toronto. Usually, Dad or Warren deliver the boxes, but because I had to be in the city for the wedding rehearsal, I offered to drive in early with Rufus to do the rounds today.

I breathe deeply into the scents of warm butter and brown sugar wafting out the back door of the bakery kitchen and my mouth starts to water. "You're welcome. It smells amazing in there."

See Ellie? I talk to people.

"Can I get you something?" Her name tag reads M.K. "Pastries...coffee? I can't let you in through the back, but I can bring something around. Or you can pop into the patisserie if you have a minute."

Patisserie, not bakery. That's a difference between Toronto and Ashbury. "Thanks, but I'm good," I say automatically.

"Well, next time, then. On the house."

"Thanks, will do. Enjoy the vegetables and stuff." Giving her a nod, I back away with reluctant steps. It really does smell good, but I'm not the bakery–or patisserie–type. Give me a cookie shop, though, and I'd have a problem.

Pain au Chocolate is the last shop in the strip mall, with the door for deliveries at the back of the building. As I make my way back to the truck where Rufus is waiting, the sounds and smells of the city masks the aroma of pastry, or whatever else is sold inside the patisserie. Toronto is only a forty-five-minute drive from downtown Ashbury, but it's like a different world from my little hometown.

And then the door to Pain au Chocolate opens as I pass by on the way to the truck and I'm hit with another gust of warm air, this one smelling of coffee and chocolate.

The smell of coffee convinces me. It was another early start this morning and the rehearsal tonight is still to come. I open the door to the truck where Rufus is fixated on his phone. "Hey, bud, you want—?"

"You've got to see this," Rufus interrupts, holding out his phone. "It's the girl from the concert last night. They're zip-lining—naked zip-lining!" He breaks into barking laughs.

"What?" At the word naked, I snatch at the phone. The video is of a person—a woman from the looks of the hair—zip-lining through a bunch of trees. There's an obvious lack of clothes, but thankfully nothing X-rated showing. "Looks fun. Not."

"It's the girl from the concert and—"

"Want something to eat?" He's already talked my ear off today about this girl and I'm kind of sick of it.

Luckily, the mention of food grabs his attention and he hops out of the truck. "It's so cool," Rufus says as I pull open the door. "Watch, she goes upside down."

He holds the phone up for me as we step inside the bakery. Sure enough, the girl somehow flips upside down, arms dangling as she soars through the air. I look closer. "Is her hair pink?"

Rufus nods excitedly as he takes back the phone. "That's Shae. She's like the star of it. And there's Neely and Dawson, and there's another girl there this time. They go everywhere and do everything."

"Sounds exhausting. What do you want?" I look up with surprise. There's one bakery in Ashbury, owned by the sister of my best friend. The scent of bread always drives me inside whenever I walk by Pepper's shop.

This place is nothing like that.

Clean, crisp and French; Pain au Chocolate is a world away from Pepper's comfy, kitschy shop. But the place is even busier than her place, with tiny tables filled with customers with plates of croissants and Danish and more sweet things I don't recognize, most with expressions of satisfaction on their faces.

"Whoa," Rufus says, his eyes wide as he gazes at the glass display case.

A line of people wait before me but the way Rufus is staring, there's no way I can get him out now. The woman who took the box is now manning the cash register and greets a dark-haired woman pushing a stroller. "We'll bring it right over, Susie," the woman promises.

"Thanks, M.K. Hi, Reuben," Susie says cautiously as she maneuvers the stroller to a table in the back corner. Reuben, a giant of a man behind the coffee maker, stares after her as she walks by.

I recognize his glance, the look when you want something you can't have and feel a tug of sympathy for the big guy. I miss the tinkle of the bell as the door to the shop opens.

"Shae!" M.K. cries, her dark bob swinging as she waves. "You're back."

"Hey, M.K.! Straight from the airport and I made Adam stop here first. I *missed* this place." Her voice carries through the patisserie and I turn to look.

And then I look again.

Tiny figure, big eyes the colour of melted chocolate, and hair the colour of cotton candy. But it's the smile that gets me. It's far from perfect; almost too wide with a gap between her front teeth and a crooked incisor, but it seems to light up the place, like a motion sensor bulb going off at midnight.

And it's contagious.

She skips around the patisserie like some kind of Tinkerbell fairy. From the baristas behind the counter to Susie with the stroller, she has a smile and a word for every person in the place. A couple seated in the back corner has obviously never laid eyes on her before, but I watch with amazement as they respond to her ease and friendliness as though it's normal to talk to strangers.

Maybe it is.

Alex rarely talked to strangers. Sometimes she didn't even talk to my friends, preferring to scroll through her phone instead of making conversation over beers after the game.

I have no idea why I'm comparing the two, or why I watch Pink Hair with such fascination. But I do.

She finishes her sweep of the place with a hug for the big guy at the coffee maker before she disappears into an alcove at the back of the shop.

"Who's that?" Rufus demands, even more wide-eyed than when he saw the pastries.

"I have no idea." I stare after her with a mixture of relief and disappointment. The line moves forward as a customer leaves with a white box and enough take-out coffees to keep a school full of teachers going for the day.

"Oh, that's Shae," the older woman in front of me says over her shoulder. "She's our local celebrity."

"Shae—that's *her*!" I'm worried about the safety of the phone the way Rufus waves it.

"No, it's not."

"Emmett...it is!"

We've moved up another spot in line by the time Pink Hair takes her place behind me. Celebrity or not, pink hair or not, I stare straight ahead and resist the urge to glance over my shoulder. It's tough because only moments ago, I watched a video of her zip-lining upside down. While naked.

She is fully clothed now.

Rufus, on the other hand, can't help himself from staring.

He looks and looks again. It's not until the third time when he's downright gawking at her that I nudge him to stop.

And then I have to look. She's scrolling through her phone, and with the pink little hair buns and rolled-up ankles of her jogging pants, she doesn't look too much older than Rufus.

Tiny. Cute.

Definitely cute.

"Are you...?" Rufus asks her in a tremulous voice.

She looks up from her phone. "Hey," she says with a lopsided grin, almost like she knows us.

"You are!" Rufus cries. "I can't believe it. I saw you naked!"

She blinks with surprise. "Zip-lining!" Rufus waves his phone at her. "You're *the* Shae, aren't you? I've seen all your videos."

Shae—if that is who she really is—grins from ear to ear, like Rufus just handed her a million bucks. "A fan! That's so great!"

"I've seen all your videos, and follow you on Insta, and Tik-Tok—the one with the dog is so funny." Rufus is bouncing up and down, practically vibrating. I haven't seen him this excited since I gave him his first LEGO set when he was four. Shae listens with interest as Rufus details his favourite videos. This is one time where being a third wheel isn't a bad thing as I watch the expressions flash across her face.

She meets my gaze and smiles. I quickly look at the back of the person in front of us, at the display case, at the big guy manning the coffee maker. Anywhere but at her, because it must be so obvious that I'm checking her out.

I'm plain staring. Blink, Emmett, for God's sake.

Two women sitting in the corner of the shop stop by Shae on the way to the door and comment on the concert video. In this little bakery, she really is a celebrity.

Maybe it shouldn't surprise me. There's definitely something about her. A light within, or a happy glow...I can't explain it, but there's something. Just listening to her talk to Rufus makes me feel like a gust of cool spring air has slipped into a winter-stuffy barn.

"Why are you here?" Rufus finally finishes. "You were in Thailand, like, yesterday."

"We just flew back," Shae says conspiratorially. "In fact, I haven't even been home yet. I made Adam stop here because Reuben over there—" She points at the big guy behind the coffee maker. "He makes the very best lattes, always puts hearts in the foam."

I take a deep breath like I'm diving into a pool. "Good to know," I say drily. "I can't drink a coffee without a foamy heart."

When Shae turns her attention to me, it's like all the air is sucked out of my lungs. Her eyes are big and beautiful dark pools in a tiny face and the way she looks at me under her long lashes is jolting. More than jolting; it's like she sucker punched me in the stomach.

"Foamy hearts are the best," Shae says after a slight pause, enough for me to have a glimmer of hope that I'm not the only one reacting this way.

Or else she thinks I'm an idiot.

I give myself a shake to continue the conversation. "Sounds like you're a regular. I didn't get hugs when I came in."

"You could always ask nicely," she says hesitantly.

"Okay!" Without a moment's pause, Rufus launches himself on Shae.

"Rufus!"

To give her credit, she only laughs as Rufus throws his arms around her. "It's okay," she says, looking over Rufus's head at me. Or more like his shoulder—there isn't much to her, and Rufus is a tall eleven-year-old, so they're almost the same height. "I like knowing my stuff touches people. Not many of them actually get to touch me, though."

Another laugh and something twists inside my gut at the sound. It's been a while since I let myself be affected by a woman's laugh. Or a woman, period.

It's been a very *long* three years.

"Rufus, enough," I chide, and reluctantly, my nephew lets go.

"Thank you," she says with a big smile. "And I'm sorry if I smell a little."

"You might need deodorant," Rufus tells her. "That's what they tell me."

Her eyes dance. "I probably do. He's adorable." Her gaze shifts to me. Shifts...and holds, the dancing dark eyes slowing to study my face like she's searching for something.

I want her to find it. I want her to find me.

The mere thought takes my breath away.

"Me, she said." Rufus elbows me in the side and completely spoils the moment. "I'm adorable. Not you."

"I didn't realize it was a competition," Shae says.

"He thinks I've lost my coolness." I blink with surprise at the ease of that confession. It's never been this easy talking to a woman, not even before Alex. "Not that you have any interest in what my nephew thinks of me."

"Nephew," she murmurs. "Not son."

"Not son. I don't have any kids. Not that I'm against kids...kids are fine. Rufus is great."

Rufus the Great gives me a disgusted glance and I clamp my mouth shut.

"I think it's okay not being super cool," Shae declares. "I don't like guys who try too hard, you know. Sometimes too cool is just an excuse to be a jerk."

"I'm never a jerk," Rufus promises with an earnest smile. "And I always know how to treat a woman."

Shae looks like she's trying to hide her smile. "That is very nice to hear," she says with a sideways glance at me.

I'm about to tell her that I too, know how to treat a woman, but stop myself with the realization that while cute coming from Rufus, it'd make me look like a creep.

Possibly a competitive creep.

"You reconsidered on the coffee," a voice behind me says. With a start, I look over my shoulder to see the gap between us and the counter and M.K. staring expectantly at me. "Sorry that you had to wait."

"It's no trouble at all." I can't help but look sideways at Shae. "You were the last of my deliveries."

"I hope you enjoy the weekend. What can I get you?"

"Uh...I have no idea." I shrug as I scan the glass front display case. "You hungry, Rufus?"

"Yeah, but that stuff looks too pretty to eat." Rufus turns to Shae. "Pepper's bakery has stuff like muffins and brownies. This is...fancy."

"I'm going to take that as a compliment," M.K. says with a smile. "Maybe Shae can make a suggestion for you."

"You want me to decide?" She rubs her hands with a wicked laugh and steps forward. "First thing, you need a pain au chocolate, and a croissant, because they are famous. You also should get one of the apple tarts and some macarons and definitely one of Reuben's cupcakes. No, don't," she quickly corrects, tapping the glass at the last cupcake. It doesn't look like any cupcake I've ever eaten, decorated with a river of silver sparkles in a mound of bright pink icing with some sort of cookie sticking out of it. "Don't get that."

"Okay. But it looks pretty. Interesting, with the sparkles and the pink."

It looks like you, I almost say.

"Are you really going to deprive me of Reuben's cupcakes when I've been out of the country for weeks?" Shae blinks dramatically. "The only reason I'm back is for that cupcake."

"I thought it was the foamy hearts."

Shae's smile makes *my* heart feel like it's foamy.

"Give the man his cupcake," M.K. says with a laugh. "I'll send some home with Adam for you."

Who's Adam? The lightness plummets into darkness with a simple name.

"Fine," Shae pouts. "Give them all that." She winks at Rufus. "Make sure you eat it all at once to fully enjoy the sugar high."

"Make sure you don't, or you'll have to deal with your aunt tonight," I threaten Rufus.

I pull out my wallet to pay for the coffee and the pastries and anything else Shae wants to suggest. I feel kind of lightheaded, and the headache from earlier seems to have vanished. It's as if Shae has cast a spell over me, using smiles and laughter and foamy hearts.

The big guy deposits my latte before me with a nod. "How many for you?" he asks Shae.

"Five—and one for Mike. Thanks," she says. "And Reuben, I don't know what prompted the makeover, but you look incredible. Even though I miss the beard."

"Thank you, Shae," Reuben rumbles, his deep voice and Scottish accent making even the few words hard to decipher. "I blame Adam."

"I like to blame Adam for everything I can," she says with a grin.

Rufus grabs the box and I take my coffee, reluctantly stepping out of the way while trying to think of something witty and brilliant to say to Shae.

Rufus beats me to it. "So where are you going next?" he asks eagerly.

"Nothing is planned yet," she says. "I'm trying to talk my friends into hiking the Pacific Crest Trail. Have you heard of that?" Rufus shakes his head. "It's a trail that goes from Canada to Mexico."

"You'd walk the whole way?"

"Maybe just part of it. There's also a couple of outdoor festivals that look like fun."

"So you can get pulled up on stage again?"

She gives me a glance that I can't read. "I think that was a one-time thing." Reuben sets her tray of coffees on the counter. "Thanks," she says, pulling out her phone and snapping a picture.

"Is that for your vlog?" Rufus asks excitedly.

She nods. "I always tell the world how awesome this place is every time I come in."

"It's good to see you back, Shae." M.K. says before turning to another customer.

"It was really nice meeting you," Shae says to Rufus before her eyes flick to me. "Meeting both of you. Gotta run." Juggling the coffees, she smiles one last time before backing away. "Bye. Follow me on Instagram."

And then she's gone.

Chapter Three

Shae

FOLLOW ME ON INSTAGRAM?

As the bell on the door tinkles behind me, I fight the urge to run back in with something better. Something pithy; something fun that will make him follow me...and maybe send me a DM...

I don't even know his name.

But then I'm at the car, and Dawson steps out to take the tray from my hands, letting me slide in the back between him and Natasha because I'm the smallest.

"Was it busy?" Adam asks as he starts the car. He's worked at Pain au Chocolate for two years now, meeting his boyfriend Patrick through M.K.

I glance back over my shoulder in time to see Rufus and his uncle step outside. I watch until we pull out of the parking lot and he vanishes from my view.

It's better that way.

Out of sight, out of mind. So therefore I need to stop thinking about him. Wishing...

Wishing for what?

Something deflates inside me. Are the last few days finally catching up with me? Why else would talking to this guy for five minutes rattle me so much?

"There was a lineup," I say, turning to face the front. "And I had to use the bathroom so that took an extra minute." I don't mention foamy hearts or cupcakes, or the way the little guy—Rufus, what a great name—looked at me like I'm some kind of superhero.

I liked the way the big guy looked at me too but in a much different way. Broad shoulders, amazing eyes too; light blue with lashes as thick as mine with three coats of mascara.

You don't do relationships. I give myself a shake. My life is complicated enough and men are far from simple. Besides, love only ever has one outcome and it's hella hurt.

It's better to avoid all of it.

When Adam drops off Natasha, I watch curiously as Dawson follows her to the door of the apartment building, carrying her bags and kissing her goodbye like he won't see her for weeks. It's not the first time I've witnessed the affection between them, but it's the first time I wonder about it.

What if someone was waiting for me to come home; waiting with sweet kisses and eager to hear everything that I've done?

The car is quieter than my thoughts as Adam drops off Dawson. He used to live on the same street as Neely and me, but he and his mother moved after his father passed away in high school. It's something that the two of us have in common—no father and no siblings. It also sets us apart from Neely.

The fact that, at twenty-seven, neither Neely nor I have ever been in a committed relationship, sets us apart from Dawson. We have very different reasons for staying away from the love bug, but still, neither of us has someone who says goodbye like Dawson kisses Natasha.

"You got quiet." Neely glances over her shoulder at me. The worry is apparent in her eyes. It's difficult to read Neely's facial expressions, but I can always tell what she's thinking by her eyes. They're hazel and move from green to golden depending on her mood.

"I get quiet sometimes."

"Is your mom going to be home?" Neely doesn't have to ask what's bothering me, and I'm glad she doesn't. I'd rather have her think my silence is due to the adjustment of being home, than any regret about what I didn't say to the guy in Pain.

"I doubt it. Mike will be though. He offered to pick us up," I remind her.

"That's my job," Adam says. "You should come to the rehearsal dinner tonight. It'll give you something to do. Besides, Ellie's brother is a hottie."

I manage a smile. "I've had enough hotties for a while, thanks. And I've got a hot date with my bed tonight."

The weight of exhaustion settles fully onto my shoulders as Adam pulls into the driveway between the houses. The musical chorus of birds and the *metoo metoo* of the seagulls circling the nearby beach for forgotten French fries are loud as I pull my bags from the trunk, but can't quite drown out the sound of the slow-moving traffic along Queen Street.

"Get some rest," Neely advises as I hug her. "Busy day tomorrow."

"Can't wait. Thanks for picking us up, Adam. And say hi to Patrick." I bump my suitcase up the stairs to the front porch. "Have fun tonight." With a final wave, I open the door.

Home. Home with the glossy floors and freshly painted hallway. The smell of something warm drifts in from the kitchen. Doris, Grandpa Mike's ancient yellow Lab, is slow getting to her feet, but she comes at me with a wag of her tail and a happy dog smile. I drop the handle of my suitcase and shrug off my backpack, setting the coffees on the floor to give Doris a good hello rub.

"You made it." Mike stands in the doorway of the kitchen, his silver hair as impeccable as always, a bright yellow apron covering his clothes. He opens his arms and, leaving the dog wanting more, I rush into them with a relieved smile. The image of the guy from Pain au Chocolate vanishes as Mike's arms tighten around me. The warmth of his welcome is better than a jolt of caffeine. I might not have someone meeting me with sweet kisses, but I have someone who missed me.

A constant in my life since I was fourteen and he moved in with my mom and me when my father died. He's not my grandfather per se; technically, there was never an official marriage certificate between Mike and my grandmother. After they both lost the loves of their lives, Mike convinced my mom to let him move in.

"So we can take care of each other," he said.

It's a toss-up who benefited the most from the arrangement.

"It's good to see you home, Shae-girl." After a final squeeze, Mike lets me go but his sharp eyes study me and I know he's checking to see if my eyes are tired, if the red patches are back on my face, or if the yellow tinge has returned that makes me look like a faded lemon.

Mike was there the day the doctor told me I had Batten disease. He was the one who held me when the tears finally came, and the one who never stopped telling me I had so much to live for.

"It's good to be home," I say. It is good to be home because I miss Mike and Doris and sleeping in my childhood bed with the line of misshapen stuffed animals perched on the pillows.

But the downside of being home means I'm back under the same roof as my mother.

Ducking my head away from Mike's scrutiny, I see the latest framed photo Mike has placed on the bookshelves, of me with Neely and Dawson and the baby elephants. He must have taken a screenshot from the video and blown it up. I point at it, a tired smile crossing my face.

"I liked the elephants," he says.

"You know you can always come with me," I invite. "Neely'd you there much better than Natasha. So would I."

"My globe-hopping days are long past. I leave that for young people."

"Stop sounding so old." I pick up the coffee but leave my bags and slip past him into the kitchen. "And I'm fine, by the way. Neely takes good care of me."

I'm happy to see nothing has changed in the kitchen. Same wood cupboards, same pristine counter with Mike's KitchenAid mixer taking the place of pride beside the stove. Because Mike spends so much time here, the room has a personality and warmth, not to mention always smells good.

Mike, at seventy-four, looks like a man of sixty, and a hot one to boot. I keep telling him I'm going to get him a modelling contract for the cover of one of those silver fox romance novels. He keeps fit by daily walks and runs the local pickleball club, as well as biking most weekends. He says it's mainly to work off the calories, not to get the girls.

"Not as good as I can," he says, following me. "Come. Eat. I've got food waiting for you."

"How's mom?" I ask dutifully when I'm settled at the table after a quick washup. Doris settles on the floor beside me, watching eagerly for scraps. Mike puts a plate in front of me—his famous scrambled eggs with freshly baked bread and homemade turkey sausages.

The eggs are famous because it was the dish that led to him being sent home from MasterChef Canada. He made it to the top four finalists, but the eggs, as good as they are, just didn't cut it with the judges.

"Cybil's busy at the hospital as usual." Mike takes the lid off his coffee and dumps it in a glass filled with ice.

"I can get you an iced coffee next time," I protest as I pass a hunk of sausage to the dog.

"No need," he says, settling in the seat beside me. "They charge you fifty cents more in the store. Easy enough to do it myself. I saw you at that concert the other night." The best thing about my vlog is that Mike and my mother, if she wants to, always know what I'm doing.

The lack of privacy can also be the worst thing about it.

"I saw you dancing with that singer," he continues in his *I don't like this* tone. "Tell me, did you dance the night away with him?"

I roll my eyes. "Denzel was very nice. You'd like him—he plays Fortnite too." Mike's got a thing for superhero movies, graphic novels and video games. It's like he's a twelve-year-old boy.

Rufus from Pain au Chocolate pops into my mind and I push him roughly away before he can morph into his uncle.

"Well, good for him, but that doesn't excuse him from having his hands all over you," Mike grumbles as he pours me a glass of orange juice.

I smile ruefully as I fork up another mouthful of eggs. "No one had their hands all over me. Now you sound old."

"I sound like a man who wants his granddaughter to meet a nice man who will take care of her when I'm not around."

His words hang in the air between us. Neither of us wants to mention that Mike will most likely outlive me.

"You're just trying to get rid of me," I say lightly. "So you can have more time for your video games."

"That's all it is," he agrees with a rumble of laughter. "You tell Dawson I expect to meet him online for a rematch of the last time."

"When he kicked your butt?"

"When I allowed him to win." I grin at him over the edge of my glass of orange juice. "You've got a doctor's appointment on Tuesday," Mike reminds me.

"I know."

"Your mom says old Dr. Moseley passed away." He tosses another sausage onto my plate before starting on the cleanup.

"I heard that. Sad. But I've got a new one—Dr. somebody-or-other."

"Do you want me to go to the appointment with you?"

"And make you miss your pickleball? Never." Getting up to take my now empty plate to the kitchen, I drop a kiss on his silver hair. "I missed you."

He grabs my hand but doesn't look at me. I know his eyes have filled with tears, same as mine. For a seventy-four-year-old man addicted to Fortnite, he's surprisingly emotional. "I missed you more, Shae-girl."

And that's why I've vowed never to let myself fall in love. Because when I die, those who love me are going to be left behind to pick up the pieces. And thinking about Mike hurting is bad enough. I can't do that to anyone else.

Emmett

"ARE YOU GOING TO follow her on Instagram?" Rufus demands.

"I'm not on Instagram," I remind him. "Nor do I want to be."

"You don't know what you're missing."

I missed getting her number. Do people even exchange numbers, or do singles meet via social media, sending direct messages or posting on each other pages?

There's so much I don't know.

I met Alex in a bar; it was a simple, straightforward physical attraction that led to something more. I fell in love with her in person, not some persona that she showed the world.

Shae is a girl who lives her life in the public eye. My meltdown after Alex died brought me enough notoriety to know that I don't want that again.

Even if I did, it was five minutes. Seven tops, and most of that was Rufus talking. Why am I even comparing Shae with Alex? There's a good chance I'll never see her again, even with Rufus's plans to DM her like a pen pal. It's nice that things are so innocent with him.

It doesn't feel innocent with me.

It doesn't feel like anything I've felt before. But it was *five* minutes. We talked about nothing. She's cute but...that smile but...

But I'll never see her again, so forget about it.

I let Rufus talk about her on the way to the hotel, listening with half an ear, while I do my best to scratch out the image of Shae's smile from my mind.

As soon as I unlock the door to the hotel room, Rufus takes a diving leap onto one of the double beds and claims it for his own. I wouldn't mind if Rufus stayed with me, but Ethan wanted to spend as much time with his son as possible.

Rufus and I are in the hotel room for a grand total of three minutes before there's a knock on the door. "Dad!" Rufus cries.

"Nope, it's me," Grayson Grant says as I open the door. Because Grayson is practically family, Ellie invited him and his sister Pepper to the wedding.

"I've got the room next door," Grayson adds, handing me one of the bottles of beer that he has in hands. "Hey, little dude." He lifts his bottle to Rufus, who quickly recovers from his disappointment by scrolling through TikTok videos to find more of Shae.

"I thought you were only coming in for the wedding tomorrow." I plunk my duffle bag on the bed and start unpacking. I've spent a lot of nights in hotel rooms when I was playing ball, and the one thing that would guarantee a bad night's sleep was to have all my stuff lying around.

Grayson knows this because he roomed with me when we played ball together.

The little town of Ashbury, forty-five minutes northeast of Toronto, is one of the few Canadian towns to boast two of their own to be drafted to the MLB at the same time—myself and my best friend Grayson Grant.

St. Louis took us as a pair in the third and fourth draft pick; Grayson had a ninety-six-mile fastball and a knuckleball that was almost impossible to catch, except by me. Playing together our whole lives made an unbeatable team. Grayson made me better, and I made him look great.

Being busy keeps my mind from drifting to the fact that tonight will be the first night I've spent alone in a hotel room. I've held back from asking Grayson to share, not because he snores or has a tendency to pick up women wherever he goes—I'm embarrassed to tell him I'm afraid I'll be lonely by myself.

Grayson tips up the bottle to his mouth before answering. "I thought I might convince you to come with me to meet up with this girl I met online. She has friends." He settles into one of the chairs, resting his long legs on the edge of the bed.

"Is that why you're all dressed up?" I check out Grayson's jeans and fitted polo shirt. He's lost some of the bulk he had in his pitching heyday but unlike me, Grayson always works at looking good.

Grayson used to be the skinniest kid I knew. "All arms and legs," Dad used to say. He had a good six inches on me, but my extra forty pounds meant I could always take him in a play fight.

That had been before he started with the weights. When we were sixteen, Grayson overheard a spectator at one of our baseball games say something about how the two of us had more promise than anyone on the team. That was enough for him to get into his mind that we were going to break into the majors. I had already been slightly obsessed with the sport, but after that, for the next three years, Grayson and I lived and breathed baseball. Everything was about getting better—what we ate, how much we slept, how much we trained, lifted, threw. Even girls took a back seat, which was more of a surprise for Grayson than me.

It worked; both of us considerably bigger and stronger, we were drafted to St. Louis's farm team after graduating high school. Ten years in the minors, with Grayson starting three games with the Cardinals, and me getting fourteen games in when both of their regular catchers happened to be on the DL.

A torn UCL finished Grayson; he had Tommy John surgery, but it was never the same. And it wasn't for me either. I lasted a season without him, then met Alex and things fell apart.

"No, this is what I wear all the time." Grayson casts a disparaging look at my dirty jeans and torn flannel shirt. "How about it? You can be my wingman before you desert me for the rehearsal dinner."

"It's only a couple hours, Gray. You will survive."

"You may not survive the wedding if you don't remember how to pick up women. Lots of bridesmaids in this wedding, if I remember correctly." He gives me a wink before his face falls. "I can't believe Ellie's getting married tomorrow," he moans. "It's like my heart has a crack all the way through at the thought."

"This is my sister we're talking about, you know," I say, my eyes narrowing. "Is there something you're not telling me?"

"What? No." Grayson shifts his gaze immediately. "Nice rooms, aren't they?"

I've always been able to read Grayson like a book. "Seriously, bro? You and Ellie?"

"He's always had a thing for Aunt Ellie," Rufus pipes up, his attention still on the screen. "He flirts with her all the time when you're not around."

"Dude!"

"How did I not know about this?" I cry.

"Because he's afraid you'd beat him up." Rufus finally looks up. "Duh."

"Should I be thinking of beatings?" I ask, giving Grayson my best game face, the one I cultivated to intimidate when I was up at bat. "Again—how did I not know about this?"

"No need for any beatings! It was a long time ago," Grayson says, waving back the years. "Just a summer thing. And you were obsessed with that Morgan girl—remember?"

"No."

"You do, too. You didn't notice anything except for her legs, which were truly great, I have to say. Ellie dumped me, so don't get all bent out of shape," Grayson assures me. "And she wasn't nice about it." He clutches his chest. "It really hurt."

"Good for her."

"How can you say that? I'm your best friend and your sister broke my heart."

"Well, maybe you shouldn't have been messing around with her in the first place." I stare at Grayson sitting calmly in the chair. "Why are you telling me this now? She's getting married tomorrow."

"I need to clear my conscience. Plus, this way you'll keep me away from the microphone at the wedding." Grayson grins, totally without repentance. "Come on, dude. I couldn't resist. She was so cute back then."

"Emmett thinks Shae is cute."

Grayson whips his head to Rufus still lying flat on the bed. "Who's Shae?"

"She's very cool," Rufus says.

A grin breaks over Grayson's face. "Dude! You met a girl. So what happened? Get her number? Where's she from?"

"I have no idea," I say, rolling my eyes at their enthusiasm. "Her name is Shae and that's all I know."

"That's not true! She's everywhere online." Rufus waves his phone.

"So's everybody. The first girl in years that catches your eye and you let her leave without knowing anything about her?" Grayson shakes his head with disgust. "You're so out of practice."

"I can get a hold of her through this blog thing. Vlog," I correct.

"And come across as a psycho stalker? Not the best way to make an impression."

"I made a good first impression," I say. "I did. I think I did."

Rufus shakes his head. "You didn't. Grayson's right. You're out of practice."

I throw a pair of socks at him. "What do you know about it?"

"So who is this girl?" Grayson interjects. Rufus holds out his phone and Grayson takes it.

"She's a vlogger who goes all over the place, but she's from here. Toronto," Rufus explains. "We just met her in this bakery. Check out the video of her zip-lining, and then there's this other one. It's called ExpiryDate. I don't know what that means."

"You met her?" Grayson enlarges the screen with his fingers. "Heyyy..."

"Not her, the next one."

I hear the scream as Shae appears. "She's cute. What I can see of her."

"She's cute," I confirm.

"Wait a sec." Grayson scrolls through the site with a frown on his face. "Maybe this is the girl they were telling me that they wanted for me on The Suitor."

I groan. "Not that again."

The Suitor is a Bachelor-like reality show, focusing on Canadian singles finding love. Grayson got picked up to appear on the female version two years ago, chosen as one of the men selected to woo the Suitorette. Because he's my best friend, I was stuck watching every episode, but seeing your best friend make out with a woman every chance he got was a bit too much.

He made it to fifth place, kicked off before he got to bring the Suitorette to meet his family, and told the world he'd had his heart broken. Having had watched Grayson get his heart crushed time and time again in real life, I did feel bad for him, but happy for me that I didn't have to watch any more of it.

"Get ready for another round. This time, I'm the main event." He thumps his thumb into his chest with a proud smile. "Remember I told you I got that call last week?" When I nod, Grayson smiles widely, showcasing one of the reasons he's always been so popular with the ladies. "You're looking at the next Suitor. This time it's me looking for love, and there's twenty-five beautiful ladies vying to be the love of my life, all eagerly waiting for filming to start."

"What?" I turn with another pair of socks in my hand. "Are you serious?"

"As a stone."

"Why are stones serious?"

"It's a saying."

"It's a stupid saying. Why the hell would you want to broadcast your love life to the world again?" I demand.

"Why wouldn't I?" Grayson counters. "It's a chance to find love."

"And you're such a romantic," I mutter.

"I am," he insists. "Not everyone can be as lucky as you."

"You consider me lucky?"

"I do. You had that time with Alex, the love of your life." Grayson turns to me. "You don't consider that lucky?"

"Actually, no," I drawl. "Because she *died.*"

"You *found* love," Grayson insists. "So that means you'll be able to find it again. Maybe with her." He tosses Rufus's phone onto the bed and heads for the chair, swerving at the last minute to check out the bakery box. "Is that why your room smells so good?" he asks, lifting the lid with a whistle. "Don't tell Pepper," he says to Rufus, taking a bite out of the pain au chocolate. "She gets mad if I eat bread that's not hers."

"Don't eat the cupcake," I say. "That's mine."

"Why?" Grayson asks through a mouthful of pastry. "This is really good."

"I wouldn't know, since you ate it all." I cringe as he finishes the pastry with another mouthful of beer.

"You done here? Let's go down to the bar." Grayson's suggestion manages to pull Rufus's attention from his phone. "We can talk strategy."

"Maybe tonight will be the night *you* become a man," Rufus cheers. "Or tomorrow night. Maybe you'll meet someone at the wedding."

"No way." I shake my head, still thinking of Shae. "It's a family wedding. Who's going to be there for me?"

Chapter Four

Shae

WHEN I WAKE UP the next day, the time on my phone shows that I slept well into the afternoon. I'm meeting Dawson and Natasha at the church in a few hours for James's wedding. But even though I have things to do, I roll onto my back with my phone and open Instagram.

I take a picture of my room—the few stuffed animals still on my bed with the bookshelves in the background, filled with framed photos blocking the spines of my books; mysteries and thrillers and shelves of non-fiction titles dealing with grief and loss and how to be kind to yourself.

A picture of my father sits on the top shelf. I make sure it's not in the shot.

I add the hashtags *#home #muchneededsleepin* and *#weddingdayfun* and press share. Then I go through the previous posts and reply to my people, either with comments or emojis, or even the all-powerful like button.

What would it be like not to share everything? I've been an influencer for long enough for it to be second nature—the constant pictures and comments and hashtags, always courting followers and dreaming up new ways to collect more.

What if I stopped? Would anyone care what happened to me?

It's not something I like to think about, because it's going to be a reality someday. I've already planned out what Neely will post, the pictures she'll use, who needs to be tagged. It's not something I like to think about, but it's necessary.

What if I gave it up *before* anything happened? Could I live without the obligation to post and be seen?

What would it do to me? I'd go back to being the Girl Who is Going to Die, just like I was in high school.

I don't want to be that person.

It's bad enough that this room still looks like it's frozen in time. I haven't changed anything since I left for my first trip—backpacking through Europe for the summer before Dawson and Neely started university. I didn't bother with post-secondary education; what's the point of more learning when I'd be dead before I could get a degree? But over the years, I'd taken a few courses.

I like history. I like learning about the past. It's what motivates me to make sure I have something for others to look into when I'm gone. Someday, a new generation of travel vloggers will look back and wonder how I did things. They'll learn from my mistakes.

Hopefully, they'll learn not to stay in that hostel in Prague.

I sit up and swing my legs over the bed. Today will be a challenge—I'm still tired from the trip and the jetlag will catch up in a few hours, which means I have to push through it. Weddings are always interesting—

Bittersweet, is more like it. They make me happy because it's nice to see others happy but it's easy to slide into melancholy because of the whole dying thing. But I can usually push aside what I'll be missing because I pull the happiness from life, rather than focus on the sadness. That's why I find any excuse to go to a wedding, even if I don't know the happy couple well enough to get an invite.

Like one of my favourite memories; we were in India in 2018 and managed to crash Nick and Priyanka's wedding. That was one of the most amazing nights, except for the next day when Neely came down with Delhi belly and missed the tour of the Taj Mahal.

I love the idea of two people finding their soul mate; watching them pledge to love and honour each other until the end of their lives. Another trip, we were bicycling in the south of France and stumbled across a wedding. It was beautiful, with the bright blue sky and fields of lavender surrounding the area. I'll never forget that groom because he had the biggest smile on his face as he sobbed with happiness. I made Neely and Dawson hang around until I could talk to him.

I posted a photo of the happy couple as well.

I like love stories. I love romance. If things were different, I think I would be a die-hard romantic, searching the world for my true love.

But the reality is that even if I found my true love, what good would it do? If I were to get married, and promise to love and cherish and all the stuff...knowing that I'm dying? It seems wrong somehow, like I'm keeping some secret. Unfair. I know how it's going to end, and it doesn't matter how optimistic I can be—that's how it's going to end.

I don't want to promise to love someone 'til death do us part, because I know it's only a matter of time before death will do us part, and there's nothing I can do to change that.

I glance at the picture of my father. My mother promised to love him, and look what good that did to her?

I focus on my breathing, just like my therapist suggested. I'm going to the wedding of people I care about. It's not about me; it's nothing about me. It shouldn't make me sad.

Everything in this house seems designed to make me sad.

When I drag myself out of bed, the house is quiet. This, along with the absence of Doris, tells me Mike is out walking the dog. I know if I wait, he'll make me something to eat when he gets back.

I don't expect to see my mother in the kitchen, sitting at the table with her e-reader and a bowl of grapes.

"Morning," she says with a raised eyebrow. "Or rather afternoon. Mike said you were home."

"I emailed you the itinerary." I slide past her to the coffeemaker and pour myself a mug, taking a sip as I stand with the refrigerator door open, looking for something to tempt me. The fridge is empty, save for half a leftover chicken and a stack of plastic containers.

"Yes, I got that. Thank you. Neely stopped by this morning. Her mother thought you might appreciate some of the leftover lasagna from the rehearsal dinner last night."

"That's Mama S. Always trying to feed me up."

Mom sniffs in response. Even though we've lived next to the Scalzo's for almost twenty years, she's never warmed up to Neely's mother.

I don't remember the last time she warmed up to anyone.

My relationship with my mother is...difficult to explain. She's my mother, so I love her, but there have been many, many times in my life that I haven't liked her.

I wonder sometimes what it would have been like if my father had been alive when the doctors told me I was going to die. Would my mother have been able to deal with it with him by her side, or would she have tuned out like she did after Dad died?

My father would have been fine. He dealt with everything and always came out smiling.

Except, obviously, a faulty heart.

My mother is the polar opposite of me and my father; tall and rigid, with a constant frown on her face and living by a set of rules that she never seems to tell anyone. I know I break them all because there's the aura of disappointment that comes over her whenever I'm around. Thanks to that fact, I'm different when I'm around her. Less open...less happy.

"What time is the wedding?" she asks. No questions about the trip or the flight or anything about what I've been doing for the past ten weeks. Nothing about being glad to see me, or how I'm feeling.

She's a *nurse* and she doesn't even ask how my fatal disease is making me feel.

"Four o'clock."

"Are you going with anyone?"

"Dawson and Natasha." Even my voice is different, clipped and curt; precise like I'm cutting hair. "Neely is a bridesmaid."

"I know. I'm sure she'll look lovely. I meant, are you taking a date?"

"Why would I take a date?"

My dad was the fun one; the one who gave spontaneous hugs and always had a smile on his face. Everyone says I'm just like him—which I can see, but I have no idea how he ended up with my mother. She's...she's not me. Or rather, I'm not her.

Except for one thing: neither of us has any interest or inclination for love.

"I thought maybe—"

"Why would you think anything about that? I've only been gone a couple of months, not long enough to have some great epiphany that I need a man in my life."

"I didn't say you needed a man—"

"I should hope not, since you've spent my whole life showing me that I don't need anyone."

The chair scrapes loudly as she stands up. "I don't know why I bother," she mutters.

I don't say a word as she leaves the room. The faint tinge of hospital smell lingers after she goes, the scent that always makes my stomach curl because it means tests and sadness and death.

I was a well-known figure in the hospital for a lot of years. First, there were the visits to my father after we would get the phone calls that the end was near. There were three of those calls where we rushed to get there in time; each time he pulled through, only to die alone in the middle of the night.

After he passed away, it was my turn to get to know the hospital staff; appointments with different doctors, tests, tests, and more tests while they tried to find out what was wrong with me.

"An optimistic timeline would be seven years," Dr. Moseley had explained to my mother as I sat stunned in the chair beside her. No one touched me, save the nurse who squeezed my hand after she took my blood.

That's my idea of a nurse. Someone nurturing, someone who cares.

"I'm going to die, then."

Dr. Moseley glanced at me over the rim of his glasses. I'd hated the man from the first time I'd laid eyes on him. Even at fourteen, I sensed he had no humour, no compassion, no *humanity* that would help make the diagnosis easier on me.

"Yes," he said brusquely. "But there is time—"

I got up and walked out of the room. To this day, I have no idea what Dr. Moseley said to my mother.

We don't talk about my illness. It's the wedge that has been steadily pushing us apart for the past thirteen years, and best ignored by the both of us. For her, I'm sure it's because she stopped caring about me when she heard I was going to die. For me, I'm afraid of her locking herself in her bedroom again, like she did after my dad died.

After Dad died, I was virtually alone in the house for six weeks, fed by Neely's mother, until Mama S. tracked down Mike.

I don't like thinking about that time of my life, mainly because I've never forgiven her for abandoning me. But sometimes I need to remember when I meet someone like Denzel or even Rufus's uncle. Because I know what can happen when you love someone so much, and then they die. People change when they grieve, when they're in pain. And the last thing I want to do is cause someone I love any more pain.

So I get away before they love me. Before I die and they turn into my mother—cold and alone.

"You should bother because you're my mom," I whisper into the empty room.

♥

Emmett

I've been to Ellie's future in-laws' place once before, for James's birthday, and my only memories are the smell of garlic and tomato sauce, framed family pictures on every available surface—even the bathroom—and the colour blue. And food. Lots and lots of food.

James, my soon-to-be brother-in-law, comes from a seemingly huge Italian family, and when Rufus and I arrive the morning of the wedding for pictures, the house is again overflowing with family, from the toddler being chased by a barefoot woman, to great-Nonna, deaf in one ear and insisting on shouting her every thought. I walk in on the middle of his brothers, Davis and Adam, having their own shouting match. Something about shoes.

"Emmett!" Mrs. Scalzo, who insists that I call her Mama S., greets me with a big hug. It's been years since I was the recipient of a mother's hug, but even then, my mother never hugged me like Mama S. "You're here. And Rufus." Rufus has a dazed expression on his face as Mama S pulls him in for a tight embrace. "Come, eat something, and then we'll start pictures in the backyard."

Forty-five minutes later, my pants are straining from a huge lunch. During last night's dinner, I ate more than a small family, and now this. I don't know how I'm going to be able to do up the buttons on my tuxedo jacket.

I take my spot between Rufus and brother Adam and paste a smile on my face. "I'm already tired of smiling," Adam complains good-naturedly. "We already did a bunch of family photos before Neely left."

Neely is James's sister. I met her for the first time last night at the rehearsal dinner. She seems...intense. Nice enough, but the way she ran around the house last night, like a general organizing a battle, was a little frightening.

She's with Ellie and the rest of the bridesmaids at the hotel getting ready.

Under a shade tree in the backyard, I watch as James is pushed and prodded by the photographer as well as Mama S.; pictures by himself in every pose, under every tree in the yard, and then again with his wedding party, together and separate.

I'm happy to do whatever James's mother says. She might have welcomed me like some long-lost cousin, but I can tell she's got a scary side. Mama S. may look like a typical Italian *madre,* but I think she's more Mussolini than a sweet, gentle *Mamma.*

I didn't have anyone like that on my wedding day.

We had none of this. Ellie brought a pretty nightgown for Alex to wear and tried to add some blush to her pale cheeks. Ethan took a few pictures with his phone, and to this day, I've never looked at them. I stood by Alex's hospital bed and promised to love and honour a woman who would die two days later.

I was married for three days. That has to be a record.

"Who are you trolling, little man?" Adam asks peering at Rufus's phone, which is, yet again, in my nephew's hand.

"I'm not trolling, I'm—" He shows Adam the screen, which is another video of Shae. He's already shown me six different ones since we've been here.

I'm not complaining.

"Is that...?" Adam squints and looks closer. "That's Shae."

"Do you follow her too?" Rufus's eyes are so wide that it looks like he's been shocked with a bolt of electricity. "She's famous."

"Nah, not really. I just gave her a ride home from the airport."

"*What?*"

Adam takes Rufus's phone and scrolls through the video. "This is Neely. My sister." He shows Rufus an image of a blonde girl laughing as she hoses down an elephant.

"You know Shae?" Rufus's voice is hushed.

Adam points to the next house over with a smirk. "She lives right there."

I grab the back of Rufus's jacket before he can make a run for it. "Seriously?"

Adam nods. "Neely and Shae have been best friends forever. The two of them and Dawson—three musketeers, three peas in a pod, whatever you want to call it—they've gone around the world, done everything they can think of, and then some." Rufus is still staring at the neighbouring house with an awe I've only seen him reserve for a new video game. "She's coming to the wedding, you know."

"*She is?*"

"You've never met Neely?" Adam asks me, and I shake my head. "I guess that's why. They're pretty much inseparable, so you would have met Shae."

"Just last night. She wasn't here the one time I came for a party," I say, stunned at the connection. "And if she's gone as often as those videos suggest—"

"What's she like?" Rufus interrupts. "We met her yesterday, but only for a couple of minutes."

"Shae? She's a sweetheart." Adam frowns. "When did you meet her?"

"I had a delivery at this French bakery and Shae was inside when I went in to get coffee."

Adam trills a peal of laughter. "Pain au Chocolate." He slaps his chest. "That's where *I* work. I was in the car outside."

The realization that the Adam mentioned yesterday was *this* Adam brings a smile to my face. "They kept mentioning you," I confess. "I thought maybe a boyfriend."

"Shae only wishes." He shakes his head. "The girl doesn't date."

"No?" Even I can hear the disappointment in my voice.

Adam leans closer. "Methinks there's someone with a crush on my girl Shae."

"Rufus is completely obsessed—"

"I meant you."

I hold Adam's gaze for a long moment, tempted to confess all the new and confusing emotions of meeting a girl for only five minutes. "I only talked to her for a couple of minutes."

"It's okay," Adam assures me. "She's a peach, just the best person ever. And you will fall in love with her."

I laugh nervously. "I think maybe you're taking this a little too far."

Adam shakes his head. "I'm not. Everyone falls for Shae, but the problem is, she won't want you to."

"What's the supposed to mean?"

"The girl has walls as high and strong as this house. It's not my story to tell you why, but trust me, it's time they come down. And just maybe you're the guy to do it," he muses, looking at me with an appraising smile.

"I'm not into baggage," I say with a tight smile. "I have enough of my own."

"Emmett, you big hunk, you'd be lying if you said you didn't. Everyone's got something they don't want to share in their back pocket. I think you'd be good for Shae, much better than the Justin Bieber-wannabe from Thailand."

There's someone else? "Who?" Of course there's someone else.

"Never mind. Look, it's our turn to get in on the pictures, but first, a word of advice, because I love giving advice. Shae will try to push you away. *Don't let her.* That's the secret." He gives me a conspiratorial smile as he pushes off from the trunk of the tree. "This wedding is going to be more fun than I ever imagined."

Chapter Five

Shae

ORGAN MUSIC DRIFTS OUT of the open church doors as I tiptoe up the stairs of St. Frances the Mercy in my too high, very pink strappy sandals that wind around my calves, trying my best to pull myself out my pre-wedding funk. Talking to my mother earlier didn't help. It's like she pulls me down into the dark pit where she lives, and whenever I'm around her, I end up irritable and full of thoughts I don't want to let myself think about.

Like when I was retouching my hair colour to tone down the pink, I found myself wondering what colour to dye my hair for my funeral. Not that I would do it—obviously—but Neely would. Or she'd see that it was done.

Morbid, right? I think that's my mother's influence.

I have a notebook of thoughts and requests that only Neely knows about. Maybe it's not fair dumping all that on my best friend, but she insists. In fact, during an evening where we both had way too many tequila shots, she made me tell her exactly what

I wanted when I die; we picked my outfit for the visitation, decided on the perfect spot to spread my ashes, and worked on the guestlist for the wake. Neely's practical like that, plus she knows my mother doesn't have a clue what I want.

Neely is nowhere in sight at the church, presumably stashed away in some secret bride room with the rest of the wedding party, sipping champagne and reapplying lipstick. I picture her at the door looking through a crack, watching the guests arrive. I had wanted to drop by for the family wedding pictures earlier, but sleep kept me busy. I have a text of her in her bridesmaid dress, but even though Neely has been taking photos and videos for years for the vlog, she's horrible at taking selfies. It's really the only thing she's bad at.

Other than underestimating the size of James's wedding.

"This is huge." I stare around me with amazement as we enter the lobby of the church, caught in a throng of smartly dressed guests. "I wouldn't have figured James for the big wedding type of guy." I glance over at the sign propped on the easel. *James Robert Scalzo and Eleanor Katrina Pike are pleased to be joined in marriage...* "Eleanor must like the frou-frou."

"Nah, this is all Mama S.'s doing," Dawson says, blowing his nose. The containers of flowers standing guard by the doors send Dawson's allergies into high gear as we wait our turn to enter the church.

"Oh, has she already given up on Neely getting married?" Natasha asks in a sickly- sweet voice. "She's never found a guy who likes her enough to stick around, has she?"

"Have you met her? The bride?" Dawson asks just as I open my mouth to defend Neely. He waves at the sign, clueless as always at the snide remarks of his girlfriend. I swear his brain is in his pants.

I shake my head. "Neely says she's nice but hasn't had a chance to get to know her. They've only been together for a year."

Natasha rolls her eyes. "Someone's in a hurry to tie the knot. Why bother?"

"Don't get her started," Dawson grumbles.

I elbow him in his flat stomach, before tucking in the side of his shirt where it flaps out of the waistband of his trim black pants. Neely would have told him to tuck it in, while I just go ahead and do it for him. "Give me some credit. I'm not about to mention the diminishing stats for marriages these days, or the rising costs of divorce while I'm a guest at a wedding."

"No, you'd never do that," Dawson says sarcastically. "Only at my cousin's wedding. I took her as my plus one a couple of years ago," he adds to Natasha.

"I told you to take Neely."

"She was dating that guy then."

"The jealous one. I remember him. He was a jerk."

"He was, but it wasn't him. The one with the really bad hair."

"Oh, him!" My laughter stops midway at Natasha's scowl.

"You do realize how annoying it is when you two go on like this," she complains.

"Well, you should be glad Neely isn't here, or we'd be extremely annoying," I say with a big grin. Four months of travelling and dealing with Natasha's moods and I've had enough of her.

Ahead of us, a woman wearing a dress with more jungle print than all of Thailand greets an usher with a smacking kiss on both of his cheeks before he escorts her down the aisle.

"This is huge." Dawson echoes my earlier statement as we move closer to our escort down the aisle. Through the open church door, I see the pews filled with a rainbow of guests. "I've never been to a wedding this big. Not as an actual guest," he adds, throwing me a glance, obviously struck with the same memories of wedding crashing that I have.

"Neely said it's going to be an Italian wedding, but I thought she was talking about lots of food, not the people." The couple ahead of us is taken down the aisle and Adam appears, cheerful and chipper in a tuxedo.

"Hi, gang," he says, avoiding looking at Natasha. He likes her even less than we do and makes no bones about showing it. "You wait for the next one, Shae," he adds with a grin, offering Natasha his arm. The two of them start down the aisle without a word, leaving Dawson trailing behind.

"Why?" I call after them. "What about me?"

"What about you?" An usher appears before me, tall and broad-shouldered, looking a bit like—

"You!"

The guy from Pain au Chocolate stands before me, looking more delicious in his tuxedo than any of the pastries in the shop.

"Me."

I can't stop the smile spreading across my mouth, my face. It feels like my whole body is smiling. "What are you doing here?"

"You did tell me to follow you on Instagram."

"Yes, but—" I stumble, with the horrible thought that he's stalking me. "Why are you here in person?"

His blue eyes crinkle at the corner when he laughs, saving him from broody handsome into someone fun and even better looking. His dark blond hair looks like it started out slicked back but has relaxed enough to flop over his forehead. "I'm actually about to escort you down the aisle if you let me," he says with a grin. "You seem to be dressed for a wedding. Unless, of course, this is all an elaborate plan to bump into me again?"

I cock my head teasingly. "You think this is elaborate?"

"Have you seen the menu?"

"That's just Mama S.," I say with a little wave. "But since I am all dressed up, let's do this." I swing my hips and my dress swishes around my knees, the bright pink of the flowers at the hem blurring into the black. "Do you like it? Look—pockets!"

"You look beautiful."

I freeze mid-swing, exhaling in a soft huff as warmth blooms in my chest. The words are simple and sweet and–from the way he looks at me–sincere.

"Thank you," I whisper, for once at a loss for an easy comeback. He holds my gaze for a long moment and some part of me, the same part that went mushy when Denzel Duke started singing to me, melts like warm butter.

Oh no.

Adam returns to the back of the church to collect more guests. "Get a move on, Emmett," he calls, giving my escort a wink over his shoulder. "And Shae, I like the hair."

The wink brings me back to reality—that this is a man I bumped into yesterday; I don't know anything about him. Or need to.

Or should want to.

"So you know Adam?" I tuck my arm through his, resting my hand on the crook of his elbow. He covers it with his own and the simple touch sends a swarm of butterflies into my stomach. "Just so you know, if I was really stalking you, you wouldn't have a clue," I add, doing my best to ignore the flapping insects now mixing with the warm butter and making a gooey mess.

"I'm a little frightened," he says. I notice his eyes are more gray than blue today, but still with the envy-inducing lashes.

"As you should be." We start down the aisle, walking slow enough for Adam to pass us again on the way back. "So who are you? Or is this what you like to do on a beautiful Saturday afternoon?"

Beautiful. He called me beautiful.

"Brother of the bride."

"Your sister is Eleanor?" I ask stupidly. "Why didn't you tell me?"

"She's Ellie, and I didn't say anything since the topic of weddings or family or plans for the weekend hadn't come up before you ran out with your coffee." His smile is wide and white and contagious. "I'm sure if you'd stuck around a little longer, Rufus would have asked about your plans for the weekend and we would have been off and running."

"Rufus. Your nephew," I say to remind myself that he already has a life and it doesn't include me.

"He's my brother's kid, but he lives at the farm with us, and Ellie and I help my dad raise him." He wrinkles his nose in a truly adorable gesture. "It's kind of a long story."

"So in the short version, do I at least get your name?" I ask, forgetting about not wanting to know anything about him.

"Emmett Gulliver Pike. Very happy to meet you, Shae Sullison." He leans down close enough that I smell the minty freshness of his breath. "Rufus has been Googling you. I think he knows most of the TikToks by heart."

I can't help but be pleased. "I have a fan. But—Gulliver?"

"Don't ask." I don't know how a dimple can appear when he grimaces, but it does and it makes him even cuter.

"Oh, but I really have to."

"My mother was a big lover of English literature."

"And there's a lot of great English literature out there, especially ones that don't contain names that start with G and rhyme with bulliver."

"Is that even a word?"

"It sounded better in my head."

Our eyes lock. Seriously lock, like there's a padlock and key involved, and I physically can't stop smiling. I realize too late that he's stopped beside the pew where Dawson and Natasha are already seated, and they, as well as the rest of the pew, are staring at me expectantly.

"Here you are," Emmett says finally. "Groom's side."

"That's good. I hate to admit that I haven't even met your sister. Although I'm very happy for them. I've known James since I was nine. He used to tease me something crazy and was the very first person to point out that I had breasts."

"Maybe you shouldn't mention that in your speech."

"Actually, I think that was Adam, so James is safe. Give me another minute and I'll come up with something even more embarrassing to tell you."

"It might be worth talking to you before I say my speech."

"It's always worth it to talk to me."

"I'm sure you're right."

My stomach literally attempts to flip over as Emmett brushes my hand. Once again, I'm at a loss for words and clumsily slide into the pew beside Dawson.

"Who's that?" Natasha leans across Dawson, her eyes wide with admiration as Emmett walks away.

And yes, he takes a quick peek back at me.

"No one." I sigh.

"He looks like someone." Dawson looks at me expectantly.

"Brother of the bride."

"Is that it?"

"I met him yesterday," I say after a long pause. "When Adam stopped at Pain au Chocolate. I was talking to him and now he's here."

Dawson raises his eyebrows. "Did you know he'd be here?"

I give a quick shake of my head. "No idea. I wasn't talking to him that long. It's just…" I trail off as I notice the shadow of an usher escorting another guest down the aisle beside me. Of course it's Emmett, and I meet his gaze with a shy smile. "It's weird," I hiss after he passes.

"What's weird about it? It's a cool coincidence," Dawson corrects. "Or fate, if you want to go deeper."

"There's nothing *fate* about it. He's a guy I met and now he's here. End of story."

End of story.

"Okay," Dawson says mildly.

"It is okay."

"Are *you* okay?" He gives me a strange look.

"I'm fine. Great. Why wouldn't I be?"

Emmett

I LOOK BACK AT Shae after I drop her off at the pew and she's smiling at me. A real smile, not just the excited, hey-you're-here grin that she greeted me with. Everyone likes small-world stories, coincidences where your first crush ends up as your neighbour thirty years later, or as the parent of the kid your son has a crush on.

To be honest, I didn't believe Adam when he told me Shae would be at the wedding. Being next door during the pictures is one thing, but to actually attend the same wedding is another.

But then, there she was right in front of me, her skirt swishing, smiling like I made her day by being here. And I don't want to leave; I want to talk more, find out more. There's something about her...

It's very distracting.

I finish escorting the last of the guests to their seats until Mama S. gives the order for us to assemble at the front of the church. I take my spot beside Adam and face the guests.

It's easy to pick out Shae in the sea of people beaming with anticipation. She's got a great smile, plus the hair makes it even easier. It takes a moment until I realize it's because she's standing on the pew, towering over those sitting around her as she waves at an unseen person at the back of the church.

The guy beside her pulls her down, and she's swallowed by the other guests. There's an occasional glimpse of the pink hair, but there are so many other colours around her that it's hard to tell.

James's side of the church definitely favours bright, bold colours, and Shae is no exception. Although yesterday Shae's hair seemed brighter, almost fuchsia. Today it's more muted, the pink almost blending into shoulder-length dark curls.

Does she change it every day? What colour is planned for to-morrow?

Why am I thinking about tomorrow and Shae in the same sen-tence?

Adam leans over like he knows who I'm looking for. "I told you she'd be here."

The music changes before I can reply and a group of flower girls appear at the door of the church, adorable in their pink sundresses and flowers in their hair.

Rufus is at the back of the pack, escorting the oldest flower girl slowly down the aisle. I watch proudly as he smiles and nods at the guests on the aisle, trying to stay casual, even though I know he's nervous about his role.

He does great.

Until he gets to Shae's pew.

"Hi, Shae," he whispers loud enough for me to hear.

"You look so cool." Shae smiles widely. "And you're doing a great job."

Rufus's smile lights up the church.

The bridesmaids appear; three are friends of Ellie's, girls I've known for years. The other is Neely, wearing a soft pink dress, looking quite a bit different than she did when I met her last night.

"You look amazing." I hear Shae's voice again, a little louder than what's warranted for church. Neely just shakes her head as a flush coats her cheeks as she finishes the slow walk.

As the bridesmaids take their places opposite us, the music changes into the recognizable Wedding March, and I have a bad moment.

It's the first wedding I've been to since my own. My eyes fill with sudden tears as I think of Alex and how she didn't get any of this. There was no her walking down the aisle on her father's arm, no trembling anticipation as I waited for her at the front of the church.

I wanted that for her; still want it so badly that it hurts.

And then Ellie appears at the back of the church clutching my father's arm. The hurt fades away into the swell of music as my heart swells with pride and love as my sister makes her way down the aisle.

It seems like forever until I can relax.

After the ceremony, it's time for more pictures, which means I have to smile politely for over an hour, being pushed and prodded by the photographer, and all the while not putting my hands where they shouldn't be on my bridesmaid counterpart, which is Neely.

She's nice. Very cute. And she'd be running the photoshoot if anyone let her.

Which they don't, so she spends most of the time simmering at a low boil, muttering under her breath about all the ways she would do things differently.

Getting my picture taken is never a favourite activity, but I grin and bear it because Ellie is my sister, and I want her to be happy. Besides, she's got Ethan to deal with as well as Rufus. I'm proud to admit, my nephew is better behaved than my little brother.

So it takes some time for us to get to the reception, which is held at the Yacht Club with a view of Lake Ontario. And when I get here, I find the party is already started. Music fills the room the reception is in, people are mingling with drinks in hand, and at the centre of it all is a pink-haired girl on the dance floor.

I've never seen someone look so sexy doing the chicken dance. Not only doing it but leading the entire group.

Rufus appears at my side, eyes wary. "There's Shae." I nod in response, unable to take my eyes off the way she flaps her arms. "She's not related to me, right?"

"God, I hope not," I mutter, my eyes on her swinging dress and the shapely legs under it. She's kicked off her shoes somewhere.

"Good." Without another word, he's off to join the crowd surrounding Shae, which consists of a good portion of the older generation and every kid in the place.

For once I wish I had the confidence of my nephew.

Shae smiles at Rufus and laughs. Thanks to Ellie's teachings during their kitchen dance parties, he's quick to put his own spin on the chicken dance moves. And then as if she can tell I'm staring, Shae glances over her shoulder and meets my gaze.

I give her a little salute. She responds with an enthusiastic wave, gesturing for me to join her. "No way," I say with a shake of my head.

"Why is she trying to get you to dance? Doesn't she know what you look like on the dance floor?" Grayson asks, appearing at my side as quickly as Rufus had.

There's a pit in my stomach when I think of Grayson running off to join Shae as fast as Rufus did. "I'm not about to dance."

"Don't. You'll scare her off, at least until you've had something to loosen you up. That the vlogger girl? Rufus already told me she was here." With a last look at the dance floor, he turns to the bartender and asks for two beers.

"Shae. She's James's sister's friend," I say after I have my drink in hand.

Grayson raises his eyebrow. "The sister is the tall blonde, isn't she? The one in the wedding party?"

"Neely." I see her at the entrance and point her out to Grayson. "Ah."

I nudge him. "I know that voice."

"I should hope so," Grayson drawls. "I've only known you my entire life."

"She's Ellie's new sister-in-law. Shouldn't that make her off-limits?"

"Nobody said anything about sisters-in-law, and she's not mine. Besides," he says with a smirk, walking backwards away from me. "It's a wedding. You've been out of the game for too long, bro. Best time *ever* to pick up the ladies. You'd do good to remember that."

He turns and disappears into the crowd, leaving me shaking my head.

Chapter Six

Shae

I'M WINDED FROM THE dancing but have a big smile on my face as I pull myself out of the crowd gathered around me on the dance floor in the corner of the room.

"Shae, you come back here and dance with me!" Uncle Giancarlo thunders as I back away. "We must polka!"

"I'll be back," I promise. Instead of the dancing sounds of an accordion, the electric beat of MC Hammer takes over.

"Can't Touch This," Rufus shouts as he strikes a pose in the middle of the floor. Cheers ring out as the elderly guests cluster around him, and I snap a few pictures before he's hidden by the suits pulled out of mothballs and the brightly patterned dresses of Neely's family.

I love Neely's family, even creepy second cousin Marco, who drinks too much at the family Christmas party and asks the girls to sit on his lap to ask Santa for presents.

Maybe I don't love Marco.

I wend my way through the tables set for dinner with center-pieces of squat bouquets of roses, the colours ranging from the blush of Neely's dress to a fun bubblegum pink. The room is full of pink, but it's not too much.

I fit right in.

I pose for a quick selfie at Table 2 with the hashtags *#Ellieand-James* and *#Happyweddingday*. Then I take a picture of my bare feet, tagging the brand and shade of nail polish and adding *#sorefeet #toomuchdancingnevertoomuch*.

The likes and comments have already started by the time I shove my phone into the little sequined phone case I wear across my chest like a satchel.

I love my life—the travel, the adventures, meeting all sorts of interesting people. But I know I wouldn't be able to have this life without my followers, which in turn helps me get sponsors. So maybe I would still have this life, but I'd have to pay a lot more for it. I have their love and support for now, and I don't take it for granted.

If I had a longer life in store for myself, maybe I wouldn't want to be a social influencer. Maybe I'd want to be a doctor or a dancer or an artist who designs those plastic Pop Harry Potter and Star Wars characters.

I'd want to be *something*. I used to think I was born to do something.

But since none of that is in the cards, I've become a social influencer with enough followers to guarantee at least another year of trips can be paid for.

I bump into Neely on her way to where Dawson and Natasha are making good use out of the free bar.

"Look at you!" I crow, grabbing her hands to admire her. "Amazing."

Neely has spent the past three months complaining about the dress. "Who picks pink for their wedding colour?" was her most common lament. I had to agree with her; while I love the colour, I won't wear a whole dress of it. From what Neely had said, I expected a gaudy shade of fuchsia with the typical big bum bow.

Instead, Neely drifted down the aisle in a blush-coloured, sleeveless chiffon dress that kissed the floor at the back and did something miraculous with her colouring. Most days, Neely is *pretty*—there is no questioning that. Long straight blonde hair hangs down her back without a hint of wave or errant frizz, eyes a strange mix of green and hazel that look golden when she's happy, and a peaches-and-cream complexion with nary a freckle. She even tans well, like gently toasted bread. Even on her bad days, Neely can easily pull off perfect.

But today she's more than simply pretty. Someone curled her hair, a sight I haven't seen since the experiment with the flexible rods in eighth grade left her bedroom full of the stench of burnt hair and Neely swearing off curly hair forever. But now, long ringlets hang down her back, with flowers and diamante pins caught up within the mass of gold.

"Yes, you mentioned that as I walked down the aisle," Neely says in an admonishing voice. But her smile tells me she doesn't mean it. "I think the whole church heard."

"Couldn't help myself. You look *hot*. Actually, not hot," I decide with a cock of my head. "Too elegant for that. You look like the beautiful woman that you are." With an ache in my heart, I throw my arms around my friend, hugging her close. "My beautiful Neely."

"I agree with that assessment, but also that she looks hot," a drawling voice says behind me. "If I'm allowed to say something like that without offending?"

I turn to find a tall man with a killer suit and longish hair that flops into his eyes. "Why do you look familiar?" I demand.

"Why do men insist on calling women *hot* when it only objectifies their sexuality?" Neely snaps at the same time.

He raises his hands, still holding a pint glass of beer and takes a step back. "Whoa. I see I've interrupted something here, and so I'll take my leave. But to answer your question—I hope you recognize me, if you're on social media as much as you are, Ms. Social Influencer extraordinaire."

Neely turns to me with a roll of her eyes. "Guess he recognizes you."

"Do you want a picture?" I ask. It's difficult not to feel awkward when people seem to think they know me. Of course, it never bothers some of the social influencers. My life may be all over social media, but there's more to me than happy-go-lucky Shae with a thirst for adventure.

Neely came up with that description for the vlog.

"And you," —he turns to Neely and actually gives her a sweeping bow. "—Are the loveliest bridesmaid I've ever had the pleasure of watching. You are not hot, but your loveliness makes me warm under the collar. You're like a modern-day Cinderella, and I hope I get to take off your glass slippers because I give a mean foot rub." He grins mischievously, and I have to smile at the effort.

And then I wait for Neely to carve him a new one because Neely doesn't like guys who are obvious. Or make an effort. Or display an ounce of charm.

But there's something about this guy that I hope will be her type. Maybe it's the ease with which he talks to us, or the smile. Or maybe it's the suit—purple so dark that it looks black, with thin pinstripes of lilac and a shirt and tie the same shade.

Plus, he's super cute.

"You're a bit much, aren't you?" Neely asks. I stare at her, incredulous to see a hint of a smile in her eyes. Did I miss something here?

"They do call me Superman," he says with a waggle of his eyebrows. "I guess that makes me much of something."

"That's because his name sounds like a superhero," another voice from behind me says drily.

"Emmett!" Why do I sound so eager? And how can I stop the flutter in my stomach at the sight of him? I raise my hand to my mouth in an attempt to physically wipe the smile from my lips, which is pointless because my face lights up again when he smiles at me. "Nice wedding," I chirp, inwardly cringing at the overly perky tone.

"It was. You seem to be enjoying yourself." His eyes skirt down to my bare feet to my pink-painted toenails. "Your toes match the flowers on your dress."

"I hope so. The colour is Strawberry Watermelon Shine."

"Shiny. I saw you dancing."

"With Rufus. He's my new number one fan."

"I'm sure he'll be happy to hear that. Maybe too happy."

I really like the way his eyes crinkle in the corner when he laughs. "Did you eat the cupcake?" I ask forlornly, my hands clasped at my chest. "My cupcake."

"I haven't yet," he admits. "It's still waiting. Maybe we can share."

"You'd share your Reuben-made cupcake with *me*?"

"Yes," Emmett says simply, and something about his tone stops my playfulness cold. Not because he's serious or upset, but the way he looks at me when he says it. Almost like he's willing to share the world with me.

I've seen looks like that before and they're very off-putting. They make me want to push the look aside and pretend it never happened.

I can't seem to do that right now.

Oh no.

"So, Superman," Neely says to break the awkward moment when Emmett and I are staring at each other. "What's your real name? Clark Parker?"

Superman smiles widely, his teeth looking perfect and very white in the dimness of the dark bar area. "No, but you get points for a good guess. Grayson Grant, at your service. Happy that I have no power, nor responsibility."

I nod, relieved to have broken free of Emmett's spell. "That would be a *super* superhero name."

"You were on The Suitor." Neely's expression is flat and cool. "I remember that line. I'm afraid you lose points for originality."

"Ouch." But his grin is like the common cold; so contagious that Neely can't help but smile in return.

I glance at her with surprise.

I don't know if this Grayson Grant is Neely's type, but it's easy to guess he'd be mine. Easygoing and fun, not to mention great looking—an hour with Grayson and I'd forget Denzel Duke ever asked me to stay with him.

But then I glance at Emmett standing smiling and solid beside his friend. Maybe he's not as flashy but he still looks good.

Plus—butterflies when he looks at me.

Which maybe isn't a good thing.

The voice of the DJ crackles over the speaker. "Our new bride and groom would like some food. Put your hands together and give a warm welcome for the stars of this evening, Ellie Pike and James Scalzo!"

The happy couple appears at the door, with the rest of the wedding party, including Rufus, clustered behind them.

Neely and Emmett share a horrified expression and rush away without a word, leaving half-empty glasses on the bar behind them.

"I guess they need to be somewhere." My voice is shaky from the knowledge that Neely isn't perfectly fulfilling her role as bridesmaid, as much as from Emmett's gaze. Neely always does what she's supposed to. It's how my life runs so smoothly.

I glance sideways at Grayson as cheers fill the reception area as Ellie and James make their way to the head table. Was it he who threw Neely off her game?

Doesn't seem possible. Neely never lets herself get distracted by men.

After the enthusiastic round of applause begins to taper off, guests are quick to start the convoy into the dining room.

"This looks like our cue to take our seats," Grayson says. "And seeing as we've been left on our own, I'll escort you to your table, which will hopefully be the same one I'm at."

He slips a hand on my back and leads me into the dining room. There are no butterflies from his touch.

Emmett

MIDWAY THROUGH DINNER, I look at the back of the room where Shae is sitting at a table with Grayson and Pepper and a bunch of people I don't recognize. Their laughter carries over the rest of the room, and the sound of glasses clinking keeps interrupting the meal, as the group demands Ellie and James kiss. Once the wine begins to really flow, it seems like every five minutes brings about a ringing cry of "Kiss, kiss," until a frowning Neely changes things and makes singing a song mandatory for the bride and groom to kiss.

That doesn't stop Shae's table. They come up with dance moves to ABBA's "Mamma Mia," even changing a few of the lyrics to incorporate Ellie's and James's names.

I can't help to notice Grayson is right beside Shae as they dance.

"They seem like they're getting along," Neely says in a rueful voice. I look over to see Grayson refilling Shae's glass as she looks up at him with a wide smile.

The same smile she gave me.

"That's fine." My response is automatic but doesn't sound convincing in the least. "It's good. They'd be good together."

"Really? You're just going to watch your friend take your girl?" Neely reaches for the bottle of white wine on the table before us and drains it into her glass.

"She's not my girl."

"But you'd like her to be. I talked to Adam, who told me his plan."

"There's a plan?"

"There should always be a plan." Neely leans forward and rests her chin on her fist to look at me. Her gaze is so direct that I feel like I've been flattened on a slide so she can view me under a microscope. "So what's your story? Since we're technically family."

"If you'd like to consider in-laws family." I smile, trying to ease her intensity.

It doesn't work.

"The family grapevine says you were married—the grapevine being Adam," Neely begins with a thoughtful expression. "But she died. That must have been very difficult."

"It wasn't my finest moment," I admit.

She frowns. "Why do you say that?"

I pause, surprised at the question. Because my meltdown was in the public eye, at least in the world of baseball, it's hard to forget that it wasn't the global event that it felt like. "I'm not proud of the way I dealt with it," I say carefully.

Neely leans closer so that even though we're talking at a table filled with laughing voices, it feels intimate. "Everyone deals with grief in their own way."

"I dealt with it by taking a promising baseball career and blowing it up." I touch my fingers together, mimicking an explosion, with sound effects to boot.

Neely says nothing, only stares at me with her golden eyes. "I wouldn't tell Shae that," she says slowly.

"Why would I say anything to her?" I ask roughly. "I barely know her. I just met her. I took her cupcake. She must hate me."

Neely smiles almost serenely. "Shae doesn't hate—anything or anyone. She's the best person ever, and since you know her now, you will fall for her. Hard and fast, like always. It's like Thanos says in the Avengers movie—it's inevitable."

"You just quoted a Marvel movie." I shake my head. "You surprise me, Neely."

"I surprise myself sometimes," she says with a trace of bitterness in her voice.

"Now it's my turn to ask why do you say that?"

She gives a violent shake of her head, blonde curls flying only to fall perfectly in place. "Uh uh. I need a lot more wine to start telling secrets. A lot." For emphasis, she picks up her glass and finishes it.

"Well, let's see what we can do about that." I signal to a nearby waiter to bring another bottle. "Since we're stuck here watching the two of them have the time of their lives."

Neely's eyes seem to pop as she clutches my arm. "Do you know that movie?"

"What movie?" I ask, lost as to where the conversation just veered off to.

"Dirty Dancing."

"It's Ellie's all-time favourite movie." I roll my eyes. "She's only made me watch it thousands of times. I prefer a good action movie, but my sister has a pout on her that—"

"It's James's favourite movie too," Neely interrupts. "It's how they fell in love."

"How?" I ask stupidly.

"They were swimming in some pond and Ellie wanted to try the dance scene from the movie where Patrick—"

"I've seen the movie *thousands* of times."

"So you know," she relents. "How they kept trying to do the catch in the water but Ellie's bathing suit was so slippery so she took it off—"

I clamp my hands over my ears. "I don't need to hear that." I move them to my eyes. "And now I can't unsee it." Lowering my hands, I look suspiciously at Neely. "Where was this pond?"

"I think at your farm. Don't you ever talk to your sister?"

"I talk to her every day but not about naked dancing in the water." I tip my head back and breathe deep. "Did not need to know that."

"You should talk more," Neely says smugly. "It's a fun story."

"Where is this fun story going?" I ask ruefully. "And please tell me no one is going to be talking about it in their speeches?"

"Oh, probably. Or maybe not." Neely gestures with her chin at the table to the right of the head table. "The nonnas won't like it. Or maybe they will," she adds with a laugh. "I have a feeling the older Scalzo generation got up to some shenanigans themselves."

The waiter takes that opportunity to deliver a cold bottle of wine to us. "I need that now," I say, grabbing the bottle so I can vanquish thoughts of a naked Ellie frolicking with great-nonna in the water.

"Back to where I was going with this," Neely says, holding out her glass for me to refill. "Because dancing in the water was when they fell in love, Adam and I thought it would be fun to remake the dance for them tonight."

"Adam?" I glance at the other end of the long table where Adam is holding court with Cousin Victor, two bridesmaids and Rufus. "Not naked, right?"

Neely smiles. "No, fully clothed. You'd never know that he took ballroom dancing for years, would you? Until you see him dance. After I stopped ballet, I took it with him for a few years."

"You were a ballerina?" It explains Neely's grace and poise.

"I danced," she corrects with a tight-lipped smile. "I wanted to be a ballerina, but wanting and being are two different things."

"Oh, I know." A flash of understanding seems to pass between us. "All too well. And so does Grayson, actually."

"Oh, really?" Another glance at the table shows Grayson telling some story that has him gesturing wildly with his arms and sending the entire table into laughter. "Well, back to our dance," Neely says dismissively.

"Yours and Adam's."

"Well, that's the thing. Adam can do all the moves—perfectly. He's so good. But he can't manage the lift. I don't know if I'm too heavy—"

I've listened to my sister moan about her weight for years, so I know the exact look to give Neely. "I don't think that's the problem. What are you, a buck ten soaking wet?"

"No, but thanks." She smiles and flicks a glance at me under her eyelashes. "He might be afraid of dropping me because he *did* drop me before—"

"And you want to give him that chance again?"

"No." Neely looks me over slowly, her gaze pausing on my upper torso. "I want to do it with you. Will you help me?"

And that's how, thirty minutes later, between dinner and dessert, I find myself shuffled to the side of the dance floor as Neely and Adam do an incredible remake of the iconic dance from Dirty Dancing.

"You just have to catch me," Neely said.

"It'll be easy," she promised.

"Just stand there," she assured me.

It *sounds* simple until the end when Neely backs up to get a run at it and Adam moves out of the way for me to step in and do the lift.

We tried it three times in the hallway leading to the kitchen, and each time I did manage to catch her and lift her high up into the air. It was shaky enough for Patrick Swayze to be glaring at me from the heavens above, but I managed.

But I never imagined the terror I'd feel standing in the middle of the dance floor as Neely runs straight at me with an expression of such determined intensity that my knees shake.

She's going to kill me if I drop her.

Chapter Seven

Shae

"**W**HAT ARE THEY DOING?" I cry as Adam and Neely move together on the dance floor, perfectly in sync with the opening bars of "The Time of My Life." Because our table is shoved so far in the back corner, it's hard for me to see over the many heads between us and the dance floor, so I clamour onto my chair to get a better look.

I have ended up at the same table as Grayson.

That doesn't really surprise me, nor does the location of the table—at the far corner of the vast reception hall. A quick survey of the table tells me that this group is neither family, nor technically friends of Ellie and James; I sit with Dawson and Natasha, Grayson and his sister Pepper, Adam's boyfriend Patrick, and the spouses of some of the wedding party.

"Did you know about this?" I ask Dawson over the music.

He shakes his head. "But they did the routine back in high school, remember?"

"That's right." Open-mouthed with awe, I watch my best friend dance with her brother, every move perfect. The look on Ellie's and James's faces as they watch the dance is one I'll never forget and I pull out my phone to take a picture to show Neely later.

And then I snap a bunch of pictures of Neely to post.

As I take a selfie of myself standing on the chair, I feel a warm hand on the small of my back. "Your friend can *dance*," he says with a low whistle. "Wow."

"Isn't she amazing?" I ask proudly. "Twelve years of ballet, six of hip hop, four of tap, and ballroom on top of that. You should have seen her when she was doing all that." I give a simple shrug. "She was incredible."

"Was? She still is. Why doesn't she do it professionally?" Grayson's eyes are wide and admiring, and I feel a flicker of hope for Neely. As much as Grayson seems tailor-made for me—even Natasha whispered it to me in the middle of the pasta course—Neely needs some fun. It can't be fun taking care of me all the time, as much as I tell her I don't need it.

"Car accident," I tell him with a rueful shrug. "She wasn't really hurt but it did something to her balance. It would have been fine for most people, but Dancing Neely is no mere mortal." I sigh heavily. "Just incredible. I went to all her recitals."

"You didn't dance?"

"Oh, I did, but I stopped when—I was fourteen when I stopped." The memory of my tears and pleading as my mother insisted on pulling me from all my dance classes still lingers in my mind, even after all this time.

"She should talk to Emmett," Grayson says, keeping his hand on my back as we watch the dance move to the crescendo. "He took a ball to his head, ended his career. Well, that and other things helped." He gives me a sad smile. "All I had to deal with was a torn UCL that ended things."

"You're a ballplayer?"

"Were. Both of us." He leans closer. "You should Google us. There's a thing—both of us drafted at the same time, same team, from the same town."

"That's so cool. I'll check you out; both of you. But first—a selfie." I lean down and snap a picture of Grayson and me. "Your Suitor fans will love it."

"Maybe you can—what the hell is Emmett doing?"

I focus on the dance floor just in time to see Emmett switch spots with Adam as Neely backs up to do the leap into the air. "What...?"

Neely runs...she jumps, and Emmett catches her perfectly, balancing her easily as he lifts her above his head.

"Oh my God," I shriek, snapping pictures as I watch Emmett hold Neely for a long minute, his hands on her waist, her sheer skirt draped before him like a curtain.

I'm in awe of the grace of the two of them, even though I can't help the painful twinge that *I* want to be the one Emmett is holding like that.

Neely deserves to have fun. And if it's Emmett she's interested in...

I brush off Grayson's help and step off the chair. I tell myself it's only the wine that makes me stumble on the landing.

Ellie rushes onto the dance floor to tearfully embrace Neely and Emmett, and then Adam.

"That was amazing." Pepper, Grayson's sister, is soft-eyed and smiling. "Ellie's always loved that movie. We used to watch it all the time."

"I know." Grayson rolls his eyes. "You used to make Emmett and me watch it over and over and over."

After the show-stopping dance display, dessert is served, along with the speeches. I love hearing the stories of how people met. I don't know what is my most favourite—when friendship leads to love, or when they can't stand each other at the start.

It seems to me that when two people are fated to be together, love will find a way. Which is why I need to be vigilant, especially around a guy like Emmett, to make sure there's no way love can get to me.

Emmett doesn't make a speech. I watch as he listens to the maid of honour and best man speak, then Neely, because of course Neely needs to speak at her brother's wedding.

When she's finished, Emmett leans close enough for their shoulders to touch. I wonder what he's saying to her.

She smiles in response and my stomach twists at the sight. I've never liked the same guy as Neely—as close as we are, we're very different and therefore have different types.

Actually, I don't have a type, other than he needs to make me laugh, and Neely hasn't been interested in anyone for a while.

Dawson leans across me to snag the bottle of wine.

Neely hasn't been interested in anyone because she's fixated on Dawson. And Dawson, as cute and adorable as he might be, is completely clueless. Although, if Natasha and his other girlfriends have anything to say about it, Neely might be too deep for Dawson.

So, if my perception of Emmett is right, then he and Neely would be perfect for each other.

Great.

Speeches over, the lights dim and the DJ takes the microphone again to announce the first dance, and Ellie and James take the floor.

Grayson leans over to me in the middle of the song. "Ellie's really great," he says speaking loudly over the music. "In case you're wondering. I don't know how close you are to James."

"He's like a brother to me," I admit. "So it's good to know."

"It's like that with Ellie and me," he says. "Except when I was seventeen and she seduced me in their barn."

"She seduced you?" I glance at Ellie dancing in James's arms and back to Grayson with a raised eyebrow. "You don't seem the type to let the woman make the first move."

"Are you kidding? I love that." He gives me a sly smile. "So if that's what's stopping you..."

I laugh instead of responding.

The lights stay low and the music slows as the DJ invites the wedding party to join Ellie and James on the dance floor. I turn back to the table to avoid watching Emmett leading Neely away from the head table as Rufus skids to a stop beside my chair.

"Will you dance with me?" he asks breathlessly.

"Don't you have a flower girl who's waiting for you?" The last thing I want is a heartbroken little girl about to burst into tears when she sees me with her date.

Rufus shakes his head. "Aunt Ellie told me to find someone to dance with because the flower girls are too little. I found you."

"You did find me." With a smile, I stand up, only to have Rufus hold up his hand.

"Wait. Emmett says I have to do this right." To my delight, Rufus does a little bow. "May I have this dance?" he asks politely, channelling his inner Mr. Bingley.

"You may. Do I have to put on my shoes?"

As I get to my feet, Rufus looks me up and down. "No shoes, because then you'll be taller than me."

I would tower over him with my heels, but without I'm only a shade taller. "That won't be a problem soon. You'll grow."

"Not soon enough for those shoes," he guffaws.

"Looking good, little dude," Grayson calls after us.

As Rufus leads me by the hand to the dance floor, my eyes find Emmett and Neely a few feet away moving around the floor.

"Did your uncle know you were going to dance with me?" Rufus' hand clamps onto my lower back and begins to lead me in slow circles, pretty confidently for someone so young. When I was his age, I stood two feet apart from the boy and barely touched his shoulders.

"He suggested it," he says with a big grin that shows a mouthful of teeth that are going to need braces in another year or two. "And he told me not to scare you off because he wants to dance with you next."

"He does, does he?" The thought produces a swirl of delight—and then dread. Emmett isn't Grayson and I have a suspicion that saying goodnight to him isn't going to be as easy as it was with Denzel.

"How would someone scare you off?" Rufus cocks his head, looking like he really wants to know the answer.

"It's pretty hard to scare me," I confess, lowering my voice. "But I wouldn't like it if a guy was a jerk, or arrogant. Confident—yes. But cocky and arrogant are a no-go."

"Good to know." Rufus nods. "Emmett's not a jerk."

"I got that impression. What about Grayson?"

"You can't like Grayson!" His voice is louder than it needs to be and a couple next to us glances over.

"I didn't say I liked him," I hiss. "He seems like a nice guy... I thought maybe for Neely."

"Oh. Well, that's okay then."

"I'm so glad you approve."

As Rufus opens his mouth, most likely with another question, Emmett and Neely glide up. "The dance was amazing," I tell her. "Adam looks like he's still dancing every day."

"Except that he can't fit into those tight pants anymore." Neely glances at Emmett with a defensive expression. "What? He's my brother. I'm the only one who can say anything about his pants."

Emmett lifts his hand from Neely's waist. "I didn't say a word."

"You did very well too," I say to Emmett.

"I stood there and caught her," he says ruefully.

Neely pats him on the shoulder. "Thank you for catching me. Unfortunately, not everyone could have managed that."

I meet Neely's eye. "Adam," we say in unison.

"You should see the comments you got," I add. "The Instagram page blew up. You know we're going to have a ton of copycatters that you're going to have to comment on. And maybe judge."

"You posted that?" Emmett asks with a frown.

"I didn't tag you, or even use your name," I say quickly. "I don't do that without permission. You can't really even see your face. Just your arms and...muscles." I smile foolishly, not wanting to let on how much I approved of how he worked those muscles.

"You seem very strong," Neely says with all seriousness and I smile to see a flush spread across Emmett's face.

"You really do," I add.

Obviously not liking where the conversation had ended up, Rufus not so subtly moves me a few feet away from them. "Tell me more about your vlog," he asks eagerly. "I watched that zip-lining video sixteen times. Were you seriously, all-the-way, naked? Because I couldn't see anything."

"How old are you Rufus?"

"Eleven, almost twelve."

"Then I'm glad you couldn't see anything. We made sure everything was covered in the video."

"That one girl screamed so loud. I want to try zip-lining, but I don't know about the naked part, especially with girls around." He makes the same face Emmett did when I invited him onto the dance floor during the Chicken Dance.

"You should keep your clothes on," I advise. "I try to as well. This was just a one-time thing."

"Who's the guy who plays the video games?" Rufus asks. "The old guy, not Dawson."

"That's my sort of grandfather, Mike. He's very good at Fortnite."

"Not better than me." The rest of the song is peppered with questions about the videos that I've posted.

"Do you want to do a selfie?" I ask when I can get a word in. "I can tag you if you think that's okay with your dad." I automatically glance at Emmett.

"Emmett's not my dad—he is." Rufus points across the room at a shorter, sleeker version of Emmett sitting at the family table with an older, gray-haired man. He has the same eyes as Emmett, so I guess father.

"That's right. Uncle Emmett."

"Emmett won't want you to tag him because of all the baseball stuff," Rufus says. "I tell him no one cares anymore but I don't think he believes me."

"What about the baseball stuff? He played with Grayson, didn't he?"

"They were awesome," Rufus's voice is reverent. "And that they were both drafted at the same time, to the same team."

"Grayson said that." I make a mental note to Google for more info. "That is cool."

"There was talk of naming the ball diamond in Ashbury after them, but Emmett said no." Rufus makes another face. "I told him it would be cool, but he says he doesn't need the attention."

As the song ends, I pull out my phone and pose with Rufus. "Post it later," Neely calls. "Let's switch partners."

Rufus seems happy to dance with Neely, which leaves me with Emmett. "Is that okay?" Emmett asks me.

"Are you asking me to dance?" I ask with a coquettish tilt to my head. "Because Rufus set the bar pretty high when he asked me."

"I'm not letting that kid beat me in anything." With a move that's as good as when he caught Neely, Emmett pulls me close so that my body has no choice but to mould into his. A jolt rushes through me, lingering tremors as if I've stuck my finger in a light socket. "Dance with me." The look in his eyes makes my breath stutter in my chest. "Please."

His arm is strong and tight and his hand is warm as it closes over mine. "Okay," I whisper, hoping I don't melt into a puddle.

Oh no.

Emmett

SHE SMELLS GOOD. SHE smells amazing.

Cookies and flowers and...strawberries? Maybe it smells like strawberries because of the pink—I surreptitiously sniff at Shae's hair.

No, definitely strawberries.

I've danced with my share of girls and women, and Neely, just a few minutes ago, but none of them felt like this in my arms. It's like she belongs there.

I can't help the smile spreading across my face.

"I see you're at Grayson's table," I say cautiously. The fabric of Shae's dress is slippery, and I tell myself that's why I tighten my hold.

"And Pepper."

I've been the recipient of too many "Tell me about Grayson," "What's he like?", "Is he interested in me?" queries in my life. For Shae to mention Pepper right off the bat makes my heart sing.

"I like her," Shae adds. "Grayson, too. He's...interesting."

"How interesting?"

Shae leans back so she can look me in the eye, slipping her hand out of my grasp to rest it on my shoulder, casual-like, as if she doesn't feel the electricity coursing between us.

Maybe she can't. Maybe it's just me.

"Are you asking if I'm interested in Grayson?" Shae's gaze is steady and direct, her eyes such a dark brown that it's hard to tell where the pupils begin.

Her waist is so tiny, with the tempting little swell of buttocks so close to my reach. I clasp my hands together like I'm handcuffed and feel the slide of her tiny hand across my shoulder.

"Are you?" I ask, not wanting to hear the answer.

"No," she says with a serious expression. Then she grins. "Are you?"

"No." My shoulders relax as I begin to breathe again. "He drools when he sleeps. And his taste in beer is horrible."

"Is that what you're looking for? Good taste in beer?"

"I prefer bourbon actually, but it's a start." I haven't touched bourbon in years, but I still can taste the smokiness on my tongue. Bourbon never got me in trouble—rye did. Rye and ginger; rye and Coke; straight up shots of the stuff.

The thought of it makes my stomach clench.

"I don't drink much hard stuff," Shae says.

"As long as you don't drink those sticky sweet wine coolers, we're fine." I fight for casual and I think I make it. Especially when Shae makes a face.

"I was impressed with your dancing," she says, and I'm happy to switch the topic.

"I'm impressed if you think that was dancing."

"Seriously, I've seen Adam and Neely pull off that move a bunch of times and it's never looked that graceful."

"Thank you."

"Grayson mentioned that you both played baseball. I never thought of baseball players being very dance-like."

"We're not. Especially catchers, like me. Lots of squatting."

"That must be why you have such a nice bum." Shae snaps her eyes closed with a sigh. "I said that out loud, didn't I?"

"Yes, you did," I say with a wide grin.

"Sometimes my filter doesn't work properly."

"No need for a filter with me."

She raises her eyebrows. "The night is still young."

Silently, we sway together like we're back in grade six at a school dance. Only Mrs. McDonald isn't here supervising, so if my hand slides down an inch...

"I feel like we need to talk," Shae whispers, one of her arms tightening around my neck.

"I like it like this," I murmur into her hair. "We'll have time enough to talk."

"But what if we don't? And I've been hit with this sudden urge to know everything about you." From what I see of Shae's expression, she doesn't seem that happy about it.

"I had that urge when I first saw you skipping around the bakery."

"I wasn't skipping and don't let Adam hear you call it a bakery. It's a patisserie. He's very proud of the French-ness of it, which is surprising since he failed grade ten French."

"I have a feeling you could tell me quite a bit about my new friend Adam," I say lightly.

"If you pay me enough, I'll give you everything embarrassing he's ever done," she promises.

"I'll keep that in mind."

We move in slow circles and I watch Neely talk to Rufus. "He's adorable," Shae says like she knows I'm watching them.

"I think he's starting to realize that," I say ruefully. "But he's a great kid."

"It must be fun having him around."

"Dad took him when Rufus was three when his mother moved to Paris to study art. Ethan—his father and my younger brother—had just started medical school so there was no way he could handle having a kid around. He didn't even have to ask; Dad just asked when Rufus could move in, and that was it. Anyway, his first Christmas was so great. Everyone kind of went overboard with him, because he was three and he'd always spent holidays with his mother and they weren't really big on Christmas. So Rufus kept getting more and more presents, and his eyes kept getting bigger and bigger. 'More?' he kept saying. 'There's *more*?'" I laugh at the memory of the kid with the blond hair that never laid flat and the chubby cheeks and thighs that ran and ran and ran with endless energy.

"That's cute. *He's* cute."

"So are you."

There's something about her that makes me say whatever pops into my mind. She'd be brilliant as an interrogator or even as a lawyer against a criminal on the stand. They'd tell her anything.

Shae rests her head on my chest. "Don't be like this," she says softly.

"Like what?"

"All adorable-like."

"Can't help it. It's my natural personality."

"Can you tamp it down a bit?" She glances up with an almost desperate expression. Her face is so perfectly heart-shaped that I want to cup it in my hands.

And kiss her. I really want to kiss her to see if she tastes as good as she smells.

"And go back to being curmudgeonly?" I ask instead of kissing her. I make the face that I've seen Dad make.

"Even that's cute," Shae groans.

"Do you have a problem with me being cute?" I ask, only half-joking. I think about Adam's remarks and Neely telling me Shae will try to push me away as I stare into those wide dark eyes, like pots of chocolate. I don't want her to close me off; I like the way she curls into me, her arms locked around my neck. She's so tiny that I have to bend over, but I don't mind.

I don't mind anything.

"No," she says with a rueful smile. "I like it."

Chapter Eight

Shae

WHAT AM I DOING?

My giddiness at being near him bubbles like ginger ale, and for once I push away the usual dread before they pop.

I'm dying.

Not this minute I'm not.

I sway against Emmett. I like being in his arms. One of his hands lies flat against the middle of my back and every once in a while his fingers flex against the fabric of my dress. Every time he moves his hand, I inch closer until my body is practically molded against him. I don't think he minds.

Neely says my resting face is a smile, but this smile feels bigger, brighter, better. And I can't stop it.

The rush of middle-aged women to the dance floor pulls me back to the realization that the Spice Girls have replaced the slow Ed Sheeran song. "I think the music changed," I whisper.

Emmett looks down as I reluctantly pull free of his arms. "I didn't know there was music."

The bubbles explode in my stomach and make me giggle. "Do you dance?" I ask. "Other than Dirty Dancing. Not *dirty* dancing, like Magic Mike." I trail off with another giggle, feeling suddenly light-headed at the thought of Emmett on stage in a G-string.

Don't think of him like that.

"I don't think you want to see me dance." He takes my hand, twining my fingers with his, and I want to melt. I want to sink back into his arms and dance a slow samba to Spice up Your Life.

"I think I do."

"We can put that on the to-do for another day since you seem to be into bucket lists and things like that," Emmett says, leading me away from the dance floor, back to the table. "We have all the time in the world."

My face falls. But I don't and I can't tell him that. I don't know how to.

How can I possibly explain to him that he needs to leave me alone when all I want is to crawl back into his arms? I want to hear more about Rufus and his life and what brought on the sadness in those silvery eyes and...?

I want to kiss him, too. Probably more than any of that.

I don't understand this pull towards him like I'm a fishing line he's reeling in. Men don't reel me in; I get away before I get caught in their nets, but tonight, I feel like I can't swim.

I can't move fast enough.

Literally.

When I'm a step away from the table, right behind Dawson and Pepper, Natasha rears up from her chair with an ugly expression on her pretty face. Without a word, she throws a glass of wine straight at Dawson.

Who manages to step to the side in time, leaving me in the line of fire.

"What the f—!" I cry as a splash of white wine hits me mid-chest.

"What the hell, Nat?" Dawson echoes. That's when she throws the wine glass at him and hits him in the chest. Dawson, with the quick reflexes of a natural gamer, catches it before it smashes on the floor. "Natasha!"

"Jesus!" Emmett grabs a napkin left on the table. Drops of wine dot his shirt, but I most of the liquid has landed on me. "Are you okay?"

"Yeah, but Dawson..." I'm more concerned with Dawson and Natasha than the ruin of my dress.

"If you can't keep your hands off someone for *one night*, then we're through," Natasha shrieks, her voice cutting through the music.

"What did I do?" Dawson turns to Pepper with an incredulous expression, like he missed something important. "I was only dancing with her."

"With every inch of her touching you. My God, it was sexier than anything I used to do when I was on stage. You were practically humping her."

Natasha's voice has heads turning at the surrounding tables, on the dance floor, and even at the bar across the room.

Silence at the table, and then a jumble of voices erupts.

"Calm down a second."

"I was not!"

"I'm a sexy dancer?"

"Are you okay, Shae?"

Emmett tries to blot my dress without touching anything important, but I push him away as Neely swoops in from the dance floor like an angry Maleficent flying in to avenge her honour. Rufus trails behind, almost lost in her skirt.

"Leave," Neely demands, jabbing her finger at Natasha. "You will not make a scene at this wedding. Out. Get out."

If I were Natasha, I'd be running for cover. Neely is fantastic to watch when she's angry, but I'd hate to be on the receiving end.

Instead, Natasha's chest swells like she's a balloon ready to pop. "You never liked me anyway." Is it just me, super-conscious of cameras, or is Natasha looking around for anyone taking a picture?

"You're right," Neely snaps. "I don't. You treat Dawson like garbage, and it was a pain being nice to you on the trip. Get out of my sight. And far away from this wedding."

Natasha turns to Dawson with an apoplectic expression. "Are you going to let her speak to me like that?"

Dawson holds up the glass. "You threw a glass at me."

"And me." I step up beside Neely, running a hand down my dress to spray the droplets of wine not soaked in by the heavy fabric. "This is a family wedding and Dawson was doing nothing wrong—not humping or groping or even touching the way he wasn't supposed to. I don't know what kind of dancing you used to do, but this wasn't it. Neely's right; this isn't the place. Get out."

Natasha glares daggers at us. I might not think much of her, but we spent ten weeks traveling and bonds do form.

All gone now.

"I should have known you'd pick his side," Natasha sneers.

"Of course we're picking his side," Neely drawls in an icy voice. "It's Dawson."

Natasha throws her head. "See what your little followers think about this," she mutters under her breath as she storms away.

"This is an *awesome* wedding." Behind Neely, Rufus's eyes are wide with delight. "Should I take a selfie for you, Shae?"

"Not this time," I tell him weakly.

Neely rounds on Dawson, the protective side vanishing as quickly as Natasha does. "She made a mess of everything—again!" she rages. "Just like in Kuala Lumpur, just like in Singapore. I told you not to bring her."

"She's my girlfriend. Or was..." Dawson trails off with a confused expression. "Who was I supposed to bring?"

"No one. For once, just *no one*. I'll go tell James everything is fine now." Even stalking from the table in full furious mode, Neely is still the epitome of grace.

"Neely," Dawson calls after her. Then he looks to where Natasha walked off to, clearly undecided.

"Go after her," I say, then groan when he takes off after Natasha, catching her by the arm at the bar. Can he not see what's in front of his face?

"What'd you do, Pepper?" Grayson groans.

"Nothing! I did nothing. We were dancing, perfectly innocently." Pepper glances after Dawson and giggles.

"That doesn't sound innocent."

"It was." She throws up her hands. "I can't help it if I laugh at inappropriate moments. Emmett's dad is out there, along with all of Ellie's new family. I would never do anything to embarrass myself."

Grayson cocks his head and doesn't say anything.

"Do you think Neely is okay?" Emmett asks into the awkward silence.

"I'll go talk to her," Grayson says, hurrying after Neely.

Pepper lifts her shoulders. "It wasn't that bad." She turns to Rufus. "Come dance with me little man, so the world can see I'm not a horrible person." Rufus eagerly takes her hand and they walk away, leaving Emmett and me alone at the table.

"What was that all about?" Emmett looks as confused as Dawson as we watch Grayson say something that must crack the iciness of Neely because she smiles. It widens as he takes her hand and spins her on the dance floor.

"No—what's *that* all about?" I counter with a smile of delight at how easily Grayson cracked Neely's cool demeanor. If he can do that when she's angry...

"I don't know," Emmett muses. "But she was so upset when Dawson—whatever he did."

I heave a theatrical sigh. "That is a long story. Sometimes I wish the two of them would just get it together and get it over with. But then sometimes I don't want it, because then things will change, and maybe not for the better," I finish in a small voice. I've known Neely and Dawson forever and I love them equally and in different ways, but what happens to me if they get together? They'll love each other more than me.

Some days I like that plan. I like the idea that they'll have each other when I'm gone. And some days the possibility and probability of a Neely-and-Dawson pairing when I'm not around hits me like a sucker punch.

"You don't like change." Emmett holds out a chair for me and I sit, the skirt of my dress poofing under my bum. "That's normal."

"Who does, really? But I know that it has to. Things happen. Feelings, situations change. You have to adjust. Roll with it."

"You seem like you're good at rolling with it."

A shrug. "I have to be." The last thing I want to explain is how I have to be good at dealing with my expiry date. Emmett does not need to know my life history at this moment.

Or ever.

But I can't turn away from his gaze. His eyes are the colour of the sky during a cold winter's day, but there's warmth in them. And interest. A lot of interest.

I've never seen a man look at me quite the way Emmett is looking. Goosebumps dot my arms. "You're cold," Emmett says as he notices. "Your dress—is it soaked?"

I touch the damp spot on my chest. The satin is thick and I brushed most of the wine away before it could soak in. "She hardly got me. Natasha's always been dramatic. Look at them." I lean forward, peering around Emmett's shoulders to watch Dawson and Natasha; Natasha gestures angrily and Dawson stands with shoulders slumped. "They lasted longer than I expected," I muse. "He's never been one for long term."

"How about you?" Emmett frowns slightly, starts, and stops speaking a few times before he can finish in a rush of words. "Is anyone about to swoop in and throw a glass of wine at me? Like that guy at the concert. Denis Dirk?"

"Denzel Duke." I try to hide my smile because I'm sure Emmett mangled the name on purpose. "No, he's—actually, Denzel *would* be the swooping sort."

Denzel would be one for grand gestures, I decide, like pulling me on stage to sing his new song, also about me. He asked me to stay in Thailand with him.

I don't know why that little bit of trivia popped into my head right then. Maybe I pushed it away, not wanting to deal with the thought of a great guy wanting more than a night of in-depth conversation with me.

"But no," I finish. "He's a good guy, but there would be no reason to throw wine on you."

"Is that because I'm not wine worthy, or because this Denis wouldn't feel the need to?" He shrugs at my expression of confusion. "I'm not good at this."

"Is anybody?"

"Grayson. Grayson is very good at this," Emmett says decisively.

I look out to where Neely is dancing with Grayson. Should I be nervous about her, for her? The last thing I want is for Neely's heart to be broken *again*.

"It's like I've been hiding for years." Emmett's voice is tinged with awe, like he's faced with the most beautiful sunrise. When I turn back to find him staring at me with the same awe, Neely is instantly forgotten, along with everything else. "Like I've been in the longest game of hide and seek with the perfect hiding spot and suddenly someone's found me." He gives me a lopsided smile and everything inside me gets all soft and gushy.

Wow. Just...wow.

"Emmett..." I begin, but I don't know what to say. How can any words make sense after that? "Boo." Before I can stop myself, I lean over and press my lips against his.

Oh no.

Soft. Warm. Surprised. I might have caught Emmett off guard with my spontaneity, but he rises to the occasion. His lips quickly part, deepening the kiss, and I feel the warmth of his hand against my cheek.

I want to crawl into his lap and kiss him again and again until neither of us can see straight. Instead, I freeze, my lips caught in a tableau of bad judgment, and I pull away like his lips are cold as ice rather than soft and firm all at once. Strong and gentle. Yielding and demanding—

It was just a kiss.

Only it wasn't.

"Hey," Emmett says with a sleepy smile, his hand snaking under my hair to pull me closer.

No. Oh no. Nononono…

His lips are only a breath away when I slap my hand against his chest to stop him. I've fallen completely and utterly under his spell. This guy might say he's out of practice, but he's hitting home runs with me.

"I have to dance."

Emmett blinks with confusion and pulls back, his hand dropping from the back of my neck. "Now?"

"It's the Backstreet Boys," I say, thankfully recognizing the music even though my head spins with indecision. "James's favourite along with Dirty Dancing. I have to go—" I gesture over my shoulder. "Neely will want me."

I have no idea if she wants me or not, only that I want Emmett enough to get away.

"Okay. Go then," Emmett says with enough resignation to stop a truck.

"I'll be back," I promise, moving away on shaky legs, and hoping Emmett can't see the effect he's had on me.

Because that kiss wasn't just a kiss and I need to dance away the tingles still spiraling through my body.

No.NoNoNoNO!

Emmett

N**O SOONER THAN** S**HAE** joins the group that swarms around James, Ellie appears at the table and plops on the chair beside me. "Who was that?" Ellie demands as she adjusts her dress. Layers of fabric drape over the chair, spilling onto my feet. "And I did just see her kiss you?"

"You saw that?" So it was real. It really happened. I resist the urge to touch my lips to see if Shae left a swipe of her lipstick as evidence. She kissed me—and then she ran away. Because of the Backstreet Boys.

I hate boy bands, now and forever.

"I did." Ellie's eyes dance.

"It was nothing," I say automatically.

"Really? It didn't look like nothing?"

I don't know what I think. I don't know *how to* after that. I touch my lower lip and track Shae's bobbing pink head on the dance floor. "I have no idea," I confess.

"That was Shae." Ellie's voice is full of wonder. "The one Rufus was watching on the video is *here*. How'd that happen?"

"Rufus's dream came true." I laugh. "But seriously, Shae is your new sister-in-law's best friend. Neely goes on all these trips with her too."

"I have to confess, I kind of hoped you'd hit it off with Neely." Ellie reaches for the bottle of wine still on the table and looks at the glasses for an empty one. "You seemed to get along last night, and then I saw you talking during dinner—and that dance! Emmett! I had no idea!"

"That was a last-minute thing and will never be repeated."

"You did the Dirty Dancing dance." Ellie clasps her hands together under her chin. "For me."

"I think you should save all that emotion for Neely and Adam. They did all the work. I just stood there at the end and held her up." Tears shimmer in her blue eyes. "Stop it," I plead.

"But you—"

"Want you to have an amazing wedding," I finish, trying to head off the swell of emotion. "Are you having a good time?"

"Oh, Emmett." Ellie sighs. Her smile tells me everything I want to know.

"That good?"

"It's everything I've dreamed about. Just perfect."

"I'm glad." My voice is gruff and I blink back my own shimmer of wetness. "You deserve it, El."

"When I think of what your wedding was like—"

"Don't," I say quickly. "Don't go there." I've kept my emotions in check today, but it hasn't been easy. While I think I'm over the worst of the grief, it still flares up, especially when I see happy people. Watching Ellie and James say the words I once said to Alex, but they have their lives ahead of them, while Alex...

I swallow past the lump in my throat.

"Is it bad today?" Ellie glances again at the bottles and glasses on the table before me. I came out of rehab and therapy with a healthy respect for alcohol, but not a drinking problem. Nine point nine times out of ten I can control myself; it was just that one time in my life when everything seemed to collapse at once.

"I can handle it," I say. "That's not a problem."

My sister reaches over and squeezes my hand. "Then what is?"

"I'm not getting into this with you here."

Ellie glances over her shoulder. For the first time that day, she doesn't have a line-up of people waiting to talk, to hug, to congratulate her. "You can if you need to."

"It's not me," I say reluctantly. "I keep thinking of Alex, of what she missed out on. She didn't get any of this."

"That's not your fault."

"Whose fault is it?"

"No one's, Emmett. I thought after all this time you'd realize that. Alex *died*—and it's no one's fault. It didn't matter if she was at the farm, or home with her own family, or on the road with you. Something was growing in her brain that no one knew about, and it was going to kill her. Stop feeling guilty. It sucks." Ellie shrugs. "But that's all. It wasn't your fault. Stop blaming yourself."

I stare at a smear of oil staining the tablecloth. "Easier said than done."

Ellie leans forward. "You've come so far tonight. You came and talked and smiled and danced." She laughs with delight. "You got kissed."

"That wasn't a kiss."

"Lips on lips is a kiss. And it wasn't from one of James's aunts, so you should be grateful for that." I smile at the thought. "Emmett…" Ellie trails off and worries at her lip. "I don't know if I should say this…"

"You started this," I remind her. "Better now than when your admirers come find you."

"Did you ever talk to Alex about if she even wanted to get married?"

I rear back in my chair. "Of course she did. Every woman… No," I admit, correcting myself. "I never asked her."

"She didn't want to get married," Ellie says gently.

Things shift, like the floor has tilted and I grab the edge of the table. "What are you talking about?"

"The day everything happened, the day she… I came home early in the morning just as she was coming out of your room." Ellie smiles sadly at the memory. "It was a little awkward, but we ended up downstairs having tea at about six o'clock in the morning."

"I didn't know that."

"It wasn't something I was going to bring up. Anyway, we got talking, mainly about you. You told her about M—about when she left."

Ellie hasn't spoken about our mother in years; the words Mom or Mother rarely come out of her mouth. It frustrates me, because there are times I want to talk about her, but I don't want to upset Ellie.

"I did."

"Well, Alex said that while it must have been awful for us, it was good to know about what happened because it confirmed that you were on the same wavelength about getting married. About not getting married," Ellie finishes.

I shake my head like I have water in my ears. "I never said anything to her about getting married. I wasn't ready, but then she got sick—"

"Alex thought you hadn't said anything because you *didn't* want to get married. And she was okay with that. She never wanted to settle down; she loved living on the road with you."

It's like Ellie is telling me about a stranger. I had no idea Alex felt that way. She had been happy and eager to stay on the road with me when I was playing, living out of hotels, nights spent at baseball fields watching the team. I thought that it was because she couldn't bear to be left behind or didn't want to be without me. "If she didn't want to get married, why did she say yes?"

I remember it like yesterday: sitting by Alex's bed, my head resting on her arm as I fought to hold back the tears. It had been the middle of the night and I hadn't left her hospital room since she'd been admitted. "Go home, Emmett," Alex had whispered, her hand with all the tubes stroking my hair.

"I'm not leaving you. Ever."

"I'm fine here."

One of the machines attached to her beeped irregularly and my head shot up, eyes wild. "What's wrong? What hurts?"

"I'm going to lose you." Alex's voice had been so weak that I had to lean in to hear. Tears pooled in my eyes.

"You're not. You'll never lose me. I'm not—let's get married!" The thought hit me like a bullet, but instead of causing damage, it made everything inside feel better. Lighter. In control, like I had a say of what would happen. "Marry me."

"Emmett..."

"I'm serious. Let's get married, and when you get better, we'll already be together and we can start our life. It'll be great. We can do it right here." I had already begun to plan, seeing Alex in a white dress, where to find rings, if Reverend Fuller would be able to marry us. Excitement pushed away the fear. "What do you say? Say yes," I begged, squeezing her hand. "Please, Alex."

She closed her eyes. "Whatever you want, Emmett."

The scene fades from my mind, my eyes surprisingly damp from the memory. "I didn't really give her a choice," I say slowly.

"You wanted to marry her." Ellie smiles, her eyes sad. I know she's still thinking of my wedding day.

"Well, yeah, but I thought she wanted it. And it was the least I could do. But if she hadn't been sick..." I bite my lip, not wanting to say the words I hadn't let myself admit. "I wasn't ready."

Ellie lays her hand on my arm, her rings glinting in the light. "You will be next time."

"Next time." For the first time, I think there might be a next time. Blowing out a deep breath, some of the guilt I'd been carrying for the past few years lifts. It's still hovering over my shoulders in case I want to pull it back down, but it's lighter. "I didn't know any of this."

"Sorry to tell you here."

"It's as good a place as any." I glance at the dance floor just as the music changes to a slower beat. I see Shae look back at me before she's swept away by Adam.

"Are you going to be okay?" The worry lines are back between Ellie's eyes, something I hadn't seen in a while. With my thumb, I reach out and smooth the furrow like I did when we were younger. She smiles.

"I'm going to be fine," I say honestly.

"I asked Grayson to keep an eye on you," Ellie admits.

I take a deep breath. There will be time to process what Ellie said and how it affects my memories, but it's enough for now. Tonight is for celebrating. "Yeah, about Grayson. Maybe we should talk about him." I raise an eyebrow. "Like maybe about the summer you were seventeen?"

"Oh, that." Ellie waves away my concern with a mischievous grin, the same one I see on Rufus's face. "It was nothing. A blip."

"I think you blipped him more than you know."

Ellie giggles like she's proud of herself. "Maybe. But I think he deserves it, don't you? It might show him a little compassion for those poor girls on The Suitor."

I push back my chair and stand up. "I think I deserve to dance with the bride tonight. I must be the only one who hasn't." I hold out my hand to my sister.

Ellie takes my hand and leads me onto the dance floor. "You deserve a lot of things, big brother, but at least I know I can help you with that one."

Chapter Nine

Shae

I KISSED HIM. *I* kissed Emmett. Right there at the table when his smile and his eyes and those heartfelt words made me gooey inside.

I have to get past gooey.

Over the years, I've met a lot of men—some good, some bad, and some seriously horrible. And with the exceptions of an Italian prince who tempted me with his philanthropy, and the Australian rugby player who gave the best hugs, I've never had a problem keeping my distance. It's like my heart is a rock and nothing is getting through it. I've never had a problem saying goodbye, au revoir, or sayonara with a smile.

But I've never met anyone like Emmett. Already I can tell he's good and strong and funny and honest...and wow, is he ever cute. I've gone to my share of black-tie events but never before has a man in a tux been so appealing. He makes my insides all squishy.

He makes me smile.

But I don't want squishy insides. I want my rock back, with no impulsive kissing. If there happens to be impulsive kissing, it can't lead anywhere.

Emmett is the yellow brick road; I know exactly where things are headed with him. And it's not a good idea to be travelling it.

But I still can't keep away from him.

The music pulses all night long and I do my best to lose myself within it. I dance with James and the rest of the wedding party, doing a mash-up of a salsa and a tango with Adam to a Jennifer Lopez song. I own the floor with Neely, Rufus firmly at my side, pulling her aunts and neighbours that I've known for years onto the floor. I fight off the attentions of the bartender on a break, and cousin Victor, and head back to the safety of Emmett's arms.

I stay with Emmett.

I like Emmett. He spins me away with a smile, his gaze never leaving mine but I'm happy when he tucks me against him.

I like being with him.

At the end of the night, when the lights flash on and James's tells us to go home, the thought of saying goodbye to Emmett twists my stomach into a Gordian knot.

The lights are on and staff move slowly to de-wedding-ize the room. Already, a few of the white tablecloths, stained with wine and tomato sauce, are balled on the tables and tired-looking waiters collect the many empty wine bottles and glasses. Centrepieces now line the head table and the wedding planner takes down the arch of pink balloons. The room looks as tired as my feet as I hunt for my shoes, only to find them placed neatly on Neely's chair.

I thank Ellie and James for a great night, hug Mama S., and skip over to where Neely and Dawson wait by the door with Emmett, Grayson, and Pepper. They look impossibly chummy for only meeting a few hours ago.

Neely scans the room, probably looking for me. "Let's go, let's go, let's go," I hiss, skipping past them to the door.

"Where?" Dawson demands.

"I thought we were getting an Uber home." Neely narrows her eyes at me, wondering what I've planned.

"Later. First, we're off to Fred's."

"I haven't been there in so long," Dawson muses.

Sold. I need at least one person on my side and Dawson owes me for taking a chestful of wine for him. My dress has long since dried, and Dawson returned to the party without Natasha, so it was more than worth it.

"What's Fred's?" Pepper asks, hovering alongside Dawson in Natasha's place. I'm going to have to get him alone to find out what happened. Or what is happening. "Or who is Fred?"

"I'm not walking," Neely protests. "My feet are killing me."

"I know. That's why we have a ride." With a big smile, I reach out and snag Neely's hand and tug her after me, knowing the others will follow.

Walking out of the Yacht Club, a welcome gust of cool air hits me in the face like a gentle slap. Any tiredness I might have felt vanishes, like it always does at the beginning of another adventure. It might have been a good wedding, but I'm ready for the next bit of fun.

I step forward, gesturing at the gleaming limousine parked by the door. "Our ride," I say grandly.

"Shae, no way." Neely grinds to a halt. "James will kill us."

"He'll never have to know. They want to leave at one-thirty, which gives us twenty-five minutes for my friend Benjamin here to drive us to Fred's and get back for the bride and groom. Right, Benjamin?" I smile widely at the driver holding the door open for us.

"Anything you say, Miss Shae," he says, his whiter than white teeth gleaming.

"See?" I spread my arms wide.

"Seriously?" Dawson groans. "You're a horrible influence on everyone. Do you know," he turns to Benjamin. "she made me go zip-lining with her? *Naked*!"

The patter of eleven-year-old feet skids to a halt behind us, followed by Ethan's heavier footsteps. "Are we taking that back to the hotel?" Rufus cries. "Cool." Without waiting for an answer, he crawls into the car.

"Rufus, no!" Emmett calls after him.

"What's going on?" Ethan asks. Up close, Emmett doesn't look as much like his younger brother, but the similarities are there. From what Emmett has said tonight, he thinks a lot of Ethan.

"We're wasting time standing around waiting. You can lecture on the way." Without a backwards glance, I duck into the car.

"Sounds good to me," I hear Grayson say.

Tiny lights illuminate the seats facing each other. It smells clean and leathery and for a moment, I regret my idea, not wanting to ruin the experience of taking the wedding night limo ride for Ellie and James. But it's too late—one by one, with a mixture of wariness and excitement, the others follow me into the car. Neely is the last one, like I knew she would be and sits by the door, not even trying to keep her dress from wrinkling. It's a tight squeeze with all of us, but it's a short ride.

I ignore the resentful stare thrown my way. "We're in," I call to Benjamin. "Good to go. We can't drink the champagne," I add as the bemused driver starts the engine. "And don't make a mess."

"This isn't a good idea," Neely frets as the car pulls away from the Yacht Club. "James is going to be so mad at us."

"We're stealing the car." Beside her, Emmett wears a pinched expression on his face and something about it doesn't sit right with me.

"We're not stealing, we're borrowing," I clarify, avoiding his eyes, which are now more steely blue than silvery.

"That's not much of a distinction. Ellie is expecting the car to be outside waiting for her and I don't want her to be disappointed."

It's the mention of his sister that gets me. And so I cave—me, who once kept an Australian accent for twenty-four hours, who wrangled a first-class seat on a flight to Abu Dhabi for the three of us by pretending I was afraid of flying, and who posed as the actress Cristin Milioti to get us into a party at the Venice Film Festival.

"I asked if we could borrow it," I admit.

"You asked?" Emmett sounds skeptical.

"When I was looking for my shoes, I bumped into James and Ellie, and they were moaning about the fact they still had so many people to say goodbye to," I say in a rush. "I said the limo was here, Ellie asked if I could make sure the driver was okay waiting, and did he want anything. Then I thought if it's just sitting there for a half-hour, could we borrow the car to go to Fred's while the driver was waiting, and they said sure." I smile widely. "No harm, no foul. I didn't do anything wrong."

"Why didn't you say that in the first place?" Neely throws up her hands with exasperation.

I shrug. "I thought it was more fun to see if you'd go along with me."

Emmett laughs, and I swear my heart almost breaks into song at the sound. But I'm not the only one who reacts—Ethan starts and stares at his brother in wonder.

"You...laughed."

"So? I laugh."

"No, dude, you really don't," Grayson says with a wide smile. "Not for a while, anyway."

"It doesn't mean I can't."

"I don't remember the last time I heard you laugh," Pepper marvels.

A flood of pink stains Emmett's cheeks. I get that I did a good thing, but I don't want him embarrassed by it. "I make everyone laugh at me," I say. "It's a gift."

"It really is." Neely smiles, our long friendship giving her the ability to read me like a book.

Ethan glances at me with a mixture of wonder and confusion. "Who are you?"

"It's Shae, Dad," Rufus says scornfully. "I showed you the videos." He leans over to hand his phone to his father, no doubt still on my Insta page.

Pulling out my own phone, I aim at Grayson and Pepper on the seat across from me, with Dawson caught between them. Rufus makes a leap and lands on Dawson's lap. "Smile," I order. I quickly post it with the hashtags *#greatnight* *#bedtimenot* and *#borrowingtheweddingcar*

"Who are you?" Ethan repeats, handing Rufus back his phone.

"A very good influencer, but a bad influence," Dawson says earnestly. "I told you she made me go naked zip-lining with her."

"Enough! It was your idea!"

"I didn't know it would be all-over naked."

"Is there such a thing as part-naked?" Pepper asks with a laugh.

Grayson winces and covers his crotch with his hands. "Not sure I'd be up for that," he says.

"I definitely wasn't up for it," Dawson says with a grin.

There's a pause, and the whole car bursts out in laughter, except for Rufus, who looks confused.

Emmett catches me watching and smiles and I snap a quick picture of him. No hashtag needed for this one.

This one's for me.

Emmett

"THANKS, BENJAMIN!" SHAE WAVES as the limo pulls away leaving us standing outside a tired-looking restaurant. She turns to us with a satisfied smile. "Better than walking, right?"

"And Ellie gets her car back with lots of time to spare," Ethan agrees.

It's been a while since I've spent time with my brother. When he comes home, it's for short stretches, and inevitably turns into chaos as Ethan tries to shove in as much fun stuff with Rufus as possible.

Tonight won't be an exception. Already, Rufus is champing at the bit for the famous pancakes. "Let's eat," Shae says and pulls open the door.

My first thought when I walk in is that I don't want to eat anything from this place. It smells of grease and while the surfaces are scrubbed, there's an almost visible haze of overcooked fries and melted cheese that hangs over everything. It's a small space with the counter spanning the length of the restaurant, and a row of single tables lining the window. Between them are a few four-tops; clean,

I begrudgingly notice, with shining cutlery set on the folded paper napkins.

Ashbury—population seven thousand, nine hundred—has three restaurants, all of which are places I've never hesitated frequenting, even with the limited menu. Fred's Diner, spelled out in neon cursive on the door, has me pausing to glance over at Neely to make sure this is the right place.

I look at Neely, not Shae, because I already know Neely is the more level-headed in this trio. I'm not sure about Dawson yet.

A second look at the door shows that the 'r' in Fred's is partially faded, which makes it look like "Fed's." Great.

"Hi, Dee!" Shae chirps with a big smile for the waitress.

"Is it okay if we make one big table?" Dawson asks.

"Help yourself," Dee says. "It's not like we're busy." It's hard to guess her age in the dim light but I'd guess she's been through most of the eighties. The sleeve of tattoos is visible under her T-shirt and the glint of the piercings is obvious in her nose and ears. She gives a half-hearted wave to Shae, her sullen expression not changing.

"I'm going to potty." Shae skips away as I help Dawson pull three tables together.

"So what is this place?" Grayson asks Neely under his breath.

Neely shrugs like she knows exactly what this place looks like to outsiders. "The three of us spent a lot of time here in high school. It was sort of our spot."

I can hear the nostalgia in her voice, and because of that, I push down my reticence and take a seat at the enlarged table with another look around. Two tables are full; a couple sitting by the washroom, and an older man, possibly homeless, nursing a cup of coffee. Dee stands behind the counter talking to the very big guy manning the stovetop.

Crowded around a table still wearing suits and fancy dresses, I have never felt more out of place. I shrug out of my tux jacket and hang it on the back of my chair as Rufus leans his elbows on the table and glances around, an excited gleam in his eye.

The kid will never be able to sleep tonight.

"Interesting friends you've got," Ethan mutters from across the table. The three of us sit at one end of the table, with an empty chair gaping like a missing tooth between me and Dawson. Shae's seat—if she takes it.

"Yeah," I say, surprised that I already consider them friends. Neely is practically family, but I'd be up to hang with Dawson. And Shae... "They're cool."

Ethan glances over his shoulder to where Shae disappeared to. "Is she...is she the first...since...?" Being males, Ethan and I lack the communication skills that Ellie was born with and so we rarely talk about our feelings. The five-year age difference had seemed insurmountable as kids, but in our twenties, when it would have leveled out, I had been off playing ball and Ethan was studying for medical school. We don't really know each other.

I give a quick nod. "Since Alex. But nothing..." I trail off with a shrug. I seriously have no clue about Shae. Is she interested? Yes, even my lack of recent experience tells me that.

Would she be willing to take *whatever* this is past tonight? That's what I'm not sure about. So, delaying the end of the evening is fine with me.

"She's something else." Ethan grins appreciatively.

"Yeah." Ellie wanted me to crawl out of my hiding hole and step back into the world. I don't think she intended my first steps to be with this whirlwind with pink hair and dirty feet from being barefoot all night. "She's pretty cool."

The waitress meets Neely's pointed stare. "Pancakes for all," Neely says without checking the menu. "Sides of sausage and bacon. Oh, and eggs bennie for Shae."

"The girl still eating that?" Dee grunts.

"The girl likes her eggs."

As Dee turns back to the counter, I shake my head. "Are you sure that's what she wants? She kept saying how good the pancakes are."

"The best," Dawson agrees with a shrug. "I don't understand her, but that's what she always has here."

Are all women so complicated, or is it just Shae? Alex had been plain and simple, black and white in her opinions and her fashion. I rarely saw her wearing colours, and I remember her relief that the St. Louis jersey was white so she could wear it.

Alex was the cool blue sky of a winter day, while Shae is a rainbow. With sparkles and smiley faces.

I smile at the sight of Shae bouncing from the ladies' room with a face full of happiness. How can anyone be so happy all the time?

Shae catches the eye of the couple sitting by the washrooms. "Great place for a late-night snack," I hear her say. "Jacques makes the best pancakes. Hey." For once her smile isn't contagious. "Are you okay?"

"We're fine," the man says apologetically. He looks about my age, with hair standing up like he's been constantly running his hands through it. But the woman across from him, arms crossed across her chest, gives a vehement shake of her head to Shae's question.

"Does she always talk to strangers?" I whisper to Dawson. Just from watching her at the wedding and the few minutes in Pain au Chocolate yesterday, I'm in awe of Shae's ease with people. Even before Alex, I was never the most social person. Hiding for the past few years wasn't all that difficult for me. But Shae seems as comfortable with strangers as she is with Neely and Dawson. I wonder if that's because she shares so much online.

Dawson glances over and rolls his eyes. "Yep. She's like a puppy—thinks everyone wants to be friends with her."

Neely shakes her head. "I think we should be glad that everyone wants to be her friend, or else we wouldn't have free trips to places we'd never think to go to."

"You didn't want to go to Thailand?" Rufus asks in a horrified voice.

"Of course I did," Neely soothes. "It was a great time. But not my first choice."

"I think you're going to lose your travel spot to the little man," I hear Grayson murmur. He sits close to Neely, too close for a table with so much space between the rest of us.

"Too much nakedness there," Dawson grumbles.

"There's never too much nakedness," Pepper announces with a sly grin.

I fight the urge to roll my own eyes and focus on Shae still talking to the couple by the washroom.

"He forgot my birthday!" the woman says loudly, her face pink with anger. Because the diner is so small, overhearing the conversation isn't hard.

"Oh, wow, that's never a good one," Shae commiserates. "How long have you been together?"

"Six months," they say in unison. Somehow the way he says it makes it sound like a short time, while to her, it's clearly a milestone. I don't see this guy getting out of here in one piece if his girlfriend is mad, and with Shae on her side.

Women always take the side of the girlfriend.

Shae cocks her head and I get the sense that she's enjoying this. "That's a tough one. It's always a toss-up of what to do for birthdays when it's less than a year: does he throw you a surprise party with all of your friends—most of whom he probably doesn't know yet—or hand over a Bath and Body gift card." The guy's shoulders visibly relax as he realizes Shae's not about to gang up on him. "Do you love her?"

"Yeah," he says quickly. His girlfriend gives a sharp intake of breath that mirrors the sudden clench of my heart. "Of course."

"That's the first time you've said that." Her eyes are wide, and suddenly a bit wet. "You love me?"

The first time I told Alex I loved her was late one night after a game. It wasn't her birthday, but we were definitely celebrating. Despite that I think the moment should be private, I can't stop watching.

"Of course." He reaches across the table for her hand. "This has been the best six months of my life."

"I love you too."

I watch with admiration as Shae taps the table with her fist. "Well, that's a nice birthday present, isn't it? Don't forget to have the pancakes." Giving them a wink, she moves on to the next customer. "Have you had the pancakes?" she asks the older man by the window.

"They're not in my budget tonight," he says sadly.

"It's on me."

The waitress sets a tray of drinks before Dawson as Shae slides into the chair beside me. "Can you fix the gentleman over there," she says to Dee, jerking her thumb over her shoulder, "a big breakfast with pancakes? On me."

"He's in here almost every night," Dee says with a shake of her head. "Sometimes he has enough for eggs, most nights just toast."

"Can you make sure he has food for the next week or so? He looks really thin. I'll come in and settle with Mabel."

"Make sure you do," she says in a surly voice.

"I'll chip in as well, if Jacques will let me watch him cook." Dawson flips the hair out of his eyes and gives Dee a hopeful smile. "I forgot everything he taught me before."

"It's pancakes, for God's sake. How hard can they be to make?" Neely mutters.

"You'll have to ask him," Dee says, her scowl softening at the sight of Dawson's smile. "Make sure you stay out of the way and I'm not fixing you up if you burn yourself like last time."

"But you'll kiss it better for him, won't you?" Shae asks.

Dee gives a bark of what might be laughter and thumps the rest of the glasses on the table.

Grayson turns to Shae with a look of amazement. "Who are you? You wow the wedding, help the homeless, and make love connections. Is this a usual night for you?"

She bends her pink head to suck at her straw. "I guess."

Grayson shakes his head. "You're a strange girl. But I'm impressed with the love connection thing. You should come on The Suitor and be my Obi-Wan, whispering in my ear about who's there for the right reason."

"Obi-Wan would let you figure that out yourself," Neely says without looking at him. "I think you're better off with a Yoda than an Obi-Wan."

Grayson's jaw drops open, and mine soon follows. "Are you debating Star Wars with me?" he whispers in a hoarse voice. My childhood was spent with Grayson watching his VHS copies of the Star Wars movies. I've always been a fan, but Grayson is a fanatic, collecting LEGO sets and movie posters, not to mention a full Boba Fett costume which he wears regularly on Halloween. To have him find a woman who likes it even a fraction as much as he does must be a dream come true.

"Obi-Wan is overrated. Yoda's better," Neely says flatly.

"Shae kind of looks like Yoda," Rufus pipes up. "Especially Baby Yoda."

"I'm going to take that as a compliment," Shae says with a grin. "I thought you were already on The Suitor?" she asks Grayson.

"Gray." Pepper groans. "You have to keep quiet about it."

"Are you going to be the next Suitor?" Shae's eyes are wide with surprise. I see her gaze shift to Neely and back to Grayson.

"He's not supposed to say anything," Pepper says defensively.

Grayson waves his arms. "We're all friends here."

"Maybe so, but Shae is on social media an awful lot."

I understand her wariness—while I've never been a marquee player, the video of me getting hit by the fastball went viral, as well as exaggerated rumours of my drinking. Social media can be brutal.

Going on the reality show again means Grayson is willingly open-ing himself up to scrutiny, his every move watched by thousands, if not millions.

Finding love is one thing, but I'd want my privacy when I was doing it.

Shae turns to Pepper with a stricken expression. "I wouldn't say anything."

"Please don't. They'll sue him if he releases the news first. It's in the contract."

"It is?" Grayson turns from Neely with wild eyes.

"Yes, brother. You should read the thing. I do and I'm not even your lawyer."

"We won't say anything, but you have to agree to let us post something as soon as it's official." Neely's voice is cool and busi-nesslike.

"Like an interview?" Grayson looks interested.

"Sure. Anything, really."

"Sounds good. But I'll only talk to you." He glances at Shae. "No offense, of course. But this is a good way to make sure that you'll talk to me again." For a moment I don't think the smile will work on Neely until the corners of her mouth begin to curve up.

"Oh, all right."

"Such enthusiasm. I love it!"

Pepper watches the exchange between Grayson and Neely with a worried gleam in her eyes until he turns to his sister with a wide smile. "It's all good," he assures her. "No need to worry. I can take care of myself."

Pepper rolls her eyes. "I'm not too sure about that."

"I know that feeling." Neely looks pointedly at Shae, busy taking a video of Dawson wearing a stained apron over his suit at the stovetop flipping pancakes. With all her energy, Shae must be hard to keep up with, but I don't see why she'd need someone to take care of her.

"Anyway," Pepper says, moving on from her brother and back to Shae. "I want to know how you knew that he loved her." She jerks her chin at the couple, now smiling and holding hands.

"He had this look in his eyes," Shae says simply "Like he was afraid he would lose her. Why would he look like that unless he loved her?"

I have a feeling it might not be long before I have that look in my eye.

Chapter Ten

Shae

T HE BEST THING ABOUT hanging out at Fred's is that we take over the diner. I've talked to Mike about how it stays open and neither of us can figure out how, because it's never busy. Even though the pancakes are some of the best in the city, the service is not, with Dee being the most personable of the wait staff.

Back in high school, I made the mistake of telling a few friends about my diagnosis. The news spread like wildfire, and for years, I was known as the Girl Who's Going to Die. Everyday classes were bad enough as every sneeze or cough was monitored and discussed. When I missed three days because of the flu, news spread that I had died.

But parties were the worst. At my first high school party, I was accosted by no less than fifteen people wondering just when and how I was going to die. After that, I swore off gatherings with more than four people. Instead, nights when bonfires lit up the beach, or friends gathered in parents' basements with contraband wine coolers, I'd go to Fred's with Neely and Dawson. Dee would always let us do what we wanted, like pushing the tables aside so that Neely could practice for a recital, have a raucous game of Texas Hold'em with other customers, and decorate the place with glittering hearts and flowers for Dawson's Valentine Day date with Amy Rice in senior year.

It was open all night and we wasted many an hour eating pancakes and grilled cheese, talking and laughing, and playing Uno with Dee while our schoolmates partied.

And we never told them about how good the pancakes were, so that's why I like to spread the word now.

The door to the diner swings open, bringing in a wave of street sounds as well as Adam and his boyfriend, Patrick.

"I thought we'd find you here," Adam calls. "After you ran off with the limo—*what* was that stunt? *Shae*?"

"I asked first," I protest, pausing the video of Rufus flipping pancakes, his little face tense with concentration. "Benjamin got back in time, didn't he?"

"Yes, but the look on Mama S.'s face when it rolled up." Adam breaks into laughter as Patrick pulls two chairs to the table. They've been together for almost a year, and I still can't find much that they have in common. Patrick is solid and serious, used to the physical labour of working at his family's nursery, while Adam is outgoing and vivacious and hates to get his hands dirty. Watching the two of them really goes to show that opposites do attract.

"Can we get two orders of pancakes?" Patrick calls to Dee. "Please and thank you."

"Was Mama mad?" Neely asks with concern.

"Of course not, once Ellie told her that you and Shae had borrowed the car."

"You can do no wrong in my mother's eyes," Neely chides. "Do you know how much power that gives you?"

"I love Mama S." I put my hand to my chest. "I would never abuse that power."

"We know," Adam says. "Now, is someone going to fill me in on why Natasha went stompy-stomp out of there tonight, or what?"

"I say we get a repeat of your dance," Grayson says. "There's enough room if we push the tables back."

"No lift," Neely and Emmett cry in unison. "That might have been a one-shot deal," he adds ruefully.

"You were magnificent," Adam exclaims, hand over his heart. "But it might take a little longer to learn all the moves. I'm up to for private lessons, though, if you like."

"I'm good with just the heavy lifting," Emmett says, his face falling when he realizes what he's said. "Not that you're heavy," he's quick to assure Neely.

With a bigger group and the effects of the alcohol, we're a little louder than usual, but Dee does her best to ignore us. But when Adam and Neely take to the floor backed by music from Neely's iPhone, I catch sight of Dee watching with a half-smile on her face.

"I think you're going to have a bit of a wait for your breakfast," I call to the couple by the bathroom, still holding hands. She has a wistful expression on her face as she watches Neely and Adam dance. "You should join them."

She doesn't wait to be asked twice, dragging her protesting boyfriend to the middle of the diner. Grayson replaces "Time of Our Life" with Lewis Capaldi, and cuts in on Adam, whisking Neely into his arms with the ease of a Dancing with the Stars pro.

Neely doesn't complain.

"Is it always like this with you?" Emmett asks with amazement. He gestures to the dancing, the cooking lesson, the homeless man nursing his coffee with a huge smile on his face.

I shrug. "Sometimes." I snap a few pictures. "Seeing the diner like this can only help their business."

"That's why you're basically having a party in the middle of the night?"

"I do *that* because it's fun." I meet his gaze, and my heart attempts a backflip.

"How long have you lived around here?" Emmett asks. His politeness is a far cry from how he tried to pull me back after I kissed him.

Oh, that kiss.

"Always," I say, trying to keep my gaze from his lips. "Or at least since I was five or so. Are you from the city—I guess not, because farm? Did I hear something about you being a farmer?"

As the others cavort around the diner, Emmett tells me about working with his father, about living in a small town. I watch his mouth as he talks, as his lips form the words.

He's very enthusiastic and it's catching, especially when he tells me about suggesting changing the family farm into community-supported agriculture. "And you've got subscribers that get boxes of vegetables every week?" I ask.

He nods. "And fresh eggs from the chickens, honey from Dad's bees and Pepper supplies bread."

"Sounds like a good deal." I giggle softly. "It makes me hungry to think about it."

"I don't know how you can think about food after everything they gave us at the wedding."

"I've always been a good eater. I like my food."

"I could tell from dinner."

I narrow my eyes. "Were you watching me eat from your spot at the high table? Like I'm some kind of peasant?"

His gaze shifts away from me. "Maybe. Not the way you make it sound though," he adds defensively. "Is that creepy?"

I laugh at his reaction. "I don't think you can ever be creepy, Emmett."

"No?" He reaches over and takes my hand, stilling the constant plucking at the skirt of my dress. His hand dwarfs mine, rough and calloused from working on the farm.

What does he do? I picture him bending between rows of vegetables, feeding baby cows and goats, driving a tractor with a dusty ball cap on his head.

I like that picture of him. I like it almost as much as I like how he looks in his tuxedo. I like everything—his looks, his smile, the way he smells, how he didn't step on my feet once when we danced. I like how his gaze travels over my face as if he's checking for symptoms, but I know he's not, because he doesn't know.

I like that he doesn't know I'm sick.

But part of me wishes he did.

Emmet's life is different than mine—completely and utterly opposite. When he gets up at dawn for chores, I'm racing to catch a flight. He has someone to make him dinner at night, where I eat from takeout boxes or at five-star restaurants that I'm paid to mention. He ends the day tired and satisfied, where I am hitting a party at the same time his head hits the pillow.

We wouldn't fit. It wouldn't work, even if it could.

Because as soon as I met Emmett, the countdown began. It's only a matter of time before this bubble pops; whether it's tonight or tomorrow, or maybe a week from now. There's no hope of this going anywhere.

Emmett frowns, a furrow appearing between his blue-gray eyes. "What were you thinking about just then?"

I wipe the expression from my face and give him a wide-eyed smile. Neely says my face is as easy to read as a book. "Just thinking about my empty stomach."

When the pancakes are ready, Dee calls for us to move the tables and Dawson helps Jacques plate, instructing Rufus to start carrying the plates to the table. I'm glad when he starts with the homeless man by the window and the couple by the bathroom.

"He's going to want to get tipped for this," Ethan says ruefully, watching his son comfortably maneuver around the tables.

After my breakfast is set in before me, I take a picture of my plate, two perfectly poached eggs with a thick layer of yellow hollandaise sauce. The pancakes are good, but you can't beat eggs for the protein and other health benefits.

I don't like to think about how the hollandaise sauce and thick slices of Canadian bacon offset most of those benefits.

I post on Instagram with the hashtags *#latenightsnack #Fred'sDineristhebest* and *#partyallnight.*

"Do you do that all the time?" Emmett asks, glancing at my phone with something akin to horror in his expression.

"Social media never sleeps." With a shrug, I glance at the time before I pop it back into my satchel. "And apparently, neither do I."

"Doesn't it bother you? The lack of privacy?"

I automatically begin to shake my head, then stop. "Sometimes," I admit. "I mean, it's great to have the followers and the traveling is amazing, but sometimes when people meet me, they expect to be best friends because they think they know everything about me."

"And they don't."

My chest fills with warmth at the understanding in Emmett's eyes. How would he know anything about this? "No," I say quietly. "They really don't know much about me at all."

"So tell me something about yourself," Emmett suggests. "Something that none of these followers know about you."

I'm dying.

The words are right there at the tip of my tongue. It would be the perfect time to tell him about my disease, but I can't.

I don't want to.

"My hair isn't really pink," I say, forking up a mouthful of eggs. I'm not dying tonight.

Emmett

AFTER I FILL MYSELF with food for the third time in twenty-four hours—lunch at Mama S.'s, the wedding dinner, and now with the most amazing pancakes I've ever had—we walk to the beach.

Apparently staying up all night is a thing for Shae.

Patrick offers a ride back to the hotel, but only Ethan takes him up on it, shepherding a protesting Rufus into the car. Knowing Rufus, the kid will be asleep by the time the car turns the corner, but it will be a long five minutes of complaining.

I'm not complaining.

Because I'm still with Shae, holding her hand as she wades into the cold water of Lake Ontario until the waves brush the hem of her skirt.

I like holding her hand. It's tiny and has short nails the same pink as her toenails. I never thought I'd be fascinated by toes but when I look down and see the pink half-moons under the water, it makes me smile.

She makes me smile.

Down the beach, Pepper hikes up her skirt and runs into the water with a shriek before turning to splash Adam. The open sand

and water turn us into kids, the dark sky making it seem like we're doing something wrong by being here.

Maybe we are.

On the way to the beach, Dawson and Grayson had traded off carrying Neely piggyback style after she complained about her shoes and now Grayson lets her slide to the ground.

Neely is left stumbling in the sand. "I hate these shoes!" she suddenly cries.

"You love those shoes," Shae calls, but her voice drifts away in the night air. I'm too far away to hear what Grayson says, but suddenly Neely stomps to the water's edge and throws her shoe.

Grayson has the other one and pitches it so far out that I can't see it fall.

"Did they just throw her shoes in the lake?" Shae asks with wonder.

"I think so. I guess she really doesn't like them."

Shae's heart-shaped face creases into a grin and her giggles turn into guffaws, even though there's nothing funny about disposing of a pair of shoes into Lake Ontario. It doesn't matter, because I'm laughing too.

It's almost been twelve hours since I first saw Shae in the church—both an instant and a lifetime ago. I should be hunched over with exhaustion but instead, I'm somehow more awake than usual, noticing all sorts of things. Like how the moonlight seems to float on the water and how Shae gives a little snort before she giggles.

I love her giggle.

I wonder if this is what it feels like to be on drugs.

I've been in love before, but this is different. And I know I'm not close to being in love with Shae—twelve hours here—but there's something new and fresh and exciting as hell between us.

"Come in," Shae urges, tugging on my hand. I step forward, only to jump back as the wave crests over my shoes. It's a good thing I didn't go with the rentals.

"Shoes." I gesture at my feet.

"Barefoot is better."

"I like to be able to feel my toes."

"It's not *that* cold," she says with an impish grin.

"Or maybe you've just lost the feeling in your feet."

"Could be."

"I'll warm them up. They're so small, like baby feet. One will fit in the palm of my hand."

Shae stretches out her arms and studies our entwined hands. "Are you for real?" she asks quietly.

I step into the waves and tug her close enough to lift her up. She laughs as her bare, and probably very cold, feet dangle over the water. "I don't get wet feet for just anybody."

This would be a perfect time to kiss her. In fact, my body realizes it before my head and lowers Shae so our mouths are only an inch apart. One second and I'll be able to tell if her lips are as cold as the rest of her—

"Emmett!" I turn in time to see a rainbow-coloured rubber ball fly through the air towards me and Grayson laughing. Shae squeals when I drop her, lunging for the ball and soaking her dress up to her knees.

The game is on, a mixture of rugby, touch football, and keep-away that somehow morphs into a furious round of dodge-ball.

City versus country, which isn't fair because Grayson and I have been playing ball for so long that we can anticipate each other's moves. But Shae surprises me at how quick she is, tiny feet sprinting down the sand. And Neely is fiercely competitive with a dirty streak. I don't remember the last time I've laughed so much, felt so free like the weight of grief and guilt lifted off my shoulders.

Is this what people do when they're not hiding from the world?

Adam, as the official ref, scorekeeper, and cheerleader, finally calls an end to the game. "I'm cold," he cries, hugging himself.

"Get some wood and I'll make a fire," Shae offers. She sinks onto the sand a few feet from the waves as the others scatter in search of anything flammable on the beach.

I stay with Shae.

When Neely settles beside us, Shae reaches over and pinches the fabric of her dress. "Your dress," she wails. The hem of her dress is damp and crusted with sand, the tiny pleats of the skirt impossibly wrinkled.

"It might be fixable." Neely spreads the skirt around her. "But as much as I love it, chances are I won't wear it again. It is a bridesmaid's dress. Wear it once and it hangs in your closet forever, isn't that the thing?"

"I've never been a bridesmaid," Shae muses.

Dawson dumps an armload of sticks and pieces of driftwood before Shae and she leans forward. "Need any help?" I ask.

"She's got this," Neely assures me before Shae can answer.

Adam hands her a handful of dried grasses. "I want to be a bridesmaid," he says. "Neely, you'll let me be part of your wedding party, won't you? After all, I'm your favourite brother."

"Keep thinking that." Neely gives him a smug smile. "But it's going to be a while, so don't hold your breath."

Grayson and Pepper return with their own armloads in time to hear Neely's remark. "You could come on the Suitor with me," Grayson invites. "That could speed things up."

Neely rolls her eyes. "Not this again."

I've seen Grayson work his magic on women too many times to count, and I'm impressed how Neely seems to be resisting him.

"Dawson, then," Adam says. "He loves me."

"You want to wear a dress to my wedding, you go right ahead," Dawson says, helping Shae arrange the pile of twigs and sticks into a little teepee in the sand.

Why doesn't Adam ask Shae about future weddings? But I get distracted by Shae rubbing two sticks together like she's trying to start a fire.

"Don't you have matches?" Pepper asks, watching Shae with a puzzled frown.

"When I was trying to get on Survivor, I spent weeks learning how to start a fire because that's what you have to do on the show," Shae explained, her tiny hands a blur as she rubs the sticks together. "I don't understand why so many contestants go on that show without knowing. If I could start a fire, they'd keep me around, so that was going to be my thing."

"Did you get on the show?" Grayson asks, staring at the sticks. "I don't watch reality shows—other than mine, of course."

She shakes her head as a thin stream of smoke appears. Dawson tucks the dried grass around the base as Shae purses her lips to blow on the tiny sparks. "Didn't make it past the audition," she says sadly. "It's too bad because I would have blown their minds with my fire-making skills."

"Consider my mind blown." I gesture to the slender flames now visible. "You made fire."

"I somehow feel emasculated," Grayson grumbles.

"What else can you do?" Pepper's face lights up with excitement as the tiny fire grows. "Or what else have you done?"

As the fire grows big enough to warm chilled hands, I listen to a litany of places Shae has visited, stories of exploits and adventures, of near misses and getting into trouble. The affection between the three of them is obvious, and while my friendship with Grayson is nothing to complain about, Neely, Dawson, and Shae have such a bond that it's more like family than mere friends.

I'm not surprised they follow her.

How could one woman have done so much in such a short time? Playing baseball meant that I traveled across the country, but my life can't begin to compare to Shae's. Airport to airport, suitcases dumped at hotels while they explore the culture and countryside of so many different places. And to be happy to share her life with strangers who happen to push the follow button. It blows my mind to think about it.

My experience with social media was so different that I'm having a hard time reconciling the hate and criticism I faced with the ease and joy Shae seems to feel.

Or maybe she's just happy about everything.

Her face lights up when she laughs, which she does a lot. I like the way she lets Neely and Dawson tell the stories but fills in the punch line at the perfect moment. They play off each other, finishing each other's sentences like they have some sort of hive mind.

I have a need to know Shae as well as they do.

Leaning back in the sand, I reach out my arm and smile when Shae leans against it without missing a beat in her story. The scent of strawberries surrounds me.

I never realized how much I missed this; physical contact, being with friends. And Shae—how did I last so long without spending time with a woman who fascinates me so completely? She has me wrapped up so tight that I can't think of anything else, not even what tomorrow will bring. But I try to focus on the conversation rather than how good Shae smells.

I'll have time enough to smell her.

Creepy, dude. That's way too creepy.

"You really got arrested in Peru?" Grayson is asking with disbelief.

Shae laughs without a trace of self-confidence. "Who knew you couldn't go pee behind a tree? Dawson did it, so I thought it was safe, but a park person wandered up just in time to see my bare bum." She leans to nudge Neely with her shoulder. "Thank God for this one talking her way out of it for me."

"What's your favourite place?" Pepper asks.

Each shares a different place; Costa Rica for Dawson, south of France for Neely, Thailand for Shae. "You always pick the latest place as your favourite," Neely chides.

"It was so much fun. The elephants and the zip-lining and the concerts."

"And Denzel Duke?" Pepper raises an eyebrow.

"Nothing happened with Denzel," Shae says quickly.

"He's *Denzel Duke*! How could nothing happen? Have you seen what he looks like in the Calvin Klein ad?"

"I wear Calvin Klein," Grayson cuts in.

"*Underwear* brother, not aftershave."

"It's cologne! And it smells good."

Leaving the warmth of my arm, Shae crawls across the sand to sniff at Grayson like a dog. "You kind of smell like maple syrup," she says, scrunching her nose.

"Well, *now*. I smelled good before. Didn't I?" He turns to Neely.

"You smelled good." Grayson smirks and Neely's eyes pop when she realizes what she's said. "But nothing happened with Shae and Denzel," she adds firmly, clearly hoping to lead the conversation away from her scent preference. "Shae's always been slow to start a relationship. I hope that is about to change." And then she looks pointedly at me.

Shae rolls her eyes. "Subtle, Neely, real subtle."

"I can be more direct if you like."

"No need." She looks away with a grimace, which isn't that encouraging.

"Your life must be incredible," Pepper marvels. "All the traveling, seeing so much of the world. I've only ever been to Florida and Jamaica."

"Come with us next time," Shae invites.

"I'd love to, but duty calls. My bakery. It's not much, but it's mine."

"It's a great place," I say automatically. "You've worked hard for it."

Pepper smiles at me. "Thanks, Emmett."

"You have a bakery?" Adam demands. He slaps his hand across his chest. "Me too!"

"No, you work in a bakery—a patisserie," Neely corrects. "There's a difference."

Adam waves his hand. "Tomato, tom*a*to—bakery, patisserie."

"No, owning, working for M.K. That's the difference."

Adam grimaces at his sister, and then his face lights up. "You know what we should do next?" he demands, his voice rising with excitement.

"Go to bed?" Dawson mutters.

"Let's go visit Reuben!" Adam claps his hands. "He'll be heading into Pain about now to make the croissants." He says the words in a mangled Scottish accent, which makes everyone laugh.

"I have no idea what you said, but what's a Reuben?" Grayson asks.

"Big guy I work with at Pain au Chocolate." This is said with a French accent, just as mangled.

"Is that the place where you got those awesome pastries?" Grayson turns to me. "That I, of course, didn't eat because I would never put something like that in my mouth that my dear sister didn't bake."

Pepper rolls her eyes.

"I think it's closed," Dawson points out.

"But this Reuben guy is there, and he'll let you in, won't he? It'll be an adventure," Pepper insists. "And I think I need to see it to check out my competition. We've been up all night anyway, what's another hour or so?"

And so the night continues as we make our way to Pain au Chocolate.

Chapter Eleven

Shae

THE WIDE WINDOWS OF Pain au Chocolate shine brightly against the darkness of the neighbouring shops as we arrive via taxi. Inside, the hulking figure of Reuben moves behind the counter to disappear into the kitchen.

"He's early," Adam says with disappointment as we stand outside the locked door. "I thought we could get in and give him a good scare."

"That's mean," I scold. "Reuben is a sweetheart."

"That big guy I just saw in the window?" Grayson asks with disbelief. "That's a sweetheart?"

"He really is. C'mon, I'll introduce you." Adam takes his keys from his suit pocket and unlocks the door. As soon as the door opens, I'm hit with the scent of sugar and butter, and even better—the rich, mouthwatering smell of coffee.

I can't help but think back to yesterday—Friday—and seeing Emmett standing in line. Was it instantaneous? What was it about him that drew me right in?

Because it did. One glance at his smile—

To be honest, it was the sight of his jeans, baggy but hugging everything just right. And then the way he looked at Rufus. And then the way he looked at me. It didn't hurt that he looks a bit like Captain America with the square jaw and strong shoulders.

I was smitten, right off the bat, and for once, I can't help but smile about it.

"Are you humming?" Neely demands.

"It was a sigh," I mutter. "A happy sigh. Because of the coffee."

"Reuben!" Adam calls, ushering us inside. "I'm back. And I brought friends."

The Tragically Hip sings loudly about the constellations in Bobcaygeon, masking Adam's cry. "Reuben," he shouts. "Turn the music down. He usually listens to—" The sudden silence interrupts and the kitchen door swings open.

"It's a wee bit early for you, I'd say." Reuben hovers in the doorway, an immaculate white apron covering his clothes, and a questioning expression on his face. If I was working alone in the middle of the night and someone suddenly opened the door, I'd be running for cover. But Reuben is calm and collected, plus he's the size of a Mack truck, so I guess he doesn't have to worry.

"It's a wee bit late," I correct, darting forward to give him a hug. Reuben's towering bulk leans over to pat me on the back. "I can't get used to you without the big beard. It's a whole new you. Love it."

He touches his cheek with the fashionable scruff instead of the Hagrid hair and glances over my head at the others. "It was time for it to go. Whereabouts are you coming from?"

"The wedding," Adam says with a wave of his arms. "And then we went for pancakes and then went to the beach and now we're here. Surprise!"

"I've been up for twenty-four hours," Neely says in astonishment.

Grayson smiles easily at her. "And you still look as fresh as a daisy."

On the ride from the beach, my head has slowly felt like it's filling with sand, leaving me slow to react. I have no desire to count how long I've been awake for or even think about the last time I've had a full night's sleep because it will only make it worse. I know I can catch up on my sleep. It's always like that on a trip and it's even worse when I come home, my body slow to adjust to the time zone. Neely always bugs me about extra vitamins and the green tea she swears by, but with the wedding, she hasn't had time to remind me.

I'm a big girl and fully capable of reminding myself. Pulling out my phone, I make a note in my calendar to take vitamins and notice the doctor's appointment on Tuesday morning.

I slide my phone out of sight.

"I suppose you need your coffee," Reuben says with a rueful smile. "Just so happens that I've already put it on."

"Actually, I've got someone here who wants to meet you." Adam pulls Pepper forward. She wears an ear-to-ear grin. "This is Pepper, another baker. And this is Reuben, who is a genius in the kitchen involving anything butter and pastry."

"And cupcakes," Emmett adds with a sideways glance at me. "Or so I've heard."

I brush Emmett's arm with my shoulder. "I said I'd share," I whisper.

"Share what?"

A giggle bursts out at the knowing look in his eyes and heads turn in our direction.

"Aye, yes." Reuben looks at Emmett with a flash of recognition and nods. "Tell me about this bakery," he suggests, gesturing Pepper behind the counter.

And then Reuben and Pepper are off and running, quickly disappearing into the kitchen while a grumbling Adam makes the lattes.

"This is a great place." Grayson looks around with an appreciative smile as he sits at a tiny table with Neely, so close that his knees must touch hers. I notice Neely isn't crying for personal space. Grayson seems to have worked a spell on her. "I'm not sure we'll get Pepper out of here."

"It's the best." I take a few pictures of the empty patisserie, the night sky outside the windows a dark background. "Do you think M.K. will mind if we're here?" I ask, hesitating before I post them.

"She loves me," Adam declares. "And therefore all of you, so it's fine. Don't make a mess because Reuben will make me clean it up."

"Is M.K. the owner?" Emmett asks, stirring his foam into his coffee. There are no foamy hearts but Adam still makes a good latte. I take a sip and keep my eyes on Emmett.

Maybe because it's the exhaustion of the day but it's as if there's a haze around me, clouding my sight so that I have to focus on

Emmett. I can't *not* look at him, staring at him like a lovesick teenager.

I prop my chin on my fist. I'm like one of those fangirls screaming for a peek of Denzel Duke. Pathetic.

But fun. For once I'm enjoying the rush, not caring where it's taking me, like the waves sweeping the remains of my fire back into the water.

Adam nods. "M.K. is a-*maz*-ing! But even more delicious is her fiancée Clay, who is to die for."

"Speaking of to die for, what happened to Reuben?" Neely leans forward, resting her elbows on the table. "New hair, no beard...what happened?"

I haven't heard the whole story, so I wrench my attention away from Emmett, only to feel the pressure from his foot against my mine under the table.

"I did," Adam says simply. "And a girl—sweet little thing, too bad it didn't work out. But she inspired him to make some changes in the Reuben outfit, and I have to say it worked out rather well." I catch the flick of his eyes towards the swinging door that leads to the kitchen where Pepper is no doubt peppering him with questions.

"He looks amazing," I announce. "I've never seen him wear jeans before."

Adam mirrors his sister and leans forward. "His bottom is to *die* for," he whispers. "Never saw that coming in those baggy cargos he used to wear."

Emmett hides his smile with the back of his hand. "Never thought this would be how your night turned out, didya?" I demand.

"Full circle." He nods. "I met you here almost thirty-six hours ago delivering a box of groceries."

"If you say that was the best moment of your life, I think I might vomit," Grayson says wryly.

Emmett raises an eyebrow. "I wouldn't want to take away any of your cheesy lines."

"He does have a few."

I choke on a mouthful of coffee, amazed at the ease of Neely's words. She has always been a tough nut to crack, but it seems like Grayson has blasted it open, leaving her sweet and salty nougat ready to taste.

I'm not the only one who notices Neely's new closeness with Grayson. Now that Pepper has disappeared with Reuben, Dawson shifts awkwardly, no doubt feeling like a fifth wheel.

Neely yawns suddenly, her mouth opening wide and tears filling her eyes. Mascara has smudged under her eyes, and most of the shadow has been rubbed away. The yawn is contagious and for a full two minutes, one by one, we all yawn.

"I guess it is catching," I say with a giggle.

"I don't know how much longer I'll last," Neely admits.

"It's been a long day," I agree, resting my head on her shoulder. "But a really good one."

"We have the wedding breakfast soon," Neely groans.

"Not me." I give a shiver of delight. "I'm off to bed as soon as we're out of here." Is it wrong that I give Emmett a sideways glance?

Maybe I'm taking this too far. Emmett is...Emmett is *good*. He doesn't deserve the chaos I'll bring to his life.

He catches my gaze and smiles, leaving me with a twinge of unease. I don't want to hurt him. Taking a deep breath, I lean back in the chair so our shoulders are no longer touching, instantly feeling the chill.

If I like him this much, then maybe?

I liked Denzel too. And the rugby player from Australia, and the salsa dancer from Rio, and... It doesn't matter if I like them. My feelings aren't the issue here, it's that they'll be left with the broken heart when I go.

When I die. And I like Emmett too much to cause him pain.

But I like him...

No. I snap upright like I've scalded myself.

Adam gives a theatrical groan, breaking into my reverie. "I forgot all about that. What are we doing here?"

"You suggested it," Dawson reminds him.

"I couldn't have. Drink up boys and girls so I can go home and get a few hours of beauty sleep."

"I have an idea," Neely says, looking over at me. Neely can always tell what I'm thinking like she's got some telepathic empathy or something. Even as she begins, I already know it's going to have something to do with Emmett.

"If it involves going anywhere else, count me out," Dawson grumbles. "The only place I want to go is my bed."

"Grayson was telling me about your farm," she says to Emmett, with a sly glance at me. "Why doesn't Shae visit and video something for the vlog?" She looks over at Dawson for support. "Don't you think it's a good idea?"

She's really lost the gift of subtlety tonight. But the thought of more time with him and seeing Emmett on his own turf does what Neely wants—it pulls me back into the haze of Emmett.

"It's different." I've always wondered how Neely would react if Dawson ever disagreed with her. "I think the followers would get a kick out of seeing a real-life, working farm, rather than some of the touristy ones we've been to."

"Like the lavender farm in France?" I ask. "Or the goat yoga place."

"We have goats, but there's no yoga," Emmett says quickly. "I don't do yoga."

"Is the big man afraid to be flexible?" I ask in a teasingly sweet voice.

"No, the big man is afraid his old catcher's knees will lock up and I'll end up stuck in one of those pigeon or eagle positions."

Adam gives him a pitying smile. "I don't think there's an eagle pose in yoga."

"There is!" I shoot away from the table, tottering slightly in my heels as I bend and twist to demonstrate the pose. "It's the *garudasana*. Also called the eagle pose."

"I guess I know more than I think I do." Emmett grins, leaving me tottering.

"I think you should go," Neely urges as I un-pretzel myself. "We have nothing planned and people might like to see something other than wedding and late-night shots."

"But I have such good stuff from tonight." I pull out my phone and catch Neely scowling. "But sure, if you think it's a good idea?" I ask Emmett, suddenly wary about his reaction of seeing me again.

"I think it'd be great," Emmett says with an extra dose of eagerness. "My father would love it, and so would Rufus. I might get my cool uncle status back if you show up."

"Well, that makes it all worth it."

When Pepper returns from her kitchen tour, she finds Dawson asleep with his cheek smushed against the wall. I've pushed past the waves of nausea that have slowly been starting inside me, a major tell when I'm too tired, but I won't last much longer. And Neely, always the last to give in, looks wan with the deepening shadows under her eyes from lack of sleep rather than smudged mascara.

"You only came back from Thailand yesterday," Emmett exclaims after Dawson shakes himself awake. "You must be exhausted."

"It was Friday," Neely corrects as I finally begin to count on my fingers how much sleep I've gotten since we've been back. "It's already Sunday."

"Go home," Grayson orders.

Adam quickly clears our dishes and Neely orders Ubers for us, as I try to think of something to say to Emmett. This is goodbye, but is it? Is he waiting for me to say something? But with my head suddenly spinning, I barely know my own name.

I don't want to leave it like this.

When the cars pull up, hugs are exchanged. I'm the last one in the car, with a long look at Emmett.

"Are we on for the farm?" he asks with a hopeful smile.

I nod with my own smile of relief. And then, as he prepares to shut the door of the car for me, Emmett leans down for a hasty kiss.

The Uber pulls up outside Neely's house and I climb out, my head spinning with exhaustion and the kiss. It's nothing more than our lips smushed together, but it sends me into a tailspin. Should I? Could I? I touch my lips with a tired smile.

"You're going to visit him?" Neely insists as we hug goodnight on the sidewalk.

"Monday. Because it's already Sunday now."

She nods firmly as she steps back. "He's a good one, Shae."

"I know."

"Don't...don't do what you usually do." I see the concern in her purple-shadowed eyes. "Give him a chance."

My smile fades as car headlights illuminate us and I step aside so that my mother can pull into the shared driveway. I haven't seen her since leaving for the wedding but she's the last one I want to talk to right now. I wave to Neely and head for the steps, slow on tired feet.

"You're finally home," my mother says as she catches me fumbling with the key. "Long wedding."

"We were having fun." The door turns and I step inside, welcomed by the thump of Doris's tail against my leg.

"Who's we?" Her keys rattle in the bowl on the table and she slips off her coat behind me. I try to hurry out of her way, but my fingers have trouble unbuckling the strap on my shoe.

"Neely, Dawson," I say shortly. "Adam. Some friends we made at the wedding."

I have one shoe off as Mom looms above me. "Who is he?"

"He who?" Slumped against the wall, I stare innocently up at her. I *am not* telling her about Emmett.

"It must be a guy. You always seem to find one." With a click of her tongue, she drops a hand on Doris's yellow head and turns away.

"Is that a problem for you?" It's like my mother knows exactly what button to press, and when to press it for maximum impact. Am I such an open book that she can tell that I met Emmett, and not only that, but I'm confused beyond belief? This is when I need a mother to confide in, not a cold shell still floundering in the muck of her own pain.

"As long as you don't make it a problem for them," she says crisply. "Your future is uncertain, to say the least, and the last thing you should be doing is setting some poor guy up for heartbreak."

"I just met him," I mutter, pulling off my second shoe and setting them neatly by the wall.

"You of all people should understand what it's like to lose someone."

"Yeah, I think I'm an expert on that," I say, heavy on the sarcasm. The memory of my father's funeral is as vivid as if it happened last night. My mother's blank face and how she looked right through me is something I doubt I'll ever forget.

But she always seems to forget that she wasn't the only one that he left behind.

"Do you think it's fair to him?"

"What's fair? And to who?" My stomach sinks because I know where she's going with this.

"To let him care about you. What if he falls in love with you?"

"He's not going to fall in love with me." I stare unseeing past her shoulder into the dark house. Mike left the kitchen light on, sending shadows into the living room.

"Stop encouraging him." Her voice is firm and forceful like she expects me to submit.

"I'm not encouraging him!" I throw up my arms. "I like him, okay? I like him."

I like him a lot. Too much.

Mom sucks in her breath. "Have you told him?"

"Telling someone I'm going to die is usually a conversation killer, so I try to avoid it," I shoot back, the sarcasm heavy in my voice.

"You should let him decide."

"Let him to decide to run, is that it? Is that what you would have done if you knew Dad had what I have? This death sentence? Would you have left before things got heavy? Before you got hurt?"

"I don't know what I would have done," Mom says quietly. She can't look me in the eye. "I wish I would have known though. I deserved to know."

"Well, I just met Emmett, and he doesn't deserve to know anything." Three angry stomps have me sweeping past Mom without a word, but she stops me before I get to the stairs.

"Shae? Think about him. Be fair. You're very easy to love, and you don't want to hurt him."

"Could have fooled me," I mutter.

"I don't want you to hurt anyone." How can a mother have no qualms about insisting that her daughter live without love? I've been listening to her arguments since I was fourteen when she cautioned me on getting too close to Dawson when we first met.

"You will leave him," she had said with a frightening lack of emotion. "How do you think he's going to feel when you're not there anymore after he's come to rely on you? It's going to be bad enough for poor Neely. You don't want to hurt anyone else."

It's like my father had snatched her heart out of her chest when he died, leaving no evidence other than her robot-like rationale about love.

And for years, I've listened to her. Despite everything, I've thought she's been right about this—falling in love will not work for me.

But I've known Emmett for hours and I can feel a shift of my beliefs. That alone should scare me, but instead I feel...

Free? Liberated?

Happy.

My mother wants to dictate my life because of what happened to her—how she dealt with the blow she was hit with when my father died. Because of what she did, and didn't do. How she dealt, and didn't deal with.

But Emmett is not my mother and he can only react in a better way. *If* there's something between us, and *if* it works out, and—the very biggest if—*if* my expiry is close at hand, he'll deal with it much differently than my mother did.

He has to.

"Have you ever thought about whether *I'm* the one getting hurt?" Her answering stare is blank. "Nope, guess not. Well, as lovely as this conversation is, I'm off to bed."

Her heavy sigh stops me with one foot on the bottom stair. "Jana-Shae..." She's the only one who ever calls me by my full name, and usually, it's when she's disappointed in me. Which is most of the time, it seems. "Are you feeling all right?"

"You're asking that *now*?" I shake my head and stand up straight. "I'm just peachy, so thanks for your concern. No need for it though; I'll be out of your hair soon enough."

I meant off on another trip, but she looks at me with alarm. And for once I don't feel like reassuring her.

Emmett

"**D**ON'T LET HER LEAVE before I get home," Rufus cries as he runs full speed out the door to catch the bus Monday morning.

Shae is coming to spend the day at the farm. Or at least the afternoon.

There had been a spattering of DM's between us yesterday about time and directions and inane questions from Shae, like whether goats like candy and if she could bring honey home for Mike.

Dating has been a lost art for me, and I don't like communicating via text and Instagram; I'd rather talk and touch, and I can't help but second-guess some of her replies. How do people have relationships without seeing each other in person?

Shae's last message had been sent at 3:17 a.m. with the apology that she wasn't sleeping and didn't think she'd be able to make it for ten. Could she come after lunch?

I don't care when she gets here, as long as I get to see her again. My night was as restless as hers, but I don't have the excuse of a transatlantic flight to recover from. I dive into chores this morning while fending off questions about Shae from Rufus before he leaves for school.

Dad has made himself scarce in the barns as I drift around the house waiting for her. The house feels empty without Ellie and I miss seeing her clutter of books and knitting bag in the living room. Even Hardy, the family dog, left me alone with my thoughts as I wait.

I'm tempted to send Ellie a text to ask how she's enjoying Mexico, but think twice—who really wants to hear from a brother on their honeymoon?

The radio is the only sound, save the creaks of an old farmhouse. It's the last thing Dad turns off at night and the first he turns on in the morning, and I've grown up with the same country station as the soundtrack to my life.

When I hear the roar of an engine coming fast up the lane, I practically trip over my own feet in my hurry to get outside. Amid a swirl of dust, a bright blue car parks beside my truck with a flourish with Shae's mischievous smile appearing in the window.

"That's some car," I say as she hops out, trying to keep my own foolish grin from taking over my face.

"1976 Mustang Cobra." Shae waves her arms in a game show host manner. "It was my Dad's. I hardly ever have a reason to drive it, but Mike takes care of it for me." She pulls a bag from the front seat and slings it over her shoulder before shutting the door.

"Mike's your grandfather?" I ask, wanting to be sure of something because the way Shae is smiling at me makes the ground seem uneven enough to trip me.

"My grandmother's long-time boyfriend, but they never got married," Shae says, pushing her glasses on top of her head and dancing around the car. "Granny had been married twice and apparently wasn't up for a third, even though Mike is truly amazing. You'll like him." I'm busy drinking her in and almost miss the assumption that I'll be meeting someone in her family.

As she comes forward, the breeze ruffles the hem of her knee-length sundress—cute, but not the most appropriate item of clothing when you visit a farm. At least it's better than the shoes.

"You can't wear those," I say, gesturing to her pink, slipper-like shoes.

"Can't wear what? My shoes?" She sticks out her leg and rotates her foot. "These came all the way from Malaysia."

"Do they have goat poo in Malaysia?"

She scrunched up her nose. "Not that I noticed."

"If you step in some with those shoes on, you'd definitely notice. Going barefoot here is a little different than barefoot on the beach. I'll get you some boots."

"Boots," she echoes with a grin like she's excited about it.

We step forward in unison; to hug or to kiss? Hug—Shae's arms slide around my waist and I have a sense of *rightness* holding her. Alex wasn't what anyone could call affectionate, but Shae—

Stop comparing them.

Shae buries her face into my flannel shirt and sniffs loudly. "You smell farm-y."

"It's not the best smell," I say apologetically, and attempt to pull away.

She inhales again. "But it's not bad." Hooking her arms around my waist, she leans back to look me in the face. "So this is your farm. Peaceful," she continues, looking at the fields and barns and greenhouses off to the side of the house. May is always a pretty time of year with layers of green covering the faded browns of winter. Most of the trees have a good show of leaves and the fields are dotted with tiny shoots pushing out of the dirt.

I'm proud of how the place looks today like it's on its best behaviour for a guest.

"So, hey, you didn't tell me you have a *website* for your farm."

"Why does that excite you?"

"I'm all about online presence and social media, and there you are! Nice picture, by the way. You look very cute, even with the abundance of hair."

Thankfully the picture was taken before the man bun phase. "Ellie and Dad made me pose. Something about female attention."

"And I'll bet most of your customers are female. I'd be lining up to grab one of your boxes if I was into eating fresh-grown organic vegetables."

"You like your pesticides, then?"

"I think I was more referring to the vegetables." Shae giggles. "But bribery has worked well in the past if you need me to try something."

"Good to know."

"Despite my anti-vegetable stance, I want to see your farm." She bites her lip and looks up with her big eyes. "And you. I wanted to see you."

"Yeah?" I try for casual but fireworks are going off inside me and I can't stop the smile. "Good because I wanted to see you too."

Shae steps back before I have a chance to kiss her. And I really want to.

"Let's start the tour," she says with a smile. "But first, my boots.

Ellie's rubber boots are a sharp contrast to her little dress and Shae's legs are a bit of a distraction as we walk through the fields, stepping carefully over the new hills of cucumbers and the stalks of corn that already come up to her ankles. "It looks a little different in the fall," I say. "A lot more green. We've finished the second seeding of spinach—" I stop when I see how she's looking at me. "What?"

"I know nothing about farming and I'm afraid to ask anything because I'll sound stupid."

"There are no stupid questions," I say, echoing my father's words.

"Okay, then, how do you deliver vegetables when the ground looks like that?" She points to the thin spread of green from the field of beans.

"We do what's in season," I explain. "And what we have in the greenhouses." I gesture to the buildings in the distance.

"I thought they were barns. Do I get to see them too?"

"You can see anything you want."

Shae takes a few pictures, turning in circles to catch the view. And then she slips her hand into mine. "It's really so peaceful here," she says quietly.

"It is," I agree. "When I moved back, I was in need of peace and quiet." I hold my breath in case she asks *why* I came back. I have to remember that Shae knows nothing about me, but right now, I like it that way. There will be time to tell her everything, but it's nice not to see the usual layer of pity in her eyes.

"Peace and quiet," she echoes, staring off into the forest bordering the fields. "I've never really looked for it. My life is so *go-go-go*. But now that I'm here, I like it. I feel like I can be still here. Quiet."

"You're not usually quiet, are you? Or still."

"No." She rubs her arm, more out of reflection than warmth. "I always think I'm going to miss out on something if I'm still. There's still so much I want to do."

"You've got time."

She turns her face so I can't see her profile. "How long have you lived here?"

"I've been back for three years," I say. "But we've had the farm all my life. It was bigger." Taking a step beside her, I point at the newly built subdivision in the distance. "We used to own all that land as well, but the builder made Dad an offer he couldn't refuse. That's when Dad decided to scale back, try the organic vegetable side of things. Have to say, it worked out pretty well for him."

"Did you always plan on coming back? After baseball?"

I shrug, for once not bothered by talking about it. "I hadn't planned on doing anything but play ball. I figured I'd spend another five years behind the plate. Ten, if my knees held out. But it wasn't meant to be."

"What happened?"

I stiffen. Not yet. I want to wait as long as I can. "You don't want to hear my sad story. Come on, there's still more to see. I haven't shown you the goats yet." I turn to head down the hill and she scampers to my side.

"I like goats."

"You must not know too many of them. We have chickens too," I say. "They're not as cute."

"Of course they are!"

As expected, she falls in love with each and every one of the animals. What I didn't expect is for Marcus, the gruff and mono-syllabic farm manager, to be so smitten with her. He ends up taking her around the greenhouse while I round up the two goats that Shae let escape.

I must be smitten as well because I don't even get annoyed for having to chase the goats.

Shae takes pictures of everything and even convinces Marcus to be in a little video for her vlog. He stands red-faced with a goofy smile staring at Shae while she talks.

The sun is low in the sky as we finish the tour, hiking up the rise behind the greenhouses, the best place to see the whole farm.

"What's that?" Shae points to the pitching mound behind the house that Grayson and I built when we were sixteen. The trail of ground brick between the mound and home is spotted with dandelions and creeping Charlie, but Dad still maintains it in the hope that Rufus might want to use it.

"Grayson was a pitcher and I was a catcher. This is where we would practice."

She looks at me with admiration in her eyes. "This is how you got to the majors?"

"For a few games," I admit.

"But now you don't play anymore. What happened?"

I stare at the wall behind home plate pockmarked with spots where a wild pitch had gotten away from me. To tell Shae about why I'm not playing means telling her about Alex. I'm not ready for that. Someday...someday soon, but not today.

"That's a long story," I finally say. "Today is for the farm."

Shae hugs my arm, warming me from the chill that has begun with her question. "I want to know all of it. You saw my world the other night. Now it's your turn."

"Your world is a little different from mine."

"Considering there's no airport or even a beat-up hostel around here, I'd say yes." She meets my gaze with a hesitant smile. "But I like it."

"You don't have to say that. It's a farm. It's not for everyone."

"But it's for you?"

I think about the question before answering. For years, baseball had been my life and a big part of me resented the chores and responsibilities that took me away from it. But coming back, with my career in tatters, showed me that there was much more to this place than I ever gave it credit for. The rolling hills of green, the smells of the seasons, the satisfaction of a good harvest and even watching the animals grow—it's for me. It's my life now.

And as I nod, the last vestige of bitterness about how my baseball life turned out drifts away.

"Then it's for me too." She says it so quietly that I wonder if I heard correctly. But before I can ask, she scampers off in the direction of the maple tree, the biggest one on the property. Before I can catch up, she swings up to the lowest branch.

"What are you doing?"

"Climbing a tree. Did you ever climb trees?" She pulls herself up to the next branch as a gust of wind blows her dress, lifting the hem of her skirt enough for me to see her bright blue underwear.

"Maybe that's not the best thing to wear when you climb a tree." My eyes light on the boots she discarded at the base of the tree. "You don't even have shoes on."

"It's easier this way. Come up and join me."

"I don't think so." The last time I'd climbed a tree had been when Ethan had been seven. Mom had taken us to Grayson's and left us playing in his backyard while she was inside.

Ethan had fallen from the tree and broken his arm. I wonder if the long minutes between our screams and Mom rushing out of the house really happened, or I've imagined it, now that I know what had been going on.

It had been a simple break, but the trip to the hospital had cemented Ethan's wish to be a doctor, as well as my vow never to climb another tree. My little brother lasted a summer with an arm in a cast, but there was no way I would have.

I have a feeling it won't do any good to tell Shae to stop, and I watch warily as she climbs higher, her tiny frame allowing her to use branches that would break under my weight. "That's what makes it so fun. C'mon. We can play the scene in Twilight where Edward takes Bella up the tree."

I shake my head, even though I've seen the movies several times. It's not like I'm about to admit that to anyone. "I have no idea what you're talking about," I lie.

"Of course you don't," she says ruefully.

I position myself under the branch as she begins to climb down, my arms open to catch her in case she falls. But she moves quickly through the leaves until she sits on the lowest branch right above me.

"I'm going to jump," she warns me.

"Want me to catch you?"

"That'll be fun," she says impishly. "You had good practice with Neely at the wedding." Without a word of warning, she pushes off.

I catch her under her arms, but as she slides down, my arms instinctively tighten around her, leaving her laughing with a kick of her feet.

"You're so big and strong," she says teasingly.

"You weigh about as much as Rufus."

With a gasp, she stretches a hand around her back. "My dress—I think I'm mooning the trees."

Instead of setting her down, I shift my hold. Suddenly her legs are around my waist, my hands on her bum. "Oops."

"Why don't you tell me about this tree scene you wanted to reenact," I say in a low voice.

"Edward climbed a tree with her and they stood on a branch and stared at each other," Shae says, her dark eyes doing just that to me.

"Like what we're doing?"

She nods. "But we're standing on the ground so it's a little different. Edward's a vampire, so they got really high up."

"I'm not a vampire."

"I think that's a good thing."

"I thought girls liked the bad boys of the night."

Scrunching her nose, she shakes her head. "Sucking blood turns me off. Besides, they live forever, and I...won't." Her breath hitches in her throat. "I'd miss you."

"You hardly know me."

An expression of sorrow flashes across her face. "I'd miss you."

"No one lives forever, so you won't have to miss me."

She untwines her legs and slides to the ground, leaving me kicking myself for not taking the chance.

"What's next?" she asks quietly, standing two feet away and hugging herself as if the warm day has turned icy cold.

What just happened here?

Chapter Twelve

Shae

ON THE DRIVE OUT of the city, through the adorable small town of Ashbury and taking two wrong turns on the way to Emmett's, I convince myself to ignore my mother's warnings.

Maybe it's not fair to Emmett to let him fall for me, but it's also not fair for me to give him the cold shoulder for the day. And I've had a ball of anticipation growing in my belly since I said goodbye to him Sunday morning. I want to see him again. Plain and simple. After today, I'll figure it out, but I want today.

I'm letting myself like him today.

It's not hard because Emmett is great. Sweet and funny, direct but not rude, and he's got a way of looking at my mouth that makes me want to giggle because I know he wants to kiss me.

Maybe because it's that I want to kiss him too.

Things are going great until my one silly comment about Twilight and vampires brings home the fact that I won't be living forever, as clearly as if my mother had shouted the words out loud.

Today, for the first time in so long, I've let myself live—really live with a guy. I don't hold myself back with Emmett, and as we walk through the fields, breathing in the smell of green, I really believe that I'm not going to be one of the ninety percent of fatal Batten disease diagnoses.

Emmett makes me feel hopeful.

"He's a good one," Neely had texted before I left. "Give him a chance and don't blow this."

I take Neely's advice over my mother's, and it works until it doesn't.

Even so, with my mother's warnings that I'm not being fair ringing in my head, I take Emmett's hand as we walk back to the house, trying to repair the damage of the missed moment.

I *really* wanted him to kiss me.

The confusion in his eyes when I shook loose from his hold squeezes my heart with a painful sort of tightness. I know I'm giving him mixed signals, just like my mother always accuses me of, but I can't help it. I don't like the thought of hurting him, for any reason.

"I think that's the end of the tour," Emmett says stiffly. "Did you get enough? Will your followers like it?"

I've messed up. He was about to kiss me and I ruined it. It's a pattern, but this time it wasn't intentional and I've no idea what to do.

What would Neely do?

No, Dawson. WWDD?

"I think they'll love it," I say, wiggling my fingers within his grip. "How could they not? You'll get tons of traffic to your website and lots of women showing up and asking for you to deliver their vegetables. Maybe I shouldn't post it," I finish dramatically.

"Why?"

I mask my sigh at the coolness in his voice. "All that unwanted female attention. Maybe it is wanted—"

"It's not."

I squeeze his hand again. "I think you're going to have enough dealing with the attention from *me*."

"Is that right?" His blue-gray eyes are more gray than blue as he studies my face.

"I'm not good at this," I whisper apologetically.

"Neither am I."

I nod sharply and do what Dawson would do—pretend nothing is wrong. "What time does Rufus get home from school?"

"Rufus? Soon."

"Should I stay or should I go," I sing. "I'd love to see the little man but his father seemed nervous about it the other night."

"Ethan left last night. He..." Emmett trails off like he's searching for the words. "He worries," he finishes. "He tries, but it's hard being away. There's so much he misses, that he doesn't know. He thinks Rufus is going to drop everything and beg for you to take him around the world."

I rest my hand on my chest. "*I'd* let him in a minute," I say, "but he's got to go through Neely first, and she'd never let him drop out of school. Tell Ethan Rufus is safe for now."

"How did you meet Neely?" Emmett asks as we skirt the goats, even though I'm tempted to give them more carrots as a treat. So cute! "The two of you seem...different," he finishes with a chuckle.

"*Very*. I must drive her crazy because she's so organized and plan-y, and I'm like *squirrel*." I jerk my body like a dog distracted by an animal and Emmett laughs. "But I think that's why we're so good together. I met her in grade five. It was the first day of school and it had been raining all night. When the bell rang and everyone ran to the door, I slipped and fell and this older kid stepped on me. Literally stepped on me—there was a muddy footprint on my leg and everything. Neely was new at the school, didn't know anyone but her brothers, but she picked me up, and then she tracked down the kid who stepped on me and tore him a new one. She's been my hero ever since."

"It's like she looks after you," Emmett muses. "Not that you need it."

"Oh, I do," I agree. "She runs my vlog; helps me get sponsors, organizes itineraries, basically keeps it moving when all I want to do is do the fun stuff. I don't know what I'd do without her. I need to tell her that more often," I decide, struck by how much Neely does mean to me.

"It's always good to tell others how much you appreciate them." Emmett nods. "What about Dawson? Does he take care of you too?"

I laugh. "He's too busy managing his love life. I swear, that guy has more success with the female sex than anyone I know. I mean, he's cute and all." I sneak a glance at Emmett. "You're cuter, but Dawson constantly has women coming on to him. It's like they literally find him irresistible."

"And do you find him irresistible?" He doesn't meet my eye when he asks.

"Definitely not." I burst out with a peal of laughter. "I love him to death, but only as a friend. He's like a brother to me. There was one time in grade nine—that's how we met. I was with a group, he was with a group, and we went off together. It was *such* a bad kiss," I recall with a big smile. "I ended up laughing. Instead of being offended and storming away, he laughed too. We've been friends ever since."

I slow down as we reach the steps of the house and raise my eyebrows at Emmett.

"Well, you'd better come in," he says, his gruffness sounding exactly like I think a farmer should.

I don't even bother to hide my smile as I follow him onto the porch.

I see a lot of the outdoors when I travel, as well as the inside of enough museums and tourist attractions to hate history. I don't hate history—I don't hate anything but incurable diseases. But what I really like, what I get the most out of, is seeing the inside of a house. You can learn a lot from the way a person lives, how they set up their home.

Like Neely's house: Pictures and knickknacks cover the shelves, blankets folded on the arm of the couch suggest curling up with the cats and a book. I've always found it warm and comfortable, full of relaxed clutter of a family who likes each other.

My house, on the other hand, has no clutter other than Mike's cooking magazines. The only pictures are the ones of my trips that Mike frames, and the odd ones of my father.

I like looking at pictures of my father, comparing my dark eyes and smile to his. It makes me hopeful that I won't turn into my mother someday. Because of my mother, and despite Mike's best attempts, the house is cold, like strangers live there. It's home, but it doesn't feel like it.

Unlike Emmett's house.

I've heard the basics, that Emmett lives with his father—Peter—and Rufus; that Ellie has moved out for her marital home with James, and younger brother Ethan hasn't lived at home for years. So when Emmett holds open the door for me, I expect something of a bachelor pad, much like Dawson's basement man-cave.

"I love it," I breathe, not realizing I've spoken aloud until Emmett thanks me. There's nothing farmhouse about it, other than the rubber boots lining the wall by the back door in the kitchen. It's an open space, with the massive fireplace and flat-screen television the main focus of the sunken living room, and a gorgeous dining table made of a grayish wood that looks as if someone had just hewn it from trees in the woods. "It looks like fall."

"Ellie's influence," Emmett says with a sheepish grin. "Actually, my mother redid the place just before she left." He taps the dining room table. "Grayson's father made this. He was very good with wood. He was also very good at running off with other people's wives."

My brows knot. "Grayson's dad—"

"Ran off with my mother," he finishes.

"Whoa. How are you—? It's amazing that you're still such good friends," I say with amazement.

Seeing the inside of a person's home gives you insight into so many things. I spent the entire night with Grayson and Pepper, Emmett and Ethan, without realizing their families were connected like that.

It's not a good sort of connection either.

"It was tough at first," Emmett admits, standing awkwardly by the table as I wander towards the stairs. Framed photos line the staircase; school pictures of Ethan, Ellie and Emmett, from kindergarten to Ethan's graduation portrait. At the top are pictures of Rufus, some casual like they were taken with an iPhone as well as the stiffly posed school photos.

I'm quick to notice there are no pictures of his mother in the house.

"We didn't talk for a couple of months after it happened," Emmett continues, "which made it tough when we were playing ball together. And there was a pretty bad time when Grayson's father called on his birthday." He smiles ruefully. "That was the only time I've actually punched him."

My heart breaks for the young Emmett.

"I think that must be why Ellie and Pepper had a falling out. They couldn't handle knowing a parent was making the other one miserable. Ellie took it hard."

I step towards him and take his hand. "I can't imagine what it must have been like."

"It was..." He pauses as if searching for the word. "Tough."

"That must be an understatement."

"It was a long time ago." I wait for more, watching as Emmett searches through his memories. When a person shares information like that, there's more to come unless they forcibly change the subject, so you need to be patient. It's one thing I'm patient about.

"My last memory is her barking at me to set the table," Emmett says slowly. I squeeze his hand, letting him take his time. "I don't remember why Ellie and Ethan didn't have to help, only that I had to. I was a typical kid about it, complaining and dragging my feet, and ended up spilling a bag of milk onto the floor. She was furious—I'd never seen her so upset." There's a long pause. "She left that night."

"Not because of you," I say quickly.

He shrugs. "No, but it took a while for me to realize that. She never said goodbye. And she didn't take the dog." I follow his gaze to the well-loved dog bed beside the fireplace. "I was almost more surprised at that. She really loved that dog. I thought she loved us, too."

I open my mouth to try for something compassionate, but Emmett gives a shake of his shoulders. "Didn't expect that to come out on the first date."

"I think, technically, this might be the second," I announce. "The wedding, and all. Or, if you like, you escorting me down the aisle at the church could be the first, the reception the second. Then you've got Fred's and the beach and then Pain au Chocolate..." I count on my fingers. "This could be like the sixth date if you want."

He smiles and I see the sadness has swept from his expression. "If you want."

"If it makes you feel better about telling me stuff."

Our hands are still joined when he steps closer and pushes a strand of hair behind my ear. "I want to tell you stuff," he mutters. "Stuff I've never told anyone."

"I have that effect on people." *Keep it light, Shae. Because I'm not getting into true confessions with him now. Not now, and hopefully not ever.*

For the first time, I pretend I have all the time in the world.

Emmett's kiss is gentle at first. Almost tentative like he hasn't done this in a while. But then as I press myself against him, reaching my arms around his shoulders, he kicks it up a notch. My heart hammers against his chest as he wraps his arms around me, lifting me off my feet. My legs instinctively wind around his waist like under the tree, but there's no regret for missed opportunities this time.

I'm all in now.

There's smoothness under me and I realize Emmett has set me on the gorgeous table. And then I don't notice anything else but him until the door bursts open.

Emmett

"S HAE!"

The excitement in Rufus's voice mirrors my own while I was waiting for her to get here. That's the only reason I don't pitch him out the door after he finds us...having a moment.

The moment is over as I jump back from Shae like she's electrocuted me, my hands still flexed from being pressed on her back. Shae slides smoothly from the table as if an eleven-year-old didn't just walk in on us wrapped tighter than a roll of Saran Wrap. "Hey, Rufus!"

Rufus cocks his blond head as he stares curiously at us. "What are you doing? Were you sitting on the table?" he demands. "Because you'll get in trouble for that, and I don't want that to happen."

"No, I—"

"Were you kissing? Because that—" He stops midsentence with an expression that looks like he's doing long division in his head. "I guess that's cool."

"Glad to have your approval," I say mildly, heading to the kitchen. I leave Shae with Rufus because I need a minute.

That was...something. I take a shaky breath and stop fighting the smile that wipes my face with the force of a tidal wave.

When I glance back at Shae, she's looking a little shaky herself. Luckily, Rufus is oblivious, chattering to her about school and baseball and whatever he's into today.

"How long are you staying?" I hear Rufus ask. I turn again to see Shae with a questioning look in her eyes.

"I'll feed you." I cringe as the eagerness in my voice rings out loud and true. *Not cool, dude.* "You're welcome to stay as long as you like. Dinner...we can watch a movie after..."

"Movie?"

"We have movies."

Rufus barks with laughter. "Grandpa is a movie *fanatic*," he says. "We have *every* movie ever made."

"Maybe not every one. What's your favourite?"

"Princess Bride," she says automatically. I've never heard a person answer so quickly.

"I love that movie!" Rufus announces. "Can we watch it now?"

"Don't you have homework?" Shae asks.

"No, so we—" Rufus notices me staring and gives me a sideways glance. "Just a bit. It won't take me long."

"Why don't we watch it after dinner?" she suggests. "If that's okay with you." She glances over at me with a hopeful smile.

"Everything is okay with me right now."

Shae does her best to smoother the smile. "I thought our sixth date could be a little longer than the others."

Rufus rolls his eyes. "Oh, boy, you like each other." Swinging his knapsack over his shoulder, he hotfoots it up the stairs.

Shae raises her eyebrows. "Do we like each other?" she asks hesitantly.

"I can only speak for myself, but I think we do."

She dances fairy-like to my side and curls herself under my arm. "I think we do, too."

I laugh, with relief, with delight. How did this happen? And how is it so easy?

With Alex, it took months for love to mix in with the lust and infatuation, but it's different with Shae. It's almost like she's got some power over me, like in the vampire movie she was talking about.

Twilight. Thanks to living with a movie fanatic, I've seen more movies than I ever thought possible.

I dip my head to kiss Shae again because now that I've started, I don't want to stop. My lips barely rest on hers when the kitchen door opens and Dad clumps in, followed by Hardy, her tail sweeping excitedly at the sight of Shae.

"I really need to lock the doors," I say wryly.

Shae laughs, but once again she's quick to jump away. "Hi," she chirps to Dad.

He takes a step towards her, holding out his hand, his gray eyes studying her. "Hello, there."

"Hi." I realize she's nervous, which opens an *aww* motion inside me.

"You must be the Shae I've heard about. Although I have to admit, Rufus is much more forthcoming with information. I've heard all about the dancing at the wedding and the pancakes...seen all the videos." Dad smiles at her warmly, and Shae's shoulders relax slightly.

"He might be my number one fan." She offers her hand to Hardy for a sniff, who responds by pushing her face between her legs. Shae laughs and scratches behind the dog's ear.

"I wouldn't be surprised. But don't worry—he's eleven and this obsession won't last forever." Dad glances at me.

"Homework," I reply to the unasked question. "Shae is going to stay for dinner."

"If that's okay with you," she adds hastily.

"Of course," Dad says in a hearty voice before his brow furrows. "If we can scrounge up something to feed you."

Ellie has left the freezer full and the pantry stocked, but the only problem is that neither Dad nor I really know what to do with the food.

"Ellie liked to cook," I explain as Shae laughs at our indecision on what to have.

"I like to cook, and I learned from the best," she says, rummaging in the cupboards for a pot while Dad looks on with amusement.

"I think things are in good hands," he says. But instead of retreating to his office, or even his favourite chair in the living room, Dad takes the spot at the table, where, only moments ago, Shae had been perched, and he listens as Shae keeps up a running monologue of what she's doing in the kitchen.

It doesn't take long for Rufus to finish his homework and join us, the two of them at the table and me acting as the worst sous chef in history. Even Hardy sprawls out across the floor to watch.

"When I heard we had a social influencer visiting, I never imagined we'd get a cooking lesson," Dad says when dinner is over. Plates and bowls have been scraped clean, and even Rufus finished every vegetable in his pasta. "Are you sure you don't have a cooking vlog out there?"

"Just the travel." Shae's cheeks are pink from the compliments.

"I can't believe I liked that green stuff." Rufus shakes his head as he wipes up the last of the pesto sauce with a piece of garlic bread.

"And I showed you how to do it, so you can make it next time," she says.

"You'll have to come back and help." Smart boy. He's learning.

And so am I. "I can do dessert," I say as I put out a plate of the cookies that Mama S. gave me, along with a tub of strawberry ice cream.

"I love strawberries." The way Shae's eyes light up makes me want to raid the strawberry patch in the greenhouse.

Even Rufus wants to please and does his best at clearing the table as Dad and I start in the kitchen. "Ellie would feed us," Dad says as he fills the sink with water. "But the least Emmett and I could do was clean up."

"Mike likes to take over the kitchen," Shae shares. "I get my lesson when I'm home and then he kicks me out. It's a good deal."

Rufus has the DVD ready and waiting when the counter is clean and I'm amused by how he insists on sitting on the other side of Shae on the couch. But by the time Buttercup throws herself down the hill after Westley, Shae is leaning against me.

She smells of strawberry ice cream and garlic, an odd combination, but no less appealing.

Everything about Shae is appealing, from her laugh, to her bare feet tucked under the little skirt, to her outlook on life. But under all her bubbly cheerfulness, there's a soft spot. A vulnerable part. I get why Neely feels the need to take care of her.

"It's late," I say as Shae makes a move towards the door. "Are you okay to drive back to the city?"

"I'm fine." A yawn splits her face.

"We've got a perfectly acceptable empty bedroom room," Dad reminds me as he ushers Rufus up the stairs. "And you're more than welcome to stay."

"You are," I add. "It's no trouble."

"Stay, Shae," Rufus calls from upstairs. "You can have breakfast with me."

After a long look at me, Shae nods. "It might be nice not having to drive home in the dark," she admits. "I'll text Mike and let him know."

"Before I put you to bed, I want to show you something," I say, drawing her towards the glass doors in the living room. At the sound of them opening, Hardy's head pops up and she follows us outside onto the deck.

"Another something?" Even though her smile is wide, her eyes are tired. "I like this place."

"And this place likes you being here." I watch as Hardy manages the stairs, a little slower every year, and began her nightly sniff for raccoons. "This is one of the best parts of being out here in the middle of nowhere." The deck that Dad and I built is impressive enough, wrapping around two sides of the house and giving a great view of the valley and the lights of Ashbury. But it's not the craftsmanship that I want to show her.

"Wow." Shae's head tips back as she stares at the sky where thousands of tiny pinpricks of light dot the purple night sky. "Look at all the stars." Her ever-present phone is out, and she snaps a few pictures

"My brother has a telescope," I say, standing behind her so I can wrap my arms around her. "We used to spend hours out here on clear nights. Tonight is good, but it gets better after a storm."

Shae leans back against me with a tiny sigh. "There's so many stars. It's beautiful...but it makes me feel so insignificant. Like how can my life matter when there is so much more out there?"

"Of course your life matters."

"Those stars have been there for millions of years, and I'll be here for such a tiny fraction of that."

"But you're here now, and you're making the most of what you have. More than anyone I know."

"I have to."

I think that's what she says, but she says it so quietly that I can't be sure. And before I can ask, she points to the fence casting a long shadow across the lawn. "How did you get from there," she asks, pointing to the pitching mound, "to here? What happened?"

This is what I've been dreading since the first time I laid eyes on Shae. Telling her my story and seeing her change towards me, like everyone else changed.

"I was drunk during a game." Even saying it brings a wave of remorse crashing over me and I have to take a moment to catch my breath. "When I was up to bat, I stepped—stumbled is the better word—out of the batter's box into a ninety-eight-mile fastball.

Knocked me out, did something to my head so I couldn't play anymore. Not that my team wanted me."

Shae is silent, watching me with those dark eyes like she's waiting for me to finish. "They packed me off to rehab and my contract wasn't renewed. Instead of fighting for my career, I gave up and ran home to the farm so I didn't have to deal with the fallout. Social media was brutal." I wince at the memory.

"Which is why you like your privacy."

I expected her to question why I had been drinking, but it doesn't come. "They crucified me. I don't blame them. It was stupid, especially when you look at how much I worked to get there. How both of us worked—Grayson ran into trouble with his UCL and was still on the DL. I don't think I could have stood it if he'd been on the team. I could barely face him when I got home."

"It was an accident," Shae soothes.

"One that could have been avoided."

Could it have been avoided? If Alex hadn't died; if I hadn't been completely unprepared and unable to handle the swath of grief that knocked me sideways; if a lot had been different.

If none of that had happened, I wouldn't be standing here with Shae.

And so, instead of telling her the rest, I whistle for Hardy and take them both inside.

Chapter Thirteen

Shae

I'VE SLEPT IN MANY unfamiliar beds so it's not the reason that I wake up in the middle of the night. I'm still on Thailand time and it takes a while for my body to adjust to good old Daylight Savings Time.

So at three-thirty in the morning, just like last night, I find myself wide awake, padding down the stairs in search of something to drink.

Holding the glass against my forehead, I hope the cool water will help with the low headache that I've had since the flight home. I need sleep; I need some downtime, but like always, it's so difficult to stop. I'm afraid of missing something, terrified of not being able to finish.

I'm not sure what's on the list to finish anymore.

Drawn to the peace of outdoors, I take my water and head to the back deck where Emmett took me earlier. The dog follows me, and I'm glad for the company, smiling as she sleepily heads down the stairs to relieve herself. The shades of green in the fields and the forest blend together in the dark like it doesn't want to compete with the sky dotted with stars. In the distance, I see a lighter shade of purple from the lights of the nearby city of Whitby. The house is high enough for me to watch how the lights blend into the next town, following the lake until they reach the bigger, brighter area of Toronto.

It seems far away from here, like another world.

If I was home, there would be things to distract me even at this time of night. My laptop or books, a video game, or even attempting to make Mike's scrambled eggs, which I tried the last time I had been home from a trip.

Tonight, out here, I don't even have my phone with me.

As I prop my elbows on the railing, I can feel the muscles in my body relax. I roll my shoulders, straighten my back, listening to the cracks so loud in the quiet.

I need a long, hot bath. I need a masseuse.

Being at the farm reminds me of the first trip I did with Dawson and Neely. We toured Italy for a month and then found work at a winery in the hills of Tuscany for three weeks. It was hard work, but we had so much fun—eating and drinking with the other workers, falling into bed exhausted only to be up at the crack of dawn the next day. Even Neely enjoyed it, and she isn't much for manual labour.

Maybe I'll be a farmhand in my next life.

I like thinking about reincarnation, believing that my soul will still get to experience life even after this body fades away. Even though I try to cram as much as I can into my days, I know there's so much I'm going to miss out on. Thinking about getting another chance helps with that.

Sometimes I think about heaven, but it doesn't give me the same assurance. Hanging around on puffy clouds does not seem like my idea of fun. Plus—my head tilts back as I take a moment to contemplate the afterworld—if heaven is supposed to be *up there*, why is it that I can only see stars?

And that's where Peter finds me, staring up at the sky, the dog beside me.

"Couldn't sleep either?" he asks, making me jump. "Sorry, I thought you heard me come out." Peter is wrapped in a plaid robe, so new-looking that I suspect he gets a new one every year, and holding his own glass of water. He holds out his hand to offer me one of the cookies he's holding and the dog leaves me to sit at his feet with an adoring expression.

With a smile of thanks, I take one. "No," I say, the rich scent of chocolate mixing with the fresh smell of grass. "I'm lost in the stars." I swipe unobtrusively at my damp cheek. Falling into those thoughts has only made me sad. Drawing a shaky breath, I smile at Peter before I take a bite of the cookie.

"Beautiful out here, isn't it?" His voice is low and deep and reminds me of Mike. They seem so different, but the gentle caring they both show is there.

"It's an amazing place. You have a really wonderful family," I say honestly.

"Thank you." Peter leans on the railing beside me, close enough so that I can feel the warmth of his arm. "Forgive me if this is overstepping, but the way you say that, as well as the expression on your face, makes me think you aren't as fortunate with your family."

I swipe a hand across my face like I'm erasing my expression. "Neely tells me that's why I'm a horrible poker player—you can always tell what I'm feeling."

"Good and bad, I suppose. Neely." Peter smiles, scratching Hardy's head. "She's a firecracker, isn't she? I hope Ellie can stay on her good side."

"From what I know of Ellie, I don't think she'll have a problem."

"We've had our struggles, but I wouldn't change anything to get me where I am today. My kids, and Rufus is a joy. It's a nice life."

I glance at him with speculation. "Emmett told me you were quiet, but you don't seem like it."

Peter gives a bark of laughter. "What does he know? I've had years of kids and music and video games, all a hub of noise, and me not able to get a word in edgewise. And now Rufus. I don't suppose he ever stops talking."

"Like me, or so everyone says."

"I suspect you're quiet when you need to be. Like when there's a certain something troubling you, that you're not ready to tell my son."

"How can you say that? You just met me tonight."

"I think you'll find that I'm a pretty good judge of character."

I turn back to the sky. "You're good," I say lightly.

The chirp of crickets fills the air. The goats and chickens are quiet, sound asleep with their animal family. At home, I'm used to the hum of cars from nearby Queen Street and it's strange not to hear anything like that. No sirens, the squeak of the streetcar, faint music, and laughter from the bars.

"Will he be hurt?" Peter asks quietly.

"Not if I handle it the right way," I promise. "But the problem is that I don't know what the right way is. I'm dying."

The words pop out of my mouth like a kernel of corn escaping from the pot. Peter gives a quick intake of breath.

"I don't know how much time I have left," I continue in a soft voice, "or how I'm going to go, only that they gave me seven to ten years, and that was thirteen years ago."

There's a heavy silence on the deck. "I don't know why I'm telling you that, because I never tell anyone. I find myself drifting away from people, and they never know why until it's too late. But with Emmett...I'll tell him something. I just don't know what or when or how because—" I stop with a shaky breath. "I really like your son."

"I think he really likes you too."

"I don't want to hurt him."

"I know."

When I brush my cheeks, I find them once again wet with tears. "Shae?" Peter asks in his deep voice. When I turn, he has his arms open. I burrow into the hug without a second thought.

"I'll tell him," I whisper into the softness of his robe. "As soon as I figure out how."

"I know." Peter pats me on the back and with a squeeze lets me go. "I'll let you deal with it."

I follow Peter inside as Hardy takes her spot on her dog bed beside the couch, and then up the stairs. As he peeks into Rufus's room, I wave goodnight and slip into Ellie's. But once inside, the moonlight casting shadows through the thin curtains, I don't crawl back into bed.

Instead, I wait and listen. When the creaking of floorboards from Peter's feet stops, I count to one hundred. Then I slip out of the door again.

I pause only a few moments before I slip into Emmett's room.

Emmett

MY CLOCK READS THREE-THIRTY-FOUR when the quiet creak of my bedroom door startles me awake. And then Shae slides into my bed and curls herself around me.

"Sorry to wake you," she whispers. "I was lonely." Her bare legs are cool, and when I roll over to face her, she makes a little noise in the back of her throat.

"Are you okay?" I forgot to close my curtains last night and the moonlight streaming in is bright enough for me to see her face.

Shae nods, her gaze drifting to my shirtless chest. "Oh, wow. You don't...are you...?" She bites her lip, eyes suddenly dancing.

"Naked? You wish," I tease.

"I do wish."

I catch my breath when she touches my chest, right above my heart. I suggested Shae look through the few clothes that Ellie left to find something to sleep in and she claimed the fuzzy nightshirt with the oversized hoodie that Ellie would wear every Christmas Eve. I always thought it was the ugliest thing Ellie had, but now I rethink it. The hood flops over Shae's hair as she pushes me onto my back so she can straddle me.

There's a question in her eyes that I don't want to answer, so I pull her down to me. Our lips meet in a kiss that is so much better than the missed opportunity under the tree, especially when Shae pulls off the nightshirt in one quick move, her skin silvery-white in the moonlight.

When I open my eyes this morning, my bed is empty, but I have a smile on my face and a sense that all's right in the world.

Dad sits at the table when I get to the kitchen. "Your friend still asleep?" he asks, coating his toast with a thick layer of jam.

I shrug as I pop my toast in. "Probably. She's in Ellie's room."

"I wasn't going to ask. You're a grown man."

"Did you really think I'd bring a girl home and not tell you?"

"Well, you invited a girl to stay the night without telling me, so why is that any different? Not that it matters. I like her," he finishes.

My smile widens. "So do I."

"I brought some of those new berries in," Dad says before taking a bite of his toast. "I thought Shae might like some for her breakfast."

The morning is like every other morning; chores to do—feeding the animals, watering the new plants, gathering eggs. The only thing different is that there's a woman asleep in my house. I rush through what needs to be done and hurry back to the house, afraid she might slip away before I can say goodbye.

And tell her...I don't know what I want to tell her. How special last night was? How she makes me smile, and how I want to go on smiling.

But first I need to tell her about Alex.

I hear the radio before I open the kitchen door. Inside, I smile to find a dancing Shae wearing a pair of Ellie's shorts and a T-shirt, her pink hair pulled into tiny knobs on the side of her head and singing loudly about cold beer on a Friday night.

Hardy sprawls in the middle of the room watching. I step over the dog just as Shae twirls, a spoon in her hand, and shrieks when she sees me.

"Oh, you scared me!" Clapping her hand to her heart, she laughs with delight.

I wonder if I'll ever get tired of that sound.

"It's too loud," she says, dancing over to the radio to lower it. "But I love that song. Rufus left for school already. He made me breakfast. Well," she reconsiders. "He got out the Cheerios for me, so that's something." Standing on tiptoes, she presses strawberry-scented lips to mine. "Good morning."

"It is." I watch as she dances back to the stove to give the pot a stir. "What are you making?"

"I'll be out of here soon," she says over her shoulder. "But I wanted to make jam with those strawberries. I hope that's okay." She turns with a nervous expression. "Maybe I should have checked first. Were they meant for anyone?"

"For you," I say sheepishly. "Dad thought you'd like them for breakfast."

"Oh, I did!" Her smile spreads from her mouth to mine, contagious as always. "They were so good, and I thought they'd make good jam. There was enough left."

"You're making jam."

"I am. I found the sugar and a jar in the cupboard." She points to one of the top shelves, leaving me wondering how she got up to it. "And you had lemon, and I like to add a bit of zest when I make jam."

"Zest."

"Why are you repeating everything I say?"

I laugh with embarrassment. "In all the ways I imagined coming in the house to find you doing something, making jam was not on the list."

She stops stirring and faces me with a mischievous grin. "What did you imagine me doing?"

"You don't want to know."

"Oh, I think I do." Another stir and then she dips her finger into the pot. "Done. Do you like jam?"

"Dad lives on it."

"I did notice the collection in the fridge. I'm glad. You should offer jam to your customers, like your honey."

I watch as she carefully pours the jam into the waiting jar. "That would entail someone making it, and neither Dad nor I are about to step up for that."

"I could teach you."

"Let's start with coming back and making more. That's not going to last long around here."

Shae sets the warm jar on the cutting board to cool. "It won't last more than a week without the pectin, so make sure you eat it."

She soaks the pot in water and, as I continue to watch her, slides along the floor to where I stand. "Emmett."

"Shae." It takes everything I have not to pull her into my arms. I don't know why I resist, but something about the way she looks at me...wary, and maybe a little regretful.

"I had fun yesterday. And last night."

I reach out and touch her cheek. "Why do I get the impression there's a but coming?" I ask.

She leans into my hand, looking at me for a long moment before she smiles. It doesn't make it to her eyes. "No but. I just wanted you to know I had fun."

"So did I." Before she can say anything that will change things, I screw up my courage. "There's something I need to tell you."

"Uh oh." Shae pulls back, winding her arms around her waist like she's cold. "You really don't like jam, do you?"

"It's fine. It's nothing—well, it is," I correct with a rush of guilt. Alex can't be nothing. She was everything to me once.

And then it hits me like I've taken another fastball to the head. The last time I brought a woman into this house, she collapsed in the kitchen, only to die three days later in the hospital.

All the air leaves me with a whoosh and I stagger backward. How did I not think of that? How did I not remember...?

"Emmett?" Shae demands. "What's wrong? You're as white as a sheet."

Smiling tightly at her, I stumble to the table, with Shae right beside me. "I'm fine. It's just...I didn't tell you everything last night."

Her forehead creases. "About...baseball?"

I nod. "About why I was drinking during a game."

She sits with a concerned expression on her face. "It didn't seem like something you would do."

"It's not. It wasn't. But I'd been going through a bad time. I had a girlfriend," I say. Even though we were only married for three days, I think of Alex more of my wife than girlfriend. It somehow justifies my grief.

Shae gives an uneasy laugh. "Everyone has a past, Emmett."

"I married her. And then she died."

The word buzzes around my ears like a hungry mosquito hunting for blood. Shae sits perfectly still, her dark eyes never leaving my face. "Did you say she died?"

"She died." The words form awkwardly in my mouth, like a tongue twister. "She had a brain tumor that she never knew about. We were married for three days."

On the radio, Taylor Swift sings about lost love, and Hardy farts in her sleep. Other than that, the kitchen is silent. Shae continues to watch me as if she's waiting for me to continue. "After—"

"What was her name?" Shae interrupts in a whisper.

"Alex. Her name was Alex Tang. We'd been together for a year, with her traveling on the road with me. She didn't have any symptoms. No one knew she was sick. The one time I bring her home to meet my family..." My words trail off as the usual guilt washes over me, leaving a sourness in my belly, like a bad hangover. "She collapsed in...right there." I swallow painfully, nodding at the floor by the counter. "I wasn't here. I was getting my hair cut. Rufus found her."

Shae makes a sound in her throat.

"And then...after...I couldn't handle it." Shae jumps to her feet with a screech of chair legs but doesn't say anything. "I started drinking. Too much. And that's why I stepped into the fastball. I didn't know how to deal with my grief." I watch her pace the kitchen, her face a jumble of expressions, most of which I can't read or understand. Telling the girl you're interested in the story of your dead wife isn't in any of the first date manuals.

"She should have told you." My head jerks at the coldness of Shae's words.

"She didn't know," I stammer with surprise.

"She must have. A person knows when something is wrong with them. So don't do that," Shae says sharply. "Don't blame yourself."

"It's hard not to."

"Don't. Look, Emmett," she begins before heaving a heavy sigh. "It sucks. It's sad and it's unfair, but you did nothing wrong. You loved her." Shae chokes on the words and I stand, wondering if I should comfort her. This is different than the usual condolences, the flippant *I'm sorry* statement that sounds like they read it in a sympathy card.

This feels off. Wrong, somehow. Why is Shae so upset about a woman she never met?

"It's sad and unfair," she continues. "And I'm sorry for your loss." She delivers the last words devoid of any emotion. "You have no idea how sorry. But I have to go. I've had a really amazing time, but I have to get home."

"You're leaving?" I stare at her with confusion. "Now?"

"I'm really sorry to run out, but Mike texted me—" She snatches up her phone on the counter. "I never told him I wouldn't be home. I think he's worried."

"I don't want him to worry...okay. Do you want—?"

"When did she die?"

"Three years ago." My voice sounds like a croak to my ears and I clear my throat. "It's been three years."

"Are you over her?"

I shrug. "I don't know if you're ever over something like that, but I know I'm ready to move on."

Shae stills her flurry of movement and looks at me with an expression of such sadness that tears prick in my eyes. "That's so good," she whispers. "But you can't move on with me."

Chapter Fourteen

Shae

H IS WIFE...EMMETT HAD A wife. And she *died*.

All the while Emmett tells me about her, about what happened, inside I'm screaming *DieDyingI'mdyingShedied* until I'm convinced the words echo in the kitchen.

I need to escape before the churning frustration and fear spew out in an anguished scream. "I'll wash Ellie's things and get them back to her."

Emmett stares at me with such a sad look of disappointment that I have to blink back the wash of wetness in my eyes. Instead, I dart past him to grab my dress, carefully folded in a plastic bag in the living room. I can't get too close to Emmett because I know if I touch him, even get close enough to brush his arm, I'm going to break.

Get out of the house.

"Are you okay?" He still has a concerned expression on his face. He shouldn't be concerned about *me*! I've done enough to him. *Life* has done enough to him.

He doesn't need any more help from me.

"It's the drive. I need to get back," I say, my hand on the door and leaving the remnants of my jam-making on the counter. "I'm sorry, Emmett. Say bye to Rufus and your dad for me."

"Okay..." He follows me out the door. "Shae..."

"Thanks for everything," I interrupt, reaching on tiptoes to brush a kiss against his cheek. "I'll see you."

I make it to my car, but the tears start as I race down the lane. And I have to pull over when they begin to fall in earnest, bringing racking sobs and a wail of frustration at how *unfair* life is.

I don't remember much of the drive home but I make it in one piece, only to have Mike meet me at the door, an uncommon scowl on his face.

"You missed your doctor's appointment," he says without preamble.

"It's okay," I say as I brush past him, trying to hide my red-rimmed eyes.

"No, it's not okay. You came back from Thailand for that appointment."

"I came back for James's wedding. The appointment was just an added bonus." Dropping my bag on the floor, I keep walking. I need to hide, to find a way to stifle the screams that want to erupt despite the tears that fell on the way home.

"Jana-Shae, wait one minute."

My foot halts in mid-step. Mike never raises his voice to me. Mike, my rock, my stalwart in bad times, is never angry with me. I don't want to look at him, afraid to see the disappointment in his eyes that I saw in Emmett's.

He had a wife who died...

"You should have gone to that appointment," he barks. "You're old enough to take care of yourself, and God knows, you're off gallivanting around the world nine months of the year, but you need to be responsible. You need to take care of yourself. Have you had a decent night's sleep since you've been back?"

"I'm still jet-lagged, but it'll wear off—"

"And how deep are the shadows going to be around your eyes? You look like crap, Shae."

"I'm sorry I missed the appointment." The defensive tone in my voice makes even me cringe at how childlike I sound.

"It makes no difference to me, but you're an adult now, Shae; an adult with a *disease*. You have to take care of yourself, and that means regular checkups and no more all-nighters. Did you even think to let us know you wouldn't be home last night? I had to check Instagram to find out where you were."

I never texted him to let him know I was staying. The star picture that I posted, *#beautifulnight #farmcountry #sparklingstars #insignificant* had been the only way he knew I was okay. It seems a lifetime since Emmett held me in his arms and pointed out the constellations, and now guilt adds to everything else, making even more of a mess of my emotions.

"What's the point of meeting another doctor?" I burst out. "I know what he's going to tell me—I'm going to die! And I don't want to hear it. I really don't want to hear it." Without another word, I head for my room in a run.

Flopping on my bed hard enough to make the pillows jump, I grab the nearest one and bury my face in it. And then I scream. Harsh, fierce screams of frustration and pain that lead to choking sobs.

When it's over, when I'm left drooping with exhaustion, I open my bedroom door to find Mike standing there. He looks up at me sadly and opens his arms.

Shoulders hunched under the weight of grief, I burrow into his arms. "Oh, Shae," he soothes as the tears begin again. "What happened?"

"I like him." Each word is heavier than the one before it. "I like him a lot."

"This is Emmett, isn't it? He seems like a good guy, so it's not a bad thing."

"It is," I scream, Mike's shoulder muffling the worst of it. Downstairs, I hear the clink of Doris's tags as the dog lifts up her head at the sound.

He leads me back into my room and sits me down, his arm a blanket. "Shae, you can't let your mother's past dictate—"

"His wife died," I say slowly. "And he messed up his baseball career because of it. I can't do that to him again."

Mike sighs heavily. "You don't know it would be the same."

"But it wouldn't be easy. And he's got so much to lose—the farm, his family. Rufus." I close my eyes thinking about the tear-stained face of Rufus. "I can't hurt anyone else."

His arm tightens around me. "Shae, you know, it's up to him to take that chance." I've heard the words a thousand times, along with my mother's mantra, *"It's not fair to them."*

Is it a wonder that I'm a mess? For two people who claim to care about each other—and me—it's always been a tug-of-war between them.

"Have you told him?" Mike asks. "You didn't, did you?"

I shake my head back and forth, feeling the cotton of Mike's shirt under my forehead. "He told me about baseball last night. I thought it was a stupid mistake, and it happens. Mistakes happen. And I thought maybe... maybe this can work. I told his father, you know, in the middle of the night. Maybe he'll forget I said anything."

"Why would he forget about it?"

"No one needs to know. It's over with Emmett even before it begins."

"Is it?"

"It has to be. This morning—I made jam," I say suddenly.

"We have jam," he says without the slightest impatience.

"And Emmett came in and looked at me, and blurted out how she *died*..." My throat tightens at the word but I push on. "And I'm going to *die*..."

"You should have said something."

"How?" I spread my hands with frustration. "Oh, hey, Emmett, that's too bad your wife died, and hey, I'm going to die too? How do I say that?" I look at Mike, tears dripping down my cheeks. "I can't. This is why I can't fall in love. It's not worth it."

"Oh, Shae-girl." Mike hugs me hard. "But it is worth it. You just need to see that it can be."

Emmett

A COLD BALL OF confusion grows inside me as I watch the dust settle. Shae flew out of here in her sporty little car leaving me gaping at the speed.

She obviously didn't like hearing about Alex.

Messing up my baseball career is one thing, but learning the reason why—she didn't want to hear that? I don't understand. I don't understand any of it.

Did I miss the part of her that lacked compassion? Did I not see the red flag that would have told me to proceed with caution when dumping my past on her?

A little voice suggests that maybe the grief over Alex was only an excuse for my being an idiot. That I can't blame anything or anyone other than myself for being stupid enough for drinking before a game.

I crush a carpenter ant under the toe of my boot with enough force to decapitate it, exactly what I should do to the little voice.

Stony-faced, I return to the kitchen to clean up the mess before I head to the greenhouse. I know the ruin of my baseball career is my fault; I've accepted it. Acknowledged it. I don't deserve a defense; there's no justification for my actions.

But I like to think I deserve a little sympathy for losing someone I loved.

Maybe I got it all wrong. Maybe I got Shae wrong.

It wouldn't be the first time.

As I wipe up the smear of strawberry on the counter, for the first time I let myself think about what Ellie told me at the wedding. That Alex *hadn't wanted* to get married. It hadn't even been on her radar, and I made it happen without even asking.

I didn't even propose properly.

I lean against the counter, wet cloth in my hand, and think back to those days. A haze coats my memories, a fog layered on those three days. From when Alex collapsed in the kitchen—

Right here. It had been right here that Rufus found her.

—to when she died, only seventy-eight hours passed. The longest, and the quickest hours of my life.

I brought her here. I buried her here.

That wouldn't have changed if we didn't have the marriage ceremony; it had taken an effort to track down Alex's family. Her refusal to talk about them had masked a breach that I only got a glimpse of during the funeral. As my wife, she was my family, and I took care of everything, including flowers on her grave on holidays and the anniversary of her death. As my girlfriend, I would have done the same thing.

But marriage...

Marriage used to mean something to me, but now I have a sick feeling that I've wasted it. What if I hadn't married Alex? Would I have still ruined my career?

I push off from the counter, check that everything is back to the way it was before Shae got here, and head to the far greenhouse for some peace and quiet. Marcus and Warren will be with Dad in the fields, leaving the buildings and their silence to me.

If only I can put a stop to the thoughts racing in my mind, going as fast as Shae shot out of here.

After a day with only the thud of my boots as company, I head back to the house in a worse mood than when I left.

This morning I had been confused. Now I'm just mad. At myself, at Shae...Alex...the world.

Rufus greets me at the door, a Pizza Pocket in his hand and an eager expression on his face. "Is Shae with you?" he demands, peering around me.

"No."

"Where'd she go?"

"Probably home."

"Why?" I shrug and push past him into the kitchen. The smell of tomato sauce reminds me I missed lunch, the sick pit in my stomach masking any growling for food. "Did you make her mad?"

"Why do you assume that I did? Maybe she made *me* mad?"

Rufus stares at me with bewilderment. "But it's *Shae*."

"She's not perfect." Pulling out the empty Pizza Pocket box from the freezer, I throw it angrily into the recycling box. "Rufus, how many times have I told you not to leave empty boxes in the freezer? Or in the fridge? Or anywhere!"

"Whoa." I look at Rufus over the door of the fridge, holding out the Pizza Pocket to me. "Want it? You need it more than I do."

"No," I snap, relenting when Rufus doesn't make a move to run off but holds his ground, looking concerned. "Thanks though."

Reaching into the refrigerator, my hand hovers over a bottle of beer. It's just one, I tell myself. I don't have a drinking problem. I have a dealing with grief problem and alcohol makes it worse.

But I'm not grieving. Pulling out the bottle, as well as a can of C-Plus, I slam the door. I'm mad. Again, at myself, at Shae...the list goes on.

But I'm not angry at Rufus.

I set the can on the table and grab a bag of sour cream and onion potato chips before settling into a chair.

"Is that for me?" Rufus asks with some hesitation.

"You're not leaving, so you might as well have a drink with me."

"Cool." Stuffing the remains of the pastry into his mouth, he sits with a loud scrape of chair legs. "So what did you do?"

I squeeze the bag to open it, only to have the wrong end split, dumping chips onto the table. Figures. "Why do you assume it's me?" I ask as I scoop bits of chips back into the bag.

Rufus's forehead furrows. "Because it's a girl. And girls are mostly always right."

I give a humourless chuckle. "Aunt Ellie really did a number on you."

He drains half his can and burps loudly. "Something like this happened to me today," he says conspiratorially.

"I doubt that, but go on. What happened?"

"So, *my* girlfriend, Ava," he starts with all the confidence of an eleven-year-old with a significant other. "I thought she was going to be sitting with her friends for lunch. I sent her a text about it, because she said it in the morning, and I wanted to confirm, because that's what you do—"

I shake my head as I try to follow. Tweens have more complicated lives now than I ever did.

"—But Ms. Peony caught Ava with her phone and told her to put it away, so Ava looks at me and mouths *Sitting with Drew*. That's her best friend, so that's what I thought, and I went for lunch with Dylan and Ben. But really, Ava was saying *Sitting with you*." Rufus mouths the words dramatically and throws up his arms. "I had no idea."

"So what happened?"

"She was so *mad*! But it's good now." He shrugs his shoulder with a smirk. "I smoothed it over. I'm pretty good at that."

"Mmhmm." I don't want to get into what Rufus needs to do to fix a fight with his girlfriend. "So this was a simple miscommunication?"

"Miscommun—what? No, Ava just needs to open her mouth more when she tells me things."

I lean my head back and laugh, the laughter releasing some of the tension. Maybe that's the problem with Shae. Maybe that's all it ever is.

I'm not ready to give up yet.

Chapter Fifteen

Shae

"THERE SHE IS!" MIKE cries as I stumble into the living room the next day.

"Morning," I croak. My throat is dry and feels tight, and the light from the window makes me squint. The noise from the television starts a pounding in my head.

Dawson is on the couch beside Mike, in the slumped sitting positions that will leave him with a sore neck and stiff muscles. Neither of them looks up for more than a blink, their attention intent on the battle waging on the screen before them. The two of them are like a couple of teenagers with their video games. In fact, it was Dawson who got Mike addicted to the Fortnite game.

I have a secret video of the two of them attempting the Fortnite dance. Mike moves surprisingly well for his age.

"Afternoon," Neely corrects. She's camped on the floor with her laptop showing my latest stats and pretending not to watch the battle on screen. "The videos are up. You've already got some good numbers."

I nod, not stopping to chat until I can find some coffee. Neely follows me into the kitchen. Even with the tempting sight of freshly-baked muffins, my stomach feels queasy, still tangled from yesterday.

"You never call, you never text—I sound like a needy girlfriend." Neely takes a muffin and breaks off a piece. "So? How was it?"

"I sent you the videos before I crashed last night." I keep my back to her as I pour a much-needed cup.

"I meant, how's Emmett?"

"He showed me the farm, we had dinner, watched a movie, it was late, so I stayed." I take a gulp, the liquid burning my mouth. "And now I'm here."

I can feel Neely's gaze even before I finally look at her. "There's a whole bunch you're not telling me. Might as well get started. Did you tell him?"

"I told him a lot of things," I say shortly. I let him believe I wanted this as much as he did, and I wish I never said a word. "But no, I didn't tell him that I have an expiry date. I wasn't in the mood for pity."

Neely studies me, her golden eyes narrowed and a frown marring her pretty face. "I'm sure you're not in the mood for me to tell you that you're running scared again, but I'm going to anyway. I get why you blew off Denzel Duke, but Emmett is normal. And nice. And really cute."

"You date him, then."

"I would, but he clearly has the hots for you, so what would be the point? Besides," she pauses, avoiding my eyes. "I have a date tonight."

Her cheeks turn an alarming shade of pink, which only happens when she exercises or is embarrassed. "With Grayson?" She nods a confirmation. "Do you think that's a good idea?" I sound sharper than I mean to and immediately want to take back the words.

"Just because you're about to self-destruct with Emmett doesn't mean I'm not going to take a chance," Neely snaps.

"I'm not going to self-destruct!"

"Really? You just spent twenty-four hours with a guy and all you can say is that you had fun."

"I did have fun."

"And?"

"And nothing."

"Shae." Neely draws the word out into a sigh. "You don't have to be scared of this."

"I'm not scared. And what do you know about it?"

"I say I'm your best friend and I've seen you do everything—throw yourself out of a plane, swim with sharks, and eat potentially gross food. The only thing you're scared of is ending up like your mother. Heartbroken. Which is why you self-destruct whenever there's a good guy in the picture. You run, or you blow things out of proportion and you never, ever tell them what's going on." She pauses for effect. "Scared."

I stare at my feet, the polish chipping on my big toe. "I'm not scared. I'm just not anything. Emmett is great but..." I reach to pet Doris as she ambles into the kitchen, no doubt looking for a handout.

"What happened?" Her voice changes; I know she's trying to sound gentle but with Neely, it comes across as resigned and annoyed.

"His wife died."

"I know."

I gape at my best friend, who for once, has failed at looking after me. "A head's-up would have been nice."

"I didn't see the need."

"You didn't...Why not?"

"It wasn't my story to tell," Neely says calmly. "And I knew he'd tell you."

"How am I supposed to tell him about *me* when he just lost someone? And she was his wife! He won't think it's worth it."

"I think you're worth it." Neely looks at me like she's balancing her chequebook rather than talking about love and life and death. "You know, I want to see what you're like when you're in love," she muses. "You already glow; when you like someone you remind me of a firefly—quick and bright but it goes out too soon. If you loved someone..." She shrugs. "I'd like to see it."

"Until I burn out," I say bitterly. "Even if I wanted to tell him about my stuff, how can I after what he's been through?"

"Through what?" Dawson asks from the doorway to the kitchen. He makes a beeline to the muffins and Neely steps neatly out of his way. "Mike killed me. How can he be so good when he's old?"

I take a deep breath, happy for the distraction. "I wouldn't let him hear you say that. In his mind, Mike will always be twenty-nine."

"Maybe that's why we get along so well. So, why the powwow?" He glances from me to Neely, and back to me with a frown.

"Shae messed things up with Emmett again," Neely informs him briskly.

"Already?" Dawson groans. "I like him."

"I'm not about to keep someone around just because *you* like him."

"I like him better than Grayson," Dawson mutters.

"Not surprising," I say in a low voice.

"What's wrong with Grayson?" Neely demands indignantly.

Some days they bicker like an old married couple. Some days they can't stop laughing at stupid jokes, leaving me demanding to know what's so funny. And other times, the times I dread, is when Neely gets fed up with the unrequited love she has for Dawson and all they'll do is argue.

Like now, with Neely coolly listing all of Grayson's good points.

"He's The Suitor," is all Dawson needs to say.

My deepest hope is that once I'm gone, the two of them will find their way together. In fact, I've planned for the very thing; left letters for each of them with detailed instructions and advice how to make it work.

A breeze blows through the open window in the kitchen, still cool despite being afternoon, and smelling of Mike's geraniums.

At least it should smell of flowers. At this time of year, the kitchen is full of the scent of flowers, of fresh herbs on the windowsill, not to mention the fresh muffins.

I surreptitiously sniff the mug of coffee. I can't smell anything.

Fear rushes through me and I carefully set the cup on the counter, afraid my fingers will give out. *No.*

I can't smell anything. Can I taste? Taking another gulp of still-hot coffee, I burn my tongue, grateful I can taste the faint tinge of vanilla.

It's nothing. It's fine. I'm fine. I breathe through the panic, keeping my face still and silent so no one will know.

It's not the end. I'm not ready yet.

Taking a deep breath, I force myself to focus on a now bickering Neely and Dawson. Smiling makes me seem happy, and if I can pretend long enough, then I will be happy.

It's what has gotten me through the last thirteen years.

Dawson finally realizes I haven't shifted into referee mode and gives me a curious glance. "What—You don't look good," he catches himself with a quick frown.

"Thanks." I settle into the chair, worried that my legs will give out. Will that be next? What else will give out? What will go first? My muscles or my organs? How will my body betray me?

I stare unseeing at my phone but I sense Dawson looking at me. "What's wrong?"

"I just crawled out of bed. I don't usually wake up looking as cute and cuddly as I do." I force another smile, but Dawson isn't fooled. Neely looks at me suspiciously.

"Sarcasm." Dawson's frown deepens. "That's new."

"I can be sarcastic." I pick up a muffin to give myself something to do with my hands. Something that makes me feel normal.

"You can, but you don't."

"Maybe I'm just in a bad mood."

"When's your doctor's appointment? Have you been taking your vitamins?" Neely demands.

"I don't need vitamins!" A hunk of muffin falls to the floor as I raise my hands and Doris gobbles it up. "I don't need questions!"

They stare at each other, and then at me. "What's going on, Shae?" Dawson asks in a quiet voice. "This is more than Emmett."

"I'm tired of dying," I snap.

"So am I," Neely says coolly. She sets her laptop on the table before me. "Especially today. Here's your stats so you can see how many people love you. Trust me, those numbers would drop if they saw how pissy you're being."

"I'm not being pissy."

"Oh, no? I haven't heard one word out of your mouth that isn't *me me me*. You got dealt a really bad hand, Shae, but you're not the only one with problems. Now, if you'll excuse me, I have to get ready for my date, which I would have liked to tell you about if you weren't so self-absorbed." And with that, leaving Dawson agape, Neely sweeps out of the house.

"What's with her?" Dawson whispers.

"Me. Like always, since I'm so self-absorbed."

He peers through his glasses at me. "No, you're not. It's just...I know it's tough, but you need to remember that you've had extra time, more than they thought...maybe they can come up with something..."

"If you start talking about a cure, you know I'm going to hit you." For years, every time my health had been brought up, it's always Dawson who insists on hoping that a cure might be found.

Neely is the more practical. And it's not the first time she's accused me of being selfish. I hate the thought of her being annoyed with me, so I pull out my phone to text a quick apology. But before I can type anything, it pings, signaling an incoming text.

"Is it Emmett?" Dawson asks quietly. I look at him and Dawson must see something in my eyes. Or he's just really good at reading me. "Don't."

"Don't what?"

"Blow him off. That's what you're going to do, aren't you? I can see it on your face. You deserve this, Shae."

"But the problem is that he doesn't," I say softly. I glance at my phone. "It's not from Emmett."

Shae, the message says. *I've finally found you. I'm in Toronto for exactly eight hours and I'd love to see you. This is me sneaking into your concert.*

It's from Denzel Duke.

Emmett

As I HEAD IN from the fields the next day, I see Grayson's car parked in front of the house with a jaunty flourish, like one of those French accents. The car is long and lean, like Grayson, but dark gray. I always thought Grayson would have gone for a colourful car, like bright red or orange.

His father used to have a bright red Charger SRT8 so maybe that's why Grayson picked gray.

Rufus is at the table with Grayson, his hand stuck in the potato chip bag. "They're my chips," I say by way of a greeting, passing by to wash the dirt off my hands. My mood has improved but sinks a bit every time I check my phone and realize I haven't heard from Shae.

Which I do often enough to be embarrassing.

"Yeah, yeah." Grayson sprays crumbs as well as his words. "I brought you Pepper bread so I get some of your chips. Also, cookies from my mom." Grayson nudges the plate of thick chocolate cookies in front of me as I sink into a chair across the table from him. Mrs. Grant knows my weakness.

Grayson's mother has never been anything but nice to me, but the lingering guilt that my mother ran off with her husband makes it difficult to look her in the eyes at times.

"By the way, Pepper told me she saw Shae driving out of town yesterday," Grayson says causally. "She didn't get a good look, but thought she looked upset." Grayson and Rufus both stare expectantly at me.

"So?"

Both sets of eyebrows rise. "What's up?" Grayson asks mildly.

"There was a miscommunion," Rufus explains.

"Miscommunication," I correct. "And no, it wasn't that. Don't you have any homework to do?"

"You talked to me yesterday?" Rufus wails. "You might as well tell me because I'm going to find out anyway."

"How do you figure?"

"I'll DM Shae and she'll tell me."

"I don't even know what there is to tell. I told her about Alex," I say gruffly.

"What exactly did you tell her?" Grayson asks.

"That she died," I say sarcastically. "I told her about the baseball stuff, and then the next morning, I told her about Alex."

"The next morning?"

"She slept over because it was late," I clarify.

"In his bed," Rufus adds. "I saw her coming out in the morning. It's cool." He raises his hands defensively. "I'm cool with it and I'm the minor in the house. Geez."

I stare at Rufus. "Who are you?" I mutter.

Grayson waves an arm between me and Rufus. "We'll get back to the sleepover at a later date, but first—what did Shae say?"

"That's the thing." My shoulders slump, like the weight of the world is resting here. As much I've replayed the conversation and pushed every inane idea around my head, I still can't figure out why Shae reacted like she did. "Nothing. She asks if I was ready to move on, said it won't be with her, and then she left. Ran right out of here like the house was burning around her. I don't get it."

"That's...weird." Grayson frowns. "I thought you'd get sympathy...maybe plans for another sleepover."

"Neither happened."

"Huh. Want me to ask Neely about it?"

Now it's my turn to frown. "Is that the only reason you'd talk to Neely?"

"Well, no," Grayson says sheepishly. "I'm heading into the city to take her to dinner."

"But you're going to be on The Suitor," I say flatly, my disapproval coming loud and clear.

"We're talking about that tonight." Grayson's apparent ease of beginning a relationship with an end date is surprising. He's always been the romantic sort, giving women all the time they need, whether it's getting comfortable with dating a baseball player, returning a phone call, or even in a change room.

"Hey," he continues. "I thought this was a definite deal with you and Shae, so if not, maybe you should think twice about coming on. You can take over if this thing with Neely looks like it's going to work out."

"He needs to figure out Shae first," Rufus says. "She's the priority, not some group of emotional beauty queens who want their fifteen minutes of fame on your show."

Grayson stares. "Who are you?"

"Exactly." I help myself to a cookie, breathing in the magical scent. No one ever made me cookies—not my own mother, or Alex. Ellie was a better cook than baker, and after her rock-hard birthday cakes, Dad, Ethan, and I were happy to buy store-made cakes and cookies. There's nothing like homemade cookies, fresh from the oven. These still have a hint of warmth left. "I keep wondering if I misread the signals. Things were great when she came over Monday, but maybe..." I think about how Shae crawled into my bed in the middle of the night, slipping into my arms like she was made to be there. "It's been a while," I finish with a shrug.

"You a bit rusty?" Grayson smiles sympathetically.

"How can I not be? It's been almost three years since Alex died."

The word seems to hang in the sudden silence. "I've never heard you say that," Grayson says finally. "You say she's gone, or I lost her, like your dog ran away. It's the first time you've said she died."

"I didn't notice." I used the word when I was telling Shae, I realize. It felt strange on my tongue, but I felt surprisingly comfortable talking to Shae about it. I had felt like I could tell her anything, even things I hadn't admitted to myself. But now...

"Yeah. But it's cool. You're ready now to say it, and to do something about it. Do something about Shae, I mean."

I scowl into my cookie. "I'm not sure I can do anything except wait, I guess. How long should I do that? You are the expert, the one and only Suitor."

"For this season." Grayson chuckles wryly. "I was looking at my contract. I had to print it out and it's like a book. I had no idea that I have to do so much publicity."

"So don't do it."

"I have to. Sounds like they want me—body and soul and my firstborn too."

"Again—don't do it."

Grayson shakes his head, displaying a hint of the stubborn side that kept getting us into trouble when we were kids. "No, I'm going for it. I'm fully committed to the process."

"You sound like you're already on the show." I look around theatrically. "Are the cameras rolling already?"

"Showtime is in six weeks." He grins with satisfaction. Whatever my opinion is, Grayson really wants this.

"So that's how long it's going to last with Neely?" I ask pointedly.

"Neely." Grayson grimaces as he slowly rolls the word. "I wish I met her a year ago. Or a year from now."

"Won't you be happily suited up with someone in a year?"

"Maybe. It's bad timing because I really like her."

"She's a very likable girl."

"Yeah." His voice is morose. "It sucks really. But it's a crapshoot. There's no guarantee either the show or things with Neely will even work out. Do you know Neely's never been in a real relationship?"

"From the sounds of it, neither has Shae."

"You have to wonder about that," Grayson muses. "It's got to be all the travelling they do, don't you think? But even then, how can you not fall in love? It's not like—look at them. Neely is so gorgeous. And sweet, once you get past the control-freak side."

"I seem to remember you liking the control freak," I tease. Grayson can always lighten my mood. "Remember April Patinson?"

"That wasn't control, that was batshit possessive *crazy*," he exclaims. "Did you know she made me call her every hour on the hour when we were together? Who does that?"

"And yet you stayed with her for, what was it? Six months?"

"Five and a half." Grayson sighs. "But I was twenty-one and the sex was really good, and there was a lot of it, so what can a guy do?" He grins sheepishly.

"Put up with batshit crazy." I take another cookie. "The whole love thing bothers me," I admit. "With Shae. I mean, she's *great*. I can't think of anything I don't like about her."

"Other than the fact she ran out when she found out you're a widower?" Grayson blanches. "Sorry, bro. I've never used that word before."

"It takes some getting used to."

"Maybe that's the problem—the death thing, not you? You of all people know how hard it is to deal with grief. Maybe she has issues."

"Shae has no issues," Rufus announces. He's been sitting quietly, head swiveling from Grayson to me like he's watching a tennis game.

"Dude, every woman has issues," Grayson says. "The sooner you realize that, the better."

I barely hear as Grayson begins to regale Rufus about some of his most memorable women and their issues. Maybe Grayson has a point. Maybe Shae needs some time to work out her memories, or her past...something.

The thought perks me up.

Later, after supper, Rufus comes to me with his phone in hand. "Emmett?" he begins nervously. "I know you and Shae aren't really you and Shae, but have you looked at her Insta page? It says a lot of nice things about the farm, and the video she took with Marcus is hilarious." He pushes his phone at me.

"I'll look at it with mine," I tell him, pulling out my phone.

Rufus is right. If I didn't know better, I'd say the seven-minute video is nothing more than a love letter to Pike Place Farm and community-supported agriculture.

"Wow," I say halfway through. And then again, when the video is finished.

"You should check the website. I bet the traffic is through the roof," Rufus suggests. "And there's a spot you can leave a comment on her page, you know?"

I rewatch the video twice more before I can think of a comment to leave.

Chapter Sixteen

Shae

"I'M GLAD YOU CAME."

Denzel sits across from me in the Piano Bar in the basement of the Royal York hotel with his curls hidden under a Blue Jays hat and a huge smile on his face. As soon as I see it, as soon as I see *him*, I know meeting him is a mistake.

Getting the text from him yesterday wasn't exactly a surprise. Since I left him in Thailand, after a hastily scrawled *Bye! Thanks for the great time and LOVE the new song* written with my lipstick on the bathroom mirror, Denzel has taken to following me on Insta with a gusto that makes Rufus's uber fandom seem tame. He's liked everything I've posted and left comments and heart emojis galore, even going back and commenting on posts from six months ago.

I hadn't realized it was so serious until Dawson and I went through the recent posts yesterday and found comments about

Denzel's comments. Apparently quite a few of my followers are shipping Denzel and me.

I glance warily around the bar. It's eleven o'clock in the morning and relatively empty. My plan is to get in and out without anyone recognizing him, but the eagerness on his face makes me think I might have another problem. I wish I'd had included more of Emmett in the video I posted on the farm yesterday.

Emmett. Even thinking his name brings about a surge of wistful regret that I push away. I don't like to think about how I raced away from him. It's been two days since I've seen him and—

Not now, Shae!

"I'm still not sure how you got hold of me," I say carefully after ordering a Pepsi. Thinking about being pulled onstage still brings up a bubble of excitement, but I clearly remember never giving Denzel my contact information. "Send me a DM," I suggested several times throughout the night of heartfelt confessions.

Denzel waves impatiently. "My publicist. She thought your coverage of the tour was amazing, by the way." His smile is sweet and just a little bashful. "I liked the video of you on stage with me."

"That was incredible." I'm not sure if I'm supposed to thank him or ask for another song to be written about me, so I compromise with a wide smile. "The whole night was."

"That's why I'm here. I'm leaving for Australia tonight," he says without preamble. "Come with me."

My stomach gives a disturbing lurch of excitement, and for a moment my answer is a quick *yes.*

Denzel Duke wants me with him on the next leg of his tour, and based on the numbers Neely showed me yesterday, it would mean massive things for the vlog. All good—more followers, more sponsors, more opportunities. I could take my influence to the next level.

Plus, even more than Denzel and what this would mean for the vlog, the anticipation of leaving again is a heady thrill. I love packing my suitcase. Taxiing down the runway is one of my most favourite things to do. I get excited about the unknown, about making a plan on the fly, which is exactly what Denzel is offering.

I have a feeling he's also offering more than that, but I'm not going there. A month ago, a week ago, I would have jumped at the chance. But now, the thought of leaving makes me tired.

Maybe it's because the jetlag had me awake at three in the morning again, this time wandering around the house and hiding my phone in the cushions of the couch so I wouldn't text Emmett to apologize.

"Wow," I say, testing out my words. "That sounds amazing."

"It will be," Denzel says eagerly. "Let's go right now. I'll buy you anything you need."

My sigh is real and rueful. "Denzel. I can't just leave like that."

"Why not? You're a vlogger, you live on the road. No commitments, you said, nothing holding you here. It's perfect."

Did I really say I have nothing holding me here?

The waitress brings my drink, looking closely at Denzel. He turns his face away as I smile my thanks.

"I do have a life here," I say. "Family and friends. My dog. Doris would miss me."

"I'm not planning on keeping you forever." His face creases into a smile, heart-breaking in its beauty. "Although, I wouldn't be opposed. You and me, on the road, sneaking into places like that noodle shop."

"That noodle place was horrible." That last night in Thailand had been a fun night, but with a sinking heart, I realize that while it was but one night in a series of fun events for me, it might mean something different to Denzel.

"I thought it was great. I'd never done anything like that before. You bring out the best in me, Shae. I want to do more things like that. Things with you." He reaches across the table and grabs my hand. "You live out of a suitcase for most of the year. Live out of my suitcase for a while. Let's see where this can lead, this thing between us."

"Denzel." I stare at his hand holding mine. His fingers are long and slim, his hand soft, unlined, without the calluses and marks of manual labour.

I could feel Emmett's strength when he held me, and it gave me butterflies the way my tiny hand fit into his.

"Did I miss something?" Denzel asks, the first crack of apprehension in his voice. "There's something between us, isn't there?"

"There was," I admit. "That was an amazing night."

"But now—no?" His face falls, and he tries to tug his hand away, but I tighten my grip. "It's only been a couple of days. Is there someone else?"

I've given the *I don't do relationships* speech enough times to have regulated it to an art form, like the prose of a best seller. But the words stick in my throat.

"That's not the problem," I say finally. "Denzel, I'm dying."

He rears back from the table, an angry expression on his face. "That's not funny."

"For once, I'm not trying to be funny." I smile sadly. "I was diagnosed with Batten disease when I was fourteen. I don't know how long I have left. I could go just like that." I snap my fingers for emphasis and grimace when Denzel continues to stare at me with horror. "That was supposed to be funny."

"Are you serious?" Denzel asks in a low voice.

"Unfortunately, yes. It sucks, but I've learned to deal with it. But what I won't do is drag someone into my life. That's why I don't do relationships."

"Ever?"

"Not the serious, committed, promise rings and declarations type. If you want a one-night thing, I'm your girl." I smile wryly at him. "But I have a feeling that's not what you're looking for."

"No." His smile is there but it's strained. He doesn't know what to say and is probably now furiously racking his pretty brains to politely extract himself from this situation, like every person I've told about this.

But instead of the vague excuse to leave, Denzel surprises me.

"I don't accept that. Either you're incredibly selfless—"

"Okay, but I'm really not."

"—or you're scared."

I sit up straight. Listening to Neely is bad enough—I don't want to hear about this from Denzel of all people. "I'm not scared of anything."

He raises an eyebrow. "Are you sure about that? Not snakes or spiders or falling from a big height?"

"No," I snap."

"What about getting your heart broken?"

"Why would I be scared of that?"

"Have you ever been in love?" Denzel asks softly. "Truly, madly in love? Not loving your friend or family, but another person so much that it feels like you can't breathe without them?"

I shake my head. With everything I'd done in my life, giving my heart over to another person is something I refuse to contemplate. It's like my heart is under lock and key, and no one is getting their own key. "I can't," I whisper.

"You can," he says. "I've been in love and it was the scariest thing I've ever done. Even worse than the first time I climbed up on stage. But it was also the best. I don't think it's fair for you to cut yourself off like that because you're scared."

"You sound like Neely."

"This Neely is a smart person."

My mother's voice breaks into the conversation. The image of her curled up on her bed, piteously crying and the only thing I could do was pat her shoulder. "I miss him so much," she had wailed. My father had been dead a month, and it was like a day had barely passed since the funeral. My mother hadn't been to work since he died, hadn't been eating, or even showering. It had been up to me to look after her, even though I couldn't think about my Dad without crying.

"Don't ever fall in love," she'd ordered six months after I'd been diagnosed with Batten disease. She'd thought I had anemia, worst case lupus. Even with all of her nursing experience, she'd never imagined the doctor would give me a death sentence.

But even then, all she was concerned with was my heart. Or the hearts of others. "Trust me, I know," she'd said, hollow-eyed and lethargic. "It hurts too much to love and then lose someone. It's not fair to anyone. With this..." she'd waved her hand like my diagnosis was nothing more than a bad case of the flu. "You know how much it hurts to lose someone. Don't do it."

And then an image of a broken Emmett creeps in.

I tug my hand out of Denzel's and lean back in the booth to get as much distance between us as possible. "It's not fair."

"To who? I barely know you Shae, but I'd take any time you could give me. I'm sure someone who loves you would think the same. It would be worth it. That whole *'tis better to have loved and lost than never to have loved before* is true you know. That's why they made a poem about it. Shakespeare," Denzel says proudly.

"It's actually Tennyson," I correct gently. "Everyone thinks it's Shakespeare. Tennyson wrote it about his friend who died."

"Didn't know that. It's still true." Denzel gives me a sad smile. "I'm sorry, Shae. For everything."

"Thanks." There's not much else I can say.

Denzel raises his hand to signal the waitress for the bill. "Since you're not running away to Australia, what are you doing next?"

I stare at my hand alone in the middle of the table. "I don't know."

Emmett

I VOLUNTEER TO MAKE the handful of deliveries in the city on Friday, driven by the need to see Shae. She dive-bombed my life, and even if she doesn't want me, I deserve an explanation.

These deliveries are different than last week, so I have no reason to stop at Pain au Chocolate, other than the fact I could use a jolt of caffeine from another sleepless night. It's been like this all week, as if Shae took my ability to sleep through the night with her when she crawled out of my bed.

My pillow still smells of her but it's fading daily. What will happen when she's faded out of my life?

Plus, Pepper texted me a few days ago and asked if I could stop next time I was in town to pick up some pastries so she could compare them to hers. *And two cupcakes*, she'd typed in all caps.

As the bell over the door at the patisserie tinkles, I'm greeted by an enthusiastic whoop from behind the counter. "There's my new brother-in-law," Adam cries with a wild wave of his hand. "I thought you'd forgotten about me already."

"Not possible," I mutter under my breath, pasting a smile on my face that is no match for Adam's. "Technically, I don't think we're brother-in-law," I say out loud. "I'm not sure how that works."

"I say we're family, so deal with it," Adam states. "And even more than family, since your friendly friend Grayson showed up to take Neely to dinner last night."

"I heard about that." There's no lineup today so I take my place at the counter, nodding at Reuben behind the cash register. "Any word how it went?"

"I'd rather hear how it went with Shae." Adam gives me a mock frown. "Or why it isn't going."

"News travels fast." I give a helpless shrug. "Your guess is as good as mine."

"I told you not to let her get away! Or, wait—" Adam sucks in his breath. "Is that why you're in town? To see her?"

My cheeks feel warm under Adam's expectant gaze. "I thought I might stop by."

He claps his hands. "Then your coffee is on the house because you are exactly what that girl needs!"

"Thanks, but you don't have to do that. I need a few things actually." Pulling out my phone, I find Pepper's message. "A croissant, a pain au chocolate, éclairs, a couple of macarons and two cupcakes." I glance at the display case. Today's cupcakes have juicy-looking strawberries perched on top fluffy white icing. "Maybe a couple more cupcakes. Rufus might like those."

"And Shae," Reuben says in his heavy accent.

"Take her a cupcake!" Adam puts my coffee on the counter so he can clap his hands again.

Reuben wraps everything, except a lone cupcake, into a white box, and then hands me a small one with the cupcake. "Most of this is for Pepper," I say as I hand him my card. "I think she's aiming to be your competition. Or something."

A startled expression crosses Reuben's face, and then he smiles.

Dad instructed me to bring Mama S. a bunch of new asparagus and a quart of strawberries, so I have an easy excuse to be in Shae's neighbourhood. It's not as easy to extract myself from Mama S.'s kitchen, but I finally manage to slip across to Shae's with a bag of cookies and a jar of homemade tomato sauce.

Mike answers my knock. "Emmett, isn't it?" His expression isn't exactly welcoming, but he's not meeting me with a shotgun, either. He looks like what he is—a father figure greeting the guy who is interested in his daughter. Step-grand-daughter in this case.

I nod. "Is Shae home?" Even picking up dates when I was a teenager wasn't this awkward.

"Let me check." He pauses, his hand on the door, and turns back to me. For a moment he looks like he's about to say something, then gives a quick shake of his head. "Give me a sec."

Almost five minutes pass as I wait on the porch. Eventually, the dog comes to keep me company, pressing her body against my leg as I scratch her ears like she's giving me a dog hug.

"What are you doing here?"

My head jerks up, stomach sinking at the sound of Shae's voice, even more when I see her face. She's paler than usual, with heavy eyes etched with purple shadows. And she's not smiling. I've never seen Shae without a smile.

Something is wrong.

But my heart still leaps when I see her, and I smile widely, hoping it might be contagious.

"I was in the neighbourhood." I poke my thumb to Neely's place. "Thought I'd stop by, since I have one of these for you." I offer her the tiny box with the Pain logo etched in blue. "And some strawberries. My dad ate all the jam." The green plastic container of fresh strawberries is still warm from sitting in the cab of the truck.

Shae stares at the berries. "I'm just about to head out. After I finish…" she touches the towel covering her hair with an embarrassed grin. "I'm colouring my hair."

"Oh. Okay."

"Thank you," she says quickly. "It's good—it's just that I have something on today. Something I have to do. Now. After."

"No worries. I just thought I'd stop by, say hi. See how the jet lag is."

"It's fine." She looks everywhere but at me, her gaze finally resting on the box in her hand. "I apologize for rushing out the way I did. I had—"

"No," I interrupt. "Tell me the truth. It was Alex, wasn't it?" She stares up at me, her eyes huge. "Look, Shae, if you don't feel the same way as I do, that's fine. I can understand that. But if the thought of my dead wife—" I wince as the words come out harsher than I intended. "—got you upset, then I think I have the right to know why."

"I don't want you to be hurt," she says softly.

"What's going to hurt me? It's not like you're going to die like she did."

The plastic container of strawberries falls from her hand, sending berries rolling everywhere. The dog jumps up and scoops up the closest one. "Doris, no!" Shae exclaims, setting the cupcake down on the floor. "Don't eat that. Are they bad for dogs?" she implores.

"I don't think so." I bend over to pick up the berries at my feet.

"I'm sorry," Shae says, sounding like she's close to tears. "I wasted them because I can't—"

"They'll be fine if you wash them really well," I tell her, scooping up a few more berries. Most of them fell in the house and Shae drops to her knees to pick them up. "Except what the dog ate. I think she'll be okay, though."

"It's okay?" Shae's eyes are dark in her pale face and I start to feel a little gooey, like a soggy piece of bread.

"Of course." I hold out the container for her to drop the berries in and then help her to her feet. "It's fine. No sense crying over spilled strawberries."

"Emmett," she begins as Mike calls from inside.

"Shae, the timer went off two minutes ago!"

She clutches the towel on her head. "I really have to get this stuff off my hair," she says apologetically. "It turns a gross, funky shade if I leave it on too long."

It's like a breeze has swept through and brushed aside her concerns like Tuesday morning never happened. Her voice has lost its coolness, and her expression has lost some of its despair. I can tell there's still something bothering her, but I won't press her now. There'll be time for talking.

I hope.

"I wouldn't want you with funky hair."

She smiles gratefully. "And I really have to leave after I'm finished, but I really want to talk to you, too..."

"Are you free tonight? Rufus has a baseball game and I know he'd love to see you there."

There's a pause before she replies, long enough for maybe to think I'm wrong about things again. "Okay," she says, her eyes wide and wary. "And then we'll talk."

"All you want," I promise, my heart already leaping with anticipation at seeing her tonight.

"Shae, you're going to be late!" Mike shouts again. I step back, even though the last thing I want it more distance between us.

"I'll let you do what you need to do. But I'll see you tonight? Seven o'clock?"

"I'll be there." And before she turns, she darts forward and presses her lips against mine.

"See you." With a tap on the dog's head, I float back to the truck.

Chapter Seventeen

Shae

I SLIDE INTO THE chair at Fred's with a heaviness that's from more than a restless night. The Band-Aid on my arm, hiding the puncture spot from the needle taking what felt like gallons of blood, tugs on a hair. I drop my arm into my lap but not before Neely's eagle eye spots it.

"How was the doctor?" she asks.

My rescheduled appointment was this morning. I couldn't bring myself to tell Emmett the reason I was rushing away from him was that I had to see my doctor, let alone blurt out that I was dying.

Tonight. I'll tell him everything tonight.

"I went," I say, stacking my cutlery set out on the napkin before me. "Love being a human pincushion."

There's not much to say. My new doctor thankfully seemed to have more charm than the retired Dr. Moseley but his manner was still blunt and to the point. He said he didn't like my colour, and

I bit my tongue not to ask how he knew my original colour when this was the first time I'd met him.

I didn't mention the headache that I haven't been able to get rid of for the last few days. "He wants to run some tests. I wasn't there long." Fork over knife, knife over fork, anything to focus on, anything other than how my new doctor, Dr. Ryu, studied me across the desk in his office like he expected me to collapse right then and there.

I also didn't appreciate the sympathetic tone of the nurse who drew blood. I pictured her face after I left the lab, soft and pitying as she turned to her fellow caregivers.

"That poor little lamb. She's dying, you know. Looks healthy enough, but you never know when she'll go."

I have no idea if that even happened, but my imagination is pretty vivid.

Mabel, the daytime waitress, brings me a Pepsi. "Good to see you back," she says with a squeeze of my shoulder. Mabel has been working at the diner longer than Dee and what she loses in the speed of service, with her legs moving slower each year, she more than makes up for with her sweet nature.

"We were here the other night," I tell her as I pull the glass towards me for a much-needed shot of caffeine and sugar. "But it was a bit late for you."

"I heard about that." Mabel lifts her religiously plucked eyebrow. "You brought *boys* here."

"We bring Dawson here all the time, and he's a boy," I say with an innocent smile. The last thing I want is to talk about boys. Or Emmett. Or Emmett being a boy. I'm still reeling from seeing him earlier.

"Well, next time, make sure I'm working so I can have a boo at him. They ordered for you, you know. Grilled cheese, extra pickle." She gives a wink and heads back behind the counter.

"Thanks," I call after her.

"I'm a little scared to have Mabel check out Grayson," Neely says under her breath.

"I don't blame you." Dawson leans his elbows on the table. "It's bad enough coming in here alone and I've known her for years. I think she checks out my bum."

"Of course she does," I manage to rouse myself enough to tease. "It's a nice bum."

Dawson rolls his eyes as Neely folds her hands across the table like she's about to start a meeting. "If you're not saying anything about the doctor, then what about Emmett? Mom said he stopped by earlier. I assume that was on the way to your place."

"I thought you didn't want to hear about my *me me me*." I raise an eyebrow at Neely.

The annoyance that had caused her to storm out of my house lasted exactly one hour, when she returned, nervous for once in her life and in a dither about what to wear on her date with Grayson. I'm glad because I needed her after I met with Denzel.

"*You you you* is more interesting than my life, especially with Denzel swooping in to whisk you away." Neely raises her eyebrows. "We'll get to that in a minute."

Giving my now-auburn hair a tug, I wince. "Emmett caught me with a headful of hair dye. And then I dropped the strawberries he brought me. Not my finest moment."

Seeing Emmett had lightened my steps, but it's now the type of step you'd take on a tightrope high above the floor—careful and slow, delicate and tentative because one false move can send the rope swaying enough to make you fall.

At least I think that's how I need to proceed. I've never walked a tightrope.

"But...?" Neely raises her eyebrows expectantly.

"But I'm going to Rufus's baseball game tonight, so I'll see Emmett." I can't help but smile at the thought. "And we're going to talk."

"Talk about what?" Neely prompts.

"I don't know, maybe about the weather." I grin at her expression of exasperation. "I have no idea what I'm doing with this, so help, please. I need it."

"Don't ask me," Neely says with a shudder. "I went out with Grayson last night and I still don't understand what happened."

"If you don't understand it, maybe you're doing it wrong." I laugh, mainly at the expression of horror on Dawson's face. "What's wrong, Dawson? Afraid of being stuck in the room beside them? We had to put up with you and Natasha—"

"Britney," Neely chimes in.

"Amber," I add. "And that Charleen you picked up in Turkey."

"Why are we talking about my sex life?" he cries with confusion. "I didn't say anything."

"Yes, but your expression spoke volumes." I take another sip of Pepsi, hoping the caffeine will take the edge of the lingering headache that has suddenly stepped up the tempo, making my stomach twist and turn.

It's partly unease and partly plain nausea. While my mother's voice in my head about the unfairness of me loving someone hasn't been vanquished yet, I hope it's lost some of its power or I'm going to mess things up with Emmett again. This morning was awkward, with a head full of hair dye and not knowing how to start to tell him anything.

That I'm sick. That I'm dying. How bad I am at relationships.

And, of course, my visit with Denzel. Full disclosure here.

"Let's go back to Denzel," Dawson says, his voice accusing. "I can't believe you turned down an all-expenses-paid trip."

I shrug, trying for casual. "I've been to Australia. Now, if it was to Antarctica..." My smile is forced, but still wide and winning. "I'm still up for it if you are."

"I thought we were waiting a few months before we took off again," Neely says, her gaze shifting to the puddle of condensation around her glass.

"I know, but we could cash in on the Denzel concert going viral and—"

"I told you, I'm back at school for the summer," Neely says shortly.

I glance at Dawson who also isn't meeting my eye. Suddenly, the aura of our table takes a turn from fun and playful to cool and cagey. "I didn't know about that."

"Yes, you did, because I clearly remember having the conversation."

I honestly don't remember any conversation I had with Neely about her going back to school. But what she said about me being into myself can be true, so it's possible that we talked about it, and then it flew right out of my mind.

I'm not proud of that.

Neely has been with me from the beginning. She's given up her dreams for mine and I need to be happy for her. More importantly, I need to encourage her.

"I think that's great," I say, willing my voice to sound hearty to disguise any niggling feeling that I'm being left behind.

"We could do something in the fall," she suggests. "Or maybe we'll make it short and go before school starts."

Dawson clears his throat. "I may have a job."

"A job." Again, it's not unheard of, only that I haven't heard of it.

"Look, Shae, we've been doing a lot—Thailand, and right after Costa Rica," Dawson says with a glance at Neely that makes me wonder if the two of them planned this. "It's been non-stop and I think it might be catching up with you. I know it has for me. It might be a good idea for all of us to get some downtime. You look really tired," he finishes.

"I'm beginning to get a complex because that's all you say about me now. I'm still jet-lagged," I protest. "It takes a while."

"We're well aware of that. We're going through the same thing, but unlike you, we sleep. Take care of ourselves. I'm worried about you." Neely frowns. "You don't look good."

"I'm fine. I don't need the two of you ganging up on me."

"Have you been taking your vitamins?" she persists. "Because I know you're not sleeping. Your eyes give it away."

"I don't need your pity."

Neely rolls her eyes. "Since when have I ever shown you pity? This is concern for my friend. You should be used to it by now."

I smile tightly. "I know." The ding of the bell signaling our order is ready stops anything else I might say as I get to my feet on legs that are suddenly wobbly. "I'll help Mabel with the plates."

I got up too fast, I tell myself, blinking quickly to rid the black spots from my vision.

There's a sharp pain in my hip as I stumble into a table.

"Are you okay?" Neely asks, getting to her feet just as I lurch forward. "Shae, I think—"

The dark spots are multiplying at a rate quicker than any kid in a think tank can and it makes me nauseous. Clapping my hand over my mouth as the Pepsi I drank threatens to reappear, I forgo helping Mabel and stagger a step towards the bathroom. But my vision is covered by the dark spots and I can't see where the bathroom is, and suddenly I'm falling...

"Shae!" I hear the shout from far away, and then I can't hear any more.

Emmett

I SING ALONG TO the radio as I head back to the farm, the truck full of good smells from the pastries. About halfway home, I break down and pull out one of the cupcakes and think of Shae's expression when she bites into hers.

Reuben is truly a god of cupcakes, I admit as I lick the last bit of icing off my finger. But even if it tasted like sawdust, I'd think it was incredible right now.

The world is good today.

Or at least it will be after I talk to Shae and sort everything out. She'll have a reason for running out of the house—cold feet probably since this will be her first real relationship.

I think about the ramifications. Of being in a relationship with a woman who travels the world. I did my share of living out of a suitcase, but at least that was in the States, not across the world.

This might take some work, but I'm up for it.

It's like my head is finally screwed on straight after years of being a bobblehead, not sure of anything, especially my own emotions. I'm certain of Shae—not about what's going to happen, but that something will. I'm ready to take a step forward and after this morning, at the look she gave me, I'm sure that she's ready too.

Reasonably sure.

Shut up, I tell the doubting voice in my head. Talk to Shae first and then we'll figure everything out.

I'm more gentle with the voice that reminds me to remember Alex and my love for her. *Never forget.*

And I won't.

Rufus and Dad are at the door when I pull in, Dad coming in from the fields, and Rufus chattering away to him about something that happened at school. Both stop as I jump out of the truck with a smile and the jar of spaghetti sauce.

"Deliveries go okay?" Dad calls.

"Did you see Shae?" Rufus asks eagerly.

"How did you know I was going to see her?" I demand. I hold up the jar as I reach the door. "Mama S. sent this. I think all we need to do is warm it up."

"We can try it tonight," Dad says as he opens the door. "Should be manageable for a couple of bachelors and a sidekick."

"I'm not the sidekick, you are." Rufus laughs. But it still doesn't fully distract him. "So you talked to Shae? She's not ghosting you anymore?"

"No?" I shake my head at my own question. "I don't know. I don't know if she was because I'm not sure what ghosting is."

Rufus sighs. "You need to get into this century."

"I know what a social influencer is. I thought that was enough." I set the container of cookies on the counter, hoping that Rufus is more interested in his phone than a snack.

"You need communication for a relationship," Rufus says. "That's what Emily says."

"Emily, huh?" I meet Dad's eyes with a shrug. "What happened to Ava?"

"Old news. Emily is teaching me a lot about how to make a woman happy," Rufus confides.

"Is she now?" Dad murmurs. "I think we can all learn something from Emily."

"What did Shae say? Is she coming to my game tonight?"

"Your game." I slap my forehead, pretending to forget. "Did you have a game?"

"Har har har. You're coming, aren't you?"

"I thought I might. And I might bring a friend."

"Shae!" Rufus cheers.

"If she can make it," I add quickly, not wanting to get his hopes dashed if something changes.

"It's cool if she comes," Rufus says. "She can sit on the bench and be like a cheerleader. I think Shae would make a really good cheerleader, don't you?"

I smile as the memory of Shae with a group of wedding guests surrounding her dancing to the Chicken Dance flashes through my mind, leading to an image of Shae in the tree, and then dancing in the kitchen, making jam. "Definitely."

"Emmett?"

I pull myself out of my Shae-haze to glance down at Rufus holding his phone.

"Why is Denzel Duke at a bar with Shae?"

Rufus holds up his phone and my smile fades.

Chapter Eighteen

Shae

MY MOTHER IS THE first face I see when I wake up. She's holding my hand so I know things are bad.

"Where am I?" I say weakly. My eyelids seem to weigh a hundred pounds each and I close them gratefully.

"You're in the hospital." She uses her nurse voice rather than her regular mother voice. I know the difference because the only time I hear the soothing, gentle tone is the first five minutes when she gets home after her shift. Then she switches into mother mode and all the disappointment that goes with it. "In the emergency room."

"You passed out at Fred's." I open my eyes to see Neely and Dawson hovering behind my mother. Neely's eyes are red and swollen and Dawson looks terrified. He's always had a fear of hospitals. "We tried to catch you, but you went down so fast."

"You hit the table. Knocked it right over," Dawson adds with a bad attempt at a grin. "Everything went flying. Mabel said the sound nearly gave her a heart attack."

"Sorry, Mabel," I whisper, tears trickling out my eyes.

This is what I've always dreaded—the concern of my friends, my sorrow mixing with theirs.

How can this be happening? It's too soon. I have more to do, to see.

I don't want to go!

My throat tightens and I have trouble swallowing. Is that how I'll go—unable to breathe, to catch my breath? "How long?" I murmur.

Mom presses her lips together as she releases my hand. "I'm going to tell the doctor you're awake."

She pushes through the curtains surrounding the bed, wearing her blue scrubs. Voices and beeping alarms, the squeak of a gurney passing by crowd my bed. An IV juts out of the back of my hand leading to a bag of liquid hanging from a pole.

I wet my lips. "How long have I been here?"

"Not long. We couldn't get you to wake up at the diner. Mabel called an ambulance." Neely's voice is steady but I notice her hands clasped in front of her stomach are shaking. "Your Mom was here when they brought you in. It was—Mike's on his way."

I nod. I want to say goodbye, but I don't want them with me when I die. I'll figure out how to be alone. I can't make it any harder for them than it already is.

"Do you want me to call Emmett?" Neely asks in a soft voice.

I shake my head, the slight movement causes my stomach to roil in distress. "I don't know."

"Why don't we wait to see what the doctor says?" Neely bites her lip, her eyes shifting away from the bed, surrounded by tubes and beeping monitors. I can tell she's doing everything she can to keep from crying.

I, on the other hand, can't seem to stop myself. Dawson leans forward and brushes his hand across my cheek. "Don't cry," he whispers. "It'll be okay."

"That's what I say." My throat is unbearably tight.

"Now it's my turn." He brushes the hair off my forehead. "It's going to be okay because we love you, Shae."

My face seems to crack as tears begin to gush. "Don't say that."

"It's the truth." Neely grips my hand. "And we're here for you. Always."

Always isn't going to be that long.

A youngish doctor bustles through the curtain, his fashionable stubble masking a babyface. My mother follows close behind. "How are you doing? I'm Dr. Patel," he asks with an easy smile. "Gave yourself a nasty bump on the head, did you?"

"How long do I have?"

He frowns. "Until you're out of here? We might keep you for the day, but there's no reason for—"

"You're letting her go home when she looks like this?" Neely interrupts. "She's dying. You need to help her."

Dr. Patel steps back. "She's dehydrated and it looks like she's severely anemic. Who said anything about dying?"

"She was diagnosed with Batten disease thirteen years ago," my mother snaps and the doctor blinks with surprise. "It's a form of neuronal ceroid lipofuscinosis."

"Uh, yeah. I know what that is." He checks his clipboard with a frown. "I'm going to check my notes...run a few tests."

"Check with her doctor," Mom says, sounding for the first time like she cares.

The mention of a disease that no one in the ER has experience with really steps up my care. Soon, I'm wheeled through the halls to a private room, with Neely and Dawson following, their worried expressions deepening with every new batch of residents and interns that stick their head in the door to check out the girl who's dying. I get a new bag hanging from my pole and they've taken enough blood from my arm to make me woozy, even without the fainting.

Hours pass where I sleep uneasily, woken often by nurses coming in for more tests. Mom darts in and out of the room, unable to sit still, contacting my doctor, getting ice chips, and more importantly, using her status as to hurry things along.

I'd like to know what's going on because after a nap, I don't feel too bad for someone who's dying, other than the killer headache from the goose egg on my forehead.

But it can't help the fear that gnaws at my stomach.

Finally, hours later, the doctor appears again. I've tried to get Dawson and Neely to go home, but neither have budged and when Dr. Patel shows up, both jump to their feet and line up beside the bed.

"So I have to admit, I'm a little confused by all this mention of Batten disease," he begins, with a frown. "I tried to contact your doctor, a Dr. Moseley, but he passed away. Did you know that?"

"I met with the new one today," I tell him. "Dr. Ryu. He did some tests and I'm going back next week."

"Well, now I don't think you'll need that follow-up appointment. How long ago were you diagnosed, Shae?"

"She was fourteen," Mom says in a cold voice. "It should be right there in the file."

"Fourteen. Wow. Anyway, I'm not sure how to tell you this but..." His voice drops into a perfectly gentle soothing tone and I brace myself. "Shae, you don't have Batten disease."

There's a roaring in my ears. I can't have heard that right. "What?"

He smiles. "You don't have Batten disease. You *never* had it. Your doctor made a mistake. Shae, you're not going to die, at least not for a long, long time."

That's all I hear before the room erupts.

Emmett

I SCRUTINIZE THE INSTAGRAM post of Shae at a table with Denzel Duke. He's wearing a Blue Jays cap, and she's smiling at him. Her hair is the same pink from the wedding, so I know the picture is from the last day or so.

"It's not one of Shae's," Rufus assures me. "There's none of her hashtags." At my confused expression, Rufus points out that Shae was tagged on the photo. "She didn't take it, someone else did and it got on her page."

"I don't understand any of that." Is this why Shae wanted to talk to me? Was the expression in her dark eyes nothing but guilt, plain and simple?

"This may be nothing." Rufus waves his phone. "You know they're friends. Denzel could have stopped in Toronto, and they met for a drink. It's not like she's going to run off with him."

"You think she's going to run off with him?" I hadn't even considered that.

"No. Why would she do that?"

Because Shae is a social influencer looking for the next thing to go viral. Being whisked away by a rock star would be it.

My mind is caught in a maelstrom of thoughts as I drive Rufus to his baseball game. I haven't heard from Shae, but I sent her a text telling her where the field is, trying to stop the image of Shae at the airport, hand in hand with Denzel Duke, from blinding me.

It's not easy.

I promised to help Grayson coach that night, something I had looked forward to, but as I stand by first base, instructing the team when to steal, and when to push themselves for an extra-base hit, I keep looking expectantly at the stands to see a shock of pink hair with a cheerful smile, clapping her little hands with delight. Although I have no idea what colour her hair is now if she dyed it this morning.

I keep telling myself that she'll be there soon.

Chapter Nineteen

Shae

N*OT GOING TO DIE*
  Not going to die
Not going to die

"What?" I say.

The young doctor—I might have thought he was cute before, but now he's downright beautiful—beams at me. "I don't usually get to tell people good news in here," Dr. Patel says. "But it's right here. We did the test twice. There is absolutely nothing in your blood work to indicate that you have neuronal ceroid lipofuscinosis."

"Did I get better?" My voice is weak and hesitant, unsure. I don't know anything right now. If someone asked me my name, I'd be hard-pressed to give it to them.

Not dying.

"I don't think you were ever sick," the doctor says gently.

My mother sinks into the chair without a word, her hand covering her mouth, with Mike hugging her shoulders. Dawson stares at the doctor like he has three heads and Neely...

"How could there have been such a terrible mistake?" she cries. "We thought she was dying! For years, she's been dying. How can you just now tell us she's not?"

"I honestly don't know." Dr. Patel stands straight in the face of Neely's anger. "There could be—you're severely anemic, so it's possible that the numbers for that affected something, or were misread..." He shrugs with a rueful expression on his face. "I'm so sorry. I have no idea what happened, but I can tell you with all certainty that you do not have Batten disease."

The rush of words is like when you're driving on the highway with the window open and passing a transport truck. I can't hear a thing. All I can do is slump against the pillow and stare at Dr. Patel, fearful he's going to take the words away and tell me something else.

"She's not going to die?" Mike's voice is a gruff rumble.

"Not yet anyway. She does need to take care of herself. She's dehydrated, and her red blood count is very low so I'm prescribing an iron supplement. As well, a diet with lots of iron-rich food, like red meat and spinach—"

"She needs spinach?" Neely cries. "And to drink more water? But she's not going to die, because it was a mistake? That's what you're telling us, that someone made a mistake?" She swells like a balloon, so outraged on my behalf. "What can we do about it? Can we sue? Can we—?"

"Neely." I focus on her face, on what she's saying and the white noise in my head slowly subsides. It takes me three tries before my voice is loud enough for her to hear me before she looks to see me with my hand outreached. "I'm not going to die."

It's Dawson who grabs my hand, the confused expression transforming into one of such relief that it brings tears to my eyes. "You're not going to die."

I shake my head, tears overflowing even as my smile widens. "I'm not."

Neely makes a keening noise and as I watch, her face crumples like a used Kleenex. "You're not..." she chokes out. "Not dying...oh, Shae!"

Neely throws herself into my arms, sobs shaking her body. I've never seen her cry like this—I rarely see her cry—and it stuns me almost as much as the news. My arms tighten around her as she babbles incoherently, which of course, makes me giggle. At the rumble of my chest, Neely sits up, her face streaked with tears, snot bubbling on her nose. She swipes the back of her hand across her face, which makes me laugh more, and then she's laughing, and Dawson is there...

"I'm not going to die!"

"Not for a long time." Dawson keeps shaking his head like a wet dog, like he can't fully comprehend the news.

"Not ever!" Neely cries, her arms tightening around me.

"Not without you," I whisper. "Not without both of you."

"Wait a minute." Neely pulls back with another wipe of her nose. "We're not doing some death pact for the vlog if that's what you're thinking. There's no way—"

I laugh and wipe my eyes with the corner of the sheet. "The vlog! Dawson, take a picture of the doctor! Hashtag *#savemylife* *#hotdoctor.*"

"Why thank you. I really didn't do much," Dr. Patel says with a bemused smile. "But I'll take it. And then I have to get back to my rounds. I'll check back with you soon." He poses for Dawson, one serious, several funny. "Do you think this will help with my dating life?"

"Definitely," Dawson promises. "And we've got an in with The Suitor show, so maybe we can set you up."

"I have to call my brother before you post anything." Neely jumps off the bed, her face smeared with tears and blotches of red. "And Mama."

Mom.

As if I spoke, Dawson and Neely peel away from the bed and I see my mother, sitting stock-still in the chair, staring into nothing. Mike has his hand on her shoulder, but other than the tears that drip from her eyes like a leaky faucet, she looks like she's carved from stone.

I swallow the lump in my throat. "Mom?"

She looks at me with a blank expression. "What?"

My happiness shreds like a stale piece of bread. Even with the news, the best news of my life, I still can't provoke a reaction from her. "They told me—"

"Yes," she interrupts, standing up. "It's great news. If you excuse me for a moment, I have to check on my next shift." She slips through the curtains like a ghost.

"It's a lot for her to take in," Mike says quickly. "Give her a moment."

"Sure," I whisper, examining the IV on the back of my hand.

"But maybe I can get in on this little love fest." Mike pulls me up into a sitting position to better hug me. My tears begin again as he presses me into his chest. "My Shae-girl," he says in a choked voice. "I knew you'd be okay."

"No, you didn't." My laugh is muffled.

"I prayed for it." He pulls back and wipes the wetness on my cheeks with his fingers.

"I don't know why I'm crying," I say through my tears.

"Happiness does strange things to people." He jerks his head in the direction where my mother disappeared. "She'll come around."

I can only nod.

"I called Mama," Neely says, waving her phone at me. "I got an earful of some Italian that I couldn't understand, but the gist of it is that she wants us to come over for breakfast in the morning. She said now, but it's too late." Before she finishes speaking, she dials another number.

"Can I go home?" I wonder. "Because I'm not dying." I meet Mike's gaze and giggle. "I'm not dying."

"No, you're not." He drops a kiss on the top of my head and stands up. "I'll go check with your hot doctor."

"Listen to this." Neely holds up the phone and from a few feet away, I can hear the squawk of Adam shouting, a scream, and then silence, before the sound of sobbing.

"Adam?" Neely demands, her phone back to her ear and following Mike out of the room.

Dawson sits on the edge of the bed and picks up my non-IV hand and hugs it to his chest. "You're not dying," he says.

"I'm not." My sigh of relief is so extreme it makes me lightheaded. The world has shifted, turned upside down. What was red is

now green, what was forbidden is now free. "What do I do now?"
I ask helplessly.

"What do you want to do?"

"I don't know." The laughter bubbles out as easily as the tears
had, and now mixes with them so I'm crying and laughing all at
once. "I really have no idea."

"Get some rest," Dawson advises. "You did pass out. I don't
know if you remember that."

"I really don't." I laugh again.

"And then I have a suggestion." Dawson meets my questioning
gaze. "Call Emmett. There's no way you should mess this up now."

Emmett

S HAE DOESN'T SHOW UP for Rufus's game.

She doesn't show up, period.

The hazy picture of Denzel Duke holding her hand across the table flashes through my mind like a broken streetlight. I told Rufus not to worry, and not to DM Shae, but the way he runs to his phone at the end of every inning suggests he didn't listen to me.

On the way home, Rufus tries to explain again how someone had posted the picture on Instagram, tagging Shae so it shows up in her feed.

But it doesn't explain why she never shows up to the game.

And it's not like she didn't warn me: "Actually, Denzel *would* be the swooping sort," Shae had said at the wedding. Denzel Duke, rock star, pop star, whatever his name is, swooped in and stole her from me.

How can I compete with that?

Not that she was entirely mine, but I thought I had a chance. I wanted that chance.

To make it worse, Rufus's team loses. Badly. I think he's as disappointed about that as he is from Shae's no-show.

I can forgive her for some things, but not for letting down Rufus.

The drive home is quiet and you can smell the resentment in the car, along with a sweaty eleven-year-old. I've just pulled up to the house when my phone rings, cutting off my argument with Rufus about going straight to bed. "Hello," I bark, glaring at Rufus and jerking my chin at the house. He slams the door in response and with a sympathetic glance, Dad follows him in. "Who's this?"

"Emmett, it's Neely. Grayson gave me your number." She has to repeat it twice for me to understand her. Sounds of laughter and loud chattering interrupt her words.

"Are you at a party?" I ask sourly.

"No, well, yes! It's so great—we're at the hospital and Shae just found out she's not going to die!"

I stare at the phone in my hand. "What?"

"She's not going to die!"

I can't understand why Neely is talking about Shae like that. "So she's not with Denzel Duke?"

"No, why? Oh..." It's almost like I can see the lightbulb go on in her head. "Did they post something about him and Shae?"

"There's a picture."

"That's nothing to worry about. But, listen, Emmett, we just found out Shae isn't going to die! She's not sick after all—it was all some big mistake, which I think is criminal, but Shae isn't thinking about that, only—"

Neely's words are rapid-fire and even if I knew what she was talking about, I'd have trouble understanding her. "Neely, I have no idea what you're talking about," I interrupt.

Silence, and then the background noise abruptly fades so Neely must have stepped into another room. "Just so you know, Shae was going to tell you tonight. But then she passed out at Fred's and we took her to the hospital, which is a good thing because that's how we found out about the mistake. Although she was at the doctor's earlier, so maybe they would have caught it there. But she was planning on telling you everything, which is really hard for her, because she never tells anyone."

"Tell me what? What's going on, Neely?"

"Maybe I should let her talk to you."

"Neely Scalzo, you tell me what the hell is going on *right now*." My voice rises enough for Dad at the door to turn with surprise.

Neely's sigh of disappointment comes across loud and clear. "I told her to tell you. She never does and it always messes things up. The first thing you need to know is Shae is fine. Everything is fine."

"Everything is not fine."

"Why am I always the one who has to tell people?" Neely mutters. "Look—short version? Shae was told she had something called Batten disease when she was fourteen. She's been dying—we thought she was dying."

When I was playing ball on one of the farm teams, there had been a stadium with a horribly outdated locker room. The showers were one room, curtained cubicles crowded together, and the floor sloped so the water drained into the middle of the floor. It was lined with some material that made the sound of the water reverberate. To make it worse, the pressure was amazing, so the water fell with the force of a fastball. To shower alone was loud; to shower among the team was deafening. I remember trying to get finished as fast as I could, all the while holding tight to my bar of soap because to drop it meant it would float out to the middle of the floor.

Neely's words are the sound of the showers, and the word *dying* is my bar of soap. It's the only thing I can hold on to.

I slump against the steering wheel. "She's dying?"

"No! I mean, for years she thought she was. But tonight, after she fainted at lunch and we took her to the hospital, they found out that she's not dying after all. It's just regular old anemia, and her doctor made a horrible mistake."

I can't seem to comprehend what Neely is telling me. Hospital, dying... *Alex*, only this isn't Alex we're talking about, but Shae. Shae is dying.

"Emmett? Are you still there?"

"She didn't tell me," I say hollowly. It's like a kick to the crotch—sharp and swift and without mercy. I don't know what hurts more, the fact that there may be a world without Shae, or that she never told me about being sick.

The betrayal stings like a paper cut under your nail, dosed in lemon juice.

"She *knew* she was *dying* and she didn't tell me?" I ask, astonished that I can sound so quiet and calm. Or maybe I don't. Maybe the roaring in my ears is blocking out everything else, and I'm not hearing Neely correctly.

"No," Neely says heavily. "She never does. She's not good with relationships, Emmett, so you can't take it personally."

"I can't take it personally?" I ask incredulously. "I told her all about my wife dying, and she didn't think to mention that the same thing might be happening to her?"

I had told Shae about Alex, my mother, my family. I opened my heart and bared my soul and she never thought to mention this one little thing that changes everything?

"Your wife...Shae's not really dying," Neely says quickly. "They made a mistake. She's going to be fine. I mean, she'll die someday, but we all will, so there's nothing to worry about."

"Nothing to worry about," I echo. "Does that Denzel Duke know about this?"

"Sorry—what?" Neely stammers.

"Did I get his name right?" Rage, petty and potent, bubbles up and I can't think straight. Shae—dying and not dying. Shae, with another man. Shae, not telling me about the most important thing in her life.

"Does he know she's dying, not dying?" I demand.

"I don't know," Neely says quietly.

I don't know Neely well, but I know she's a bad liar. "Yes, you do, because you're her keeper. You know every move she makes. You know Shae told this guy that she spent one night with that she's dying, but not me."

"Emmett..."

"I deserved to know—" I say in a bleak voice. "She told me I can't move on with her." I flash back to how she ran out of the kitchen that day, leaving me confused and more concerned than I had been in a long time. "That was because she was dying."

"Yes," Neely says quickly. "But she's not anymore."

How could she not tell me? Knowing what I'd been through, how my life fell apart after Alex—how could Shae not think I'd understand? How could she not trust me?

And then the thought of Shae dying hits me like that fastball, leaving me gasping and foggy with the sharp stab of pain.

Shae, so small and white in a hospital bed, tubes and machines attached, with nurses monitoring her every heartbeat. Sitting by her bed, every sense on high alert listening for the sound of her breath...and when there wasn't one...

The burger that Dad made for dinner rises in my stomach and I gag, remembering how I lay on Alex's chest, begging her to breathe again, one more time, until the nurse pushed me away.

"I can't," I whisper. "I can't do this."

Neely is still talking when I hang up the phone.

Chapter Twenty

Shae

I'M NOT GOING TO die. I can't get tired of saying it, aloud or just in my head. I'm not going to die.

Mike finally takes Neely, Dawson, and my mother home, with the promise that he'll be back in the morning to pick me up. I love how happy they are—smiling, laughing, Neely even giving an impromptu dance.

That was before she talked to Emmett on the phone. Or tried, before he hung up.

I think that's the reason they keep me in the hospital overnight. When Neely tells me about her call to Emmett, I felt like how bread dough is punched before it rises again and my monitors did funny things, so the nurse got nervous and said they wanted to keep me overnight for observation.

Dr. Patel stops by the see me at the end of the shift and tells me he ordered a new bunch of tests. I think he takes the mistaken diagnosis a little more personally than he needs to. Maybe it's a doctor thing. But the nurse comes to my room just before midnight and takes a bunch more blood.

"Get some rest," she says after affixing the cotton ball and Band-Aid to the inside of my elbow. "You'll be out of here in the morning."

As for me, I can't be angry that they made a mistake. I could, but what would be the point? I might have dealt with thirteen years of thinking I could die at any moment, but honestly, did it do me any harm?

When I look at what my life has been like, the reality is that I wouldn't have done a fraction of those things if I didn't think I had an expiry date. So when Neely takes umbrage again on my behalf, threatening to sue and expose and stuff about malpractice lawsuits, I tell her to stop. I do join in with one final, expletive-filled curse at my former doctor, and then I let it go.

I don't know what to do about Emmett. I don't know if I can let it go with him.

I made Neely repeat the conversation over and over again, trying to understand what Emmett said to her. I don't understand the Denzel part until Dawson checks my Insta page and finds hundreds of comments from the grainy picture that *@Denzelismine* posted.

A quick comment and my own post wishing Denzel well in Australia should fix things.

But the rest...

It seems simple—like I ran when I found out his wife died, Emmett is running for cover before he's faced with the possibility of losing me too.

That's what is so frustrating—he's not going to lose me. I'm not going to die. But I can't blame him. I have no idea about what he went through. I can understand how he would be freaked out by the thought of it happening again.

I try calling, but it goes directly to voicemail.

As I toss and turn in my uncomfortable hospital bed, the lights, the alarms, and the frequency of nurses coming in to check on me, as well as thoughts of Emmett, make it hard for me to fall asleep.

But I must have eventually since I'm awoken by the squeak of shoes and open my eyes to see my mother with my chart in her hand, dressed in different-coloured scrubs from yesterday.

"Mom?"

She looks at me with a smile and I blink with shock. "Hi, sweet-ie."

Smiling? Sweetie? Something is seriously wrong with my mother.

I swallow, and a dry cough interrupts my words. Mom quickly picks up the glass of water with the bendy straw. "What are you doing here?" I croak after I take a sip.

"I wanted to see you before I start my shift. Mike will be here later to take you home. I gave him a ton of instructions." She smiles again, and this time the smile reaches her eyes. "Probably overkill."

Who is this woman? Her features are the same, with the lines around her mouth and on her forehead that deepen every year, but there's a lightness to her eyes that is new. So is the lift of her mouth. "Why?" I ask.

She gestures to the bed and I shift over to give her room to sit down, conscious of my dry mouth and possible body odour from being in the hospital for hours on end. "I had a long talk with Mike last night." She chuckles ruefully. "And, of course, you've heard about Neely giving me an earful last night."

"Sorry—what?"

"After she called...Emmett, is it? Seems like she blames me for your inability to open your heart to anyone."

My jaw drops open, leaving me gaping like a fish. "Neely said what?"

"I don't remember the exact words, but I'm sure she'll be happy to give you a recap. The gist of it is that my refusal to move on after your father's death has stunted your romantic growth. Something like that. And she's right."

"*What*?" I give my head a shake. "Did I pass out again, because how did I miss that?"

She pats my hand. "She's very protective. Neely's always been a good friend."

"The best." I look at her warily. "What do you mean, she was right?" I hold my breath, not knowing what to expect, or what I want to hear, but sensing that this might be a milestone in my relationship with my mother.

Maybe.

"Ah. Neely was right. I was wrong, for so many years." All the air drains from me in a whoosh as she continues. "I'm so sorry for my actions. Losing your father broke me," Mom admits in a quiet voice. "And then learning that I was going to lose you too made it a hundred times worse, and I couldn't find the strength to put myself back together. But you are stronger than I am. Anyone would be stronger than I am."

"Mom..."

"Neely's right. I'm so sorry for what I've done to you." She sniffs and swipes a hand under her eye. "Oh, Shae. I thought you were *dying*," she chokes, clutching my hand in a death grip. "For years, I thought I was going to lose you like I lost your father, and I've been so scared that losing you would turn me into a zombie-like when I lost him, and I've been pulling away ever since. I'm so sorry."

Even in the harsh lights of the hospital room, she looks different—she looks *at* me differently. Her eyes are warm and *loving*, free from the disappointment that has kept me away from her for so many years. "I'm so sorry I've hurt you. I didn't know how to deal with losing you."

"You're not going to lose me."

"I know. And now I understand what I've put you through for so long. I was never there for you because I was so afraid of losing you. It would devastate me to lose you."

After all these years of enduring the chasm between my mother and me, and to realize that I was right, that it *was* there but caused by a different reason, is a lot to take in.

"I'm sorry," she repeats, noticing my hesitation. "I do love you—so very much."

"I didn't think you did," I tell her honestly.

"I never showed you," she admits.

"No. You didn't." I study her carefully; the light eyes and heavier features so different from mine, but the pointed chin and heart-shaped face a match for my own. "You look like your father," people had always told me. But looking at my mother, when her lips are curved into a hopeful smile, I finally see some resemblance.

"Okay," I say finally. I know the thing to do would be to hug her, instantly forgiving her and moving on to the next chapter of our mother-daughter life, but I can't. Not yet. Too much time has passed; there's been too much ill-timed bad advice. I can't forget she told me to walk away from Emmett, that it wouldn't be fair to him to fall in love with me.

If she hadn't repeated that so many times over the years, would I have run to Emmett the first time I met him? Would he be standing right beside me now?

I'll never know.

Mom gives a quick nod and stands up, sensing my reluctance to forgive and forget. "I would like to make it up to you," she says. "But I know it will take time. I've got all the time in the world, and now, so do you. I'd like to spend some with you."

I nod, feeling a little of my anger recede. "Okay," I say, and finally smile.

Emmett

D AD MANAGED TO CORRAL Rufus into the shower but he's doing his Rufus-best to avoid getting into bed until I get there.

It's like he knows.

He doesn't say a word. When I come up the stairs with a thunderous expression on my face, trying desperately to hide my smashed heart, Rufus moves towards his room, like he's afraid to face me. And then he takes two steps towards me, to throw his arms around my waist.

"Love you, Uncle Emmett," he whispers.

The lump in my throat gets worse. "Love you too, buddy. Sorry about tonight. My head wasn't in the game."

"It's not you," Rufus says as he pulls back. "Half the team wasn't in the game, and they were actually on the field. You should go easy on Shae," he adds.

"We weren't talking about Shae."

"Yeah, but she's the reason you look like your guts have been pulled out. Love." He shrugs, a completely adult gesture that takes my breath away. "It sucks."

"That it does. Get to bed." The doorbell ringing sends a surge of hope rushing through me, quelled by the sound of Grayson's voice. "Get to bed," I repeat.

"There's drinking to be done," Rufus says in such a perfect imitation of Grayson that I can't help but laugh.

"That may be true tonight," I say as I head downstairs to have Grayson greet me, swinging a bottle by the neck.

"Ah. Superman swooping in with a bottle for me to drown my sorrow," I say.

"What's this about drowning? It's time to celebrate," he cries. "Neely told me the great news about Shae. She's going to be fine."

"Which might be a reason to celebrate had I known she *wasn't* going to be fine," I say, bypassing the table to head for the snack cupboard. Some go for ice cream when they're sad. I go for potato chips.

"She didn't tell you?" Grayson asks with bewilderment.

"She didn't tell me." I reach for the bag of salt and vinegar chips. "And if she had..." I trail off, swallowing the lump in my throat with difficulty. I can't stop picturing Shae, so tiny and white in a hospital bed. Part of me wants to run to her, but I can't.

I can't fall apart like I did before, and if I love someone like I loved Alex, I really think I will. People don't live forever.

"Could I get an explanation about what's going on here?" Dad asks as he sets three glasses on the table. "Is that too much to ask?"

I shake my head. Right now breathing is taking my entire focus, and I don't know how to find the words.

"Shae thought she was going to die, and now she's found out she's not. Celebration!" Grayson raises the bottle with a grin.

"That's great news." Dad smiles, but I get the sense the news isn't a surprise for him.

"Did *you* know?" I ask him. "Because I'm assuming *you* did," I accuse, turning to Grayson in time to see the flash of guilt cross his face.

"I thought you did too. Neely was convinced Shae told you," Grayson confesses. "Why didn't she?"

"Exactly my question." I turn to Dad, eyebrows raised.

"It wasn't my news to tell," Dad says quietly.

"So I was the only one who didn't know Shae had this death sentence." I jerk the bottle out of Grayson's hand and open it, giving myself a generous pour. "You both can get your own," I say as I stalk to the couch.

"She calls it her expiry date," Grayson offers. "According to Neely."

"That would have been helpful to know," I say. "Anything would have been, really."

"Nobody knew." Grayson follows me and sinks into the big chair.

"Everyone seems to, except for the guy in love with her." I slump forward, glass between my knees. "She even told that Dennis Drake guy. Denzel Duke," I correct. "Or whatever his name is."

"Love—wow." Grayson whistles as he follows me to the living room, bottle in his hand. "You fell harder than I thought."

I sip at the Scotch, feeling the burn as it slides down into my belly. I wish a few drinks would solve this, but I know it won't. Maybe for a while, a few hours at most. A few drinks will help me forget about everything, and the huge gaping hole inside me might repair itself.

I'm going to wake up tomorrow and Shae will still be dying.

Or not dying.

Either way, I'm not important enough for her to tell me things.

"Shae feels the same way about you," Dad says, surprising me by settling into his own chair across from the couch. "I could tell."

"Again, it might have been nice to have that information," I say bitterly. "Or *any* information."

"She's never been in love," Grayson supplies. "Neely worries about her—talks about her a lot, so I'm kind of in the know. She's never had a real relationship because she keeps pushing people away because of the whole expiry date thing. Neely says you're the only one who had a chance."

"And see how that worked out."

"Just stop that right now," Dad says. "That's enough of the wounded act. I seem to recall your behaviour after Alex died was questionable at best, and no one has ever blamed you."

"My wife died."

"And that girl has been living with the fact that her days were numbered for years. How do you think she felt about that?"

"She never told me anything about it."

"Can you imagine?" Dad asks heatedly.

"She lost her father too," Grayson says, breaking the silence. "And the way her mother handled things—you didn't know that either, did you?"

I bury my head in my hands. I didn't know anything about her. "I don't know how to get past this," I admit.

"You just do," Dad says, taking a healthy swig. "You've already gotten past so much in your life. This is just one more thing."

"I'm tired of it," I confess in a low voice. "I wanted it to be easy and fun like it was with Alex at the beginning."

"Love is never like that," Dad says.

The three of us sit in silence, taking turns filling the glasses. I think they're waiting for me to talk, but I don't know what to say. Thoughts of Alex and Shae flip back and forth, and I'm worried I might be confusing the emotions. I want to take each one out, examine it, and then stuff it into a box to stop it clogging how I react.

I know I reacted badly with Neely, but I don't know how to fix it, because I don't know how I should be feeling. It's like Shae forgot to show me a big part of herself—whatever her reasons were, it doesn't change that she's not the girl I thought she was.

And that hurts, even though I've only known her a week. Because she trusted me with so much else, and I opened up so much to her, it hurts.

So much that I can't rush to her, as much as I may want to.

Chapter Twenty-One

Shae

FTER A WEEKEND SPENT resting at home with elaborate meals for me, full of spinach and beans and lentils, with steak and beef and every iron-rich food Mike can think of, I show up at Dr. Ryu's office bright and early Monday morning to get to the bottom of things.

Tests, tests, and more tests, a CT scan, and an MRI. Dr. Ryu makes it his personal mission to discover how this mistake happened, and I have to be happy about that.

Finally, on Wednesday afternoon, I go back with my mother. We sit across the desk from Dr. Ryu as he makes us go back through my medical history one more time.

"You definitely do not have Batten disease," he says. "But I have to admit I'm very confused how Dr. Moseley thought you could have. No genetic testing was ever done?" Dr. Ryu asks my mother with a frown.

"From me, but not her father since he had passed," Mom says.

"That's odd, since neuronal ceroid lipofuscinosis is a genetic disorder. And that would have been the simplest way to confirm the diagnosis." He glances at his computer on his desk, his wide forehead a series of lines. "Do you have any idea why Dr. Moseley would make a jump to NCL? I see that there were extreme personality and behavioural changes when Shae was thirteen—" He stops as he notices the way my head whips around to my mother.

"What changes?" I demand.

"It was after your father died," she says quietly.

I throw up my hands. "Well, my father just died, so what did you expect?" I have hazy memories of the time, but I do remember getting in trouble in school more than usual. I think they brought in a guidance counselor to talk to me as well.

"She had seizures when she was seven, so there was also that." Mom ignores my question. "Dr. Moseley thought it might be a variant of late infantile NCL."

"I had seizures?" It sounds like they're talking about someone else.

"Even with that, it's quite a leap." His gaze switches to the thick file on his desk. "I have here that you knew Charles Moseley personally."

"He became a mentor of mine when I was going to nursing school." There's a defensive note in my mother's voice that I'm all too familiar with. "He thought he might be able to publish something on the case," she adds.

"On me?"

Dr. Ryu takes a deep breath through his nostrils. "I see. Do you know if he had published before?"

Mom shakes her head, and when I start to put the dots together, a slow simmer of rage begins. "Is this too big of a leap to assume he thought he could profit from me having this disease? I don't know much about medical journals, but I'm guessing it's a good thing to have your name on some report."

"Charles wouldn't do that!"

"You sure about that?"

Mom waits for Dr. Ryu to meet her gaze before she drops her eyes. "No."

"So he made it up!" The slow simmer jumps to a boil as I jump to my feet. "There was nothing wrong with me, and that quack made it all up?"

Dr. Ryu lifts his hand and I fall back into my seat, breathing heavily from my outburst. "Shae, unfortunately, we can't know that for sure."

"Because he's dead!"

"Because he has passed away, yes," he agrees.

"Isn't that lucky for him?"

He lifts his hand again. "You did have symptoms, as well oxidative stress and your dolichols may have had function issues with the modification of proteins—"

"I have no clue what you're talking about," I interrupt. "Non-doctor talk, please."

"How often did you see Dr. Moseley?" Dr. Ryu asks.

"Well." I squirm in my seat. "Honestly, once he told me I was going to die, I wasn't all that keen on seeing him."

"Four times in the last seven years," my mother cuts in with a resentful glance at me.

"I used to go twice a year when I was younger," I protest. "But then when I started traveling for the vlog..." I trail, feeling horribly guilty from the looks my mother and the doctor are giving me. Is this my fault? "I wasn't home very often and nothing ever changed, either good or bad, and honestly, I got tired of being reminded of my upcoming death."

"I can understand that." Dr. Ryu shuts my file with a decisive flap of papers. "But, it might have solved things a little sooner if you'd gone more often."

"Neely still thinks we should sue," I tell my mother on the way home from Dr. Ryu's office.

"Does Neely want to take the case?" Mom asks as she pulls into the drive.

"She's thinking of law school now, did you know that?" I say.

"No, but I think she'd make an excellent lawyer." My mother seems to have gained a new appreciation for Neely since her little outburst. Or it might be because Neely has spent a lot of time at the house in the last four days. "Is that something you want to do? Sue for malpractice?"

"I don't know." Part of me is furious at Dr. Moseley, and part of me is angry with my mother. If it wasn't for the thaw in our relationship, I doubt I could be convinced that she didn't realize what the doctor was doing.

"I'm sorry," Mom had said when the door to Dr. Ryu's office had closed behind us.

"Did you know?" I snapped.

"I had no idea," she said, her eyes clear and truthful. "I was so devastated that my baby was going to be taken from me that I couldn't think straight. And I should have. I'm a nurse, for God's sake," she adds angrily. "I should have done the research."

"You're an ER nurse, not into genetics," I concede. "And you weren't yourself."

That's the last that is said about it but it definitely dims the light that comes with not dying. At least I have a reason that such a mistake was made.

I can guarantee no other mistakes will ever be made about my health. My mother takes over the caregiving responsibilities from Neely, and her constant demands to know how I'm feeling or if I've taken my pills and how much water I've drunk in a day is kind of...nice. It's what a mother should do.

She's not alone in watching over me. I feel like everyone takes on a babysitting shift.

Neely stops by constantly, sharing all the swoon-worthy details about Grayson. Dawson comes over with the guise of helping me figure out what to do about the vlog, but it's really just to watch me while Mike is out.

But it's a good question. Do we keep things running, scaling back on our trips until Neely is out of school? Dawson tells me about the game designer position he's interviewing for, and I reluctantly admit it makes sense to put the trips on a hiatus for the time being. But the vlog is something else, along with the money I've raised over the years for research for Batten disease.

I don't know what to do about it yet, so I don't do anything.

Except for the emptiness inside me when I think about Emmett. Now that I've gotten used to the idea of not dying, thoughts about Emmett and regret quickly start to eclipse my giddy disbelief. I still find myself smiling suddenly and without reason, as I think that yes, I'll be able to have a thirtieth birthday celebration, have a baby, or get an actual job.

The smile fades when I think about working for a living. What can I possibly do?

I spend time alone in my room, looking at the webpage for Emmett's farm. It's not only because I want to look at the picture of him, but I need to learn more. I haven't given up hope yet, and I won't, but I need to find a way to get through to him.

I just haven't figured out what that's going to be.

I wonder if Emmett has forbidden Rufus from DM-ing me, because I don't get any message or comment from him. Or maybe he's angry at me.

I don't like that thought.

But one other positive outcome that's happened is that, for the first time in years, I have real conversations with my mother.

"I thought a piece of me had broken off when your father died," she admits late Tuesday night. "And I didn't know how to exist without it. I thought I was getting better, learning to deal with things, and then they gave me your diagnosis. My world kept crashing, and I couldn't understand why. I was so angry." She shakes her head in disgust. "I'm not proud of it, and I'm so sorry. The only way I kept going is with work. Thank God Mike came to live with us."

"I love Mike," I say simply. I haven't said that I forgive my mother yet, but I'm warming up to the thought. It's nice being with her. She takes off a few shifts and we spend afternoons watching talk shows and playing Yahtzee, something I hadn't done since I was a little girl.

She finally asks about Emmett on Wednesday night as we're getting ready for bed. "From what I've picked up about this Emmett," Mom begins, leaning against the doorframe of her bedroom dressed in flannel pajamas, "He's not the type to give up."

"Except on me." I poke my toothbrush at my chest, losing a gob of toothpaste in the process.

"That's because he's scared, and do you blame him? The most horrible thing he's had to go through almost happened again."

"But I'm not dying," I say, smearing the toothpaste on my nightie.

"In his head, you still might be. Like I tried to cut myself off from you. I knew deep down it didn't make sense, but I couldn't help it. I was so scared."

"So what do I do?"

Mom looks at me for a long moment. "You need a grand gesture," she decides. "Something that will slap some sense into him. Like finding out you're not dying did for me. You know those romantic comedies where the hero runs through the airport trying to catch the girl before she leaves? You need to catch Emmett before he gets too stuck in his fear."

I stare at her; my mother in her pajamas, doing her best to give me advice. I'm not sure if what she's saying makes sense, but she's *trying*. For once, she's trying to be a mother.

My smile leads to a giggle, and then an outright laugh.

"You don't think so?" My mother gives me a confused smile.

Instead of answering, I step forward and give her a hug. "Thanks," I say, burying my face in the crook of her shoulder. "I think it might work out after all."

♥

Emmett

EVEN THOUGH IT HAS to be over with Shae, I can't stop thinking about her.

Rufus won't stop asking questions. He's constantly checking Instagram to see if she's posted anything, and once he finds the unanswered texts that she's sent me, the nagging to respond begins.

I don't know what to say. I'm afraid of her dying, so I don't want to be with her.

It doesn't sound as good when I say it out loud.

But the truth is, I'm afraid of losing her. I can't go through that again. Maybe I'll never be able to love again and that thought makes me sadder than I ever thought possible.

The week drags by with usual chores. I spend most of my time in the greenhouses so I don't have to talk to people. Dad suggests that I do the deliveries on Friday, but I refuse.

It's a long week.

On Friday evening, hunger sends me into the kitchen to scrounge something for dinner. Cooking is the last thing on my mind, but Dad had Rufus helping in the fields after he got home from school, and the two of them are exhausted, lounging on the couch watching a ball game. Rufus even said he was too tired for video games.

Dad wanders in as I have the cupboard doors open, hoping for inspiration among the soup cans and jars of pasta sauce.

The jar of jam that Shae made is empty and sits in the sink waiting to be washed. I feel like throwing it out.

"We don't need to make anything quite yet," Dad says, pulling out two bottles of beer from the fridge.

"Rufus needs to eat," I say impatiently.

"There's time. Come have a drink with me." With a frown, I follow him into the living room where Rufus has disappeared. "Sit."

"What's going on?"

"Nothing." Dad sits back and rests his arm on the back of the couch. "You seem a bit uptight."

"I'm hungry," I mutter.

"How's Shae?" Dad asks. "Have you talked to her? How's she doing?"

"I have no idea," I say coolly. "You'll have to ask someone else."

"Or you can ask her?"

At that moment, Hardy barks a warning, just before the knock sounds at the front door. I frown. "Who's that?"

"Why don't you check?"

My heart leaps when I open the door, but I keep my expression neutral. There's no point in getting excited before I find out why she's here.

She's here. Shae is standing at my front door, her hair now more red than pink, but her smile as warm and wide as ever.

"Hi."

"Hello." A different car is parked in front of the house.

"My mom brought me," Shae explains when she sees me glance at it. "She wouldn't let me come alone because I've been sick. Not contagious or anything," she adds quickly. "Just stupid stuff, but I'm dealing with it since I'll be around for a lot longer now."

"I heard," I say stiffly. "I don't understand."

She looks at me with dark eyes and something cracks inside me. "That's why I'm here. I was hoping we could talk."

I cock my hand on my hip, trying as hard as I can to stuff whatever is coming up out of the crack back down. "Talk."

"Maybe we could walk and talk," she suggests. "I'm better when I'm moving."

I nod, but before I can say anything, Dad calls from the other room. "Why doesn't Shae have her mother come in here rather than wait out in the car?"

Shae's eyes light up. "That'd be great. Thanks, Peter! And we brought something for you guys as well. I'll try not to take much of your time so it won't be ruined." She turns and waves, and her mother steps from the car with a box in her hands. "I told Mike about cooking for you the other night, and when he heard I'd planned to stop by, he sent something for you. It's good. He makes the best macaroni and cheese."

"He sent us mac 'n' cheese?" I ask skeptically.

"It's your favourite, isn't it?" Her eyes blink nervously. I don't remember telling her that, but I give a quick nod. "Mom, this is Emmett," she says. "Emmett, my mother Cybil."

"Nice to meet you," I mutter, my confusion eating up good manners.

"It's lovely to meet *you*." Cybil has the same warm and wide smile as Shae.

"I have to admit, I've had a craving for this since Shae called and told me it was coming," Dad says to Cybil with a grin. "What say you have a glass of wine with me while we wait for it to warm up?"

"Sounds good to me." Without a backward glance, Cybil follows Dad into the kitchen.

"How do they know each other?" I ask with bewilderment.

"They don't. Mom, that's Peter, Peter, that's my Mom, Cybil. Talk amongst yourselves when I clear things up with Emmett," Shae calls after them, starting down the steps of the porch.

"Oh, we intend to," Cybil calls back. "Don't be alarmed if your ears are burning."

"Coming?" She holds out her hand. "Put your shoes on. Let's walk."

I do as she says because what choice do I have?

"Mom and I have worked some things out since I got out of the hospital," she explains with a happy smile as I stomp down the steps.

"What's going on?" I ask instead.

"I'm going to start from the beginning, which is what I should have done the night we met," she says with rare seriousness.

As we walk away from the house, Shae tells me about the diagnosis that changed her life. "When they told me that I had a disease that I was going to die from, I couldn't believe it. I was fourteen, and they were telling me there was no chance I was going to have a future. No school, no marriage, no family. It was...it was bad. There was a lot of anger. But eventually, I accepted this fate, and decided that I was going to do everything I could do, as quickly as I could."

"The traveling," I say. "The bucket list. That's why you call it the *ExpiryDate* list...because you thought you were going to die."

"I was going to die. I still am, only now I have more time."

Pieces click into place as easily as a jigsaw puzzle. "That's why you've never been in love."

"I saw how my mother handled my father's death, and I couldn't do that to anyone."

"You're giving yourself a lot of credit to make someone that miserable," I tell her bluntly.

I've never seen Shae at a loss for words. It takes her a few tries before she decides what to say. "I've only had my mom as an example. Even she admits it wasn't the best one. But that's why I tried to pull away, only you didn't seem to want me to. I was scared of what it would do to you, but also to me. I've never been in love before. Never wanted to...until now."

I don't respond but my heart beats a little faster.

"I was falling hard and fast for you when I spent the day here, and I had no idea what to do about it," she says softly. "It felt right, but there was still the unknown that I couldn't get my head around. And then when I heard about Alex, I jumped on it. I knew I couldn't let you be hurt again, so that was the perfect excuse for running. I told myself that it was for you, but it was really because I was scared."

Her tiny hand slips into mine. "But now something has changed for you," Shae continues. "Stop me if I'm wrong—even though I'm not usually wrong," she adds with an impish grin.

The crack gets a little wider with that grin.

"When you found out that I was dying, and then I wasn't, *you* got scared. And you ran, just like I did."

"I can't go through it again," I mutter.

She squeezes my hand. "I know it was horrible, and I don't want to ask you—but I do. I have to. I want you to take a chance again, for us."

"Shae..."

"I can't promise that I won't die," she says in a rush. "But I will promise to try really hard not to. I'll take care of myself, and I'll take care of you...if you let me. We can try not to be scared together."

I'm not sure if Shae was leading us up the hill or if I was. We stop at the top of the hill, and I stare over the fields with a much easier heart than when I started.

"I need to know something," I ask without looking down at her.

"Ask anything you want."

"What happened with you and Denzel Duke? I don't mean in Thailand," I add quickly. "That's your business. But I saw the picture of the two of you and—" I cringe even as the words come out of my mouth. I sound like a jealous boyfriend and I've never been that. But the thought of Shae— "Never mind," I say. "None of my business."

"You're right, it isn't. But I don't mind telling you," Shae says in a perfectly calm voice. "I have nothing to hide, because it's all online for everyone to see. After he pulled me onstage, I spent the night with Denzel. Talking. He really needs friends."

"I said it was your business."

"We talked all night, he eventually fell asleep and I left. As friends, or at least that's what I thought. Denzel may have had other ideas, because he showed up in Toronto and asked me to go to Australia with him. I said no. He's a great guy, but not for me," she finishes.

I had no idea how much the picture of Denzel and Shae bothered me until I heard Shae's take on it. Looking at posts of the two had been slowly driving me crazy. The knot in my stomach slowly unravels, taking with it some of my fears.

"I did tell him that I was dying," she admits. "I thought of it as a practice run for you. Because I was planning on telling you everything, only you showed up when I wasn't ready, and then I ended up in the hospital."

I study her face, looking for signs of an illness that isn't there. "Are you okay? I guess I should have asked right away."

"I'm glad you didn't. I'm so sick of everyone checking on me." Shae smiles and takes a deep breath. "Here's the sappy part. For years, I thought I was dying, and my way of dealing with that was to embrace life. Live your best day, every day, as though it's your last, all those sayings. I did it. And it's been great. I'm not stopping that."

"I don't think you could even if you wanted to," I say as she takes a pause. "That's who you are."

"It is. And if I hadn't been dying, I probably would have fallen in love a dozen times by now and had my heart broken a bunch. I think, maybe..." Shae's voice drops and she worries her bottom lip as she searches for the words. "I think I didn't jump into falling in love, not just because I was scared, but because I was waiting for you."

With her words, something explodes inside me, better than hitting any home run in front of a stadium of fans.

Shae looks up at me. "So what do you think?"

"I don't know if I can keep up with you," I say honestly.

That impish smile. "Oh, I think you can. I'm going to show you that life is still worth living."

I chuckle at her confidence and I glance up at the tree. The leaves have completely unfurled since Shae was last here. I lay a hand on the scratchy bark. "Feel like climbing a tree?"

Her smile widens so that it seems to take up her entire face. Her beautiful, sweet face, with the laughing dark eyes full of mischief. "Or you could just kiss me down here. My mom will kill me if she finds out I'm climbing trees."

I laugh as I slide a hand around her waist to pull her close. "Wouldn't want that." With my other hand, I cup her cheek, knowing somehow that this won't be easy, but it will be worth it. There's a lot of living I have to get back to. "I miss the pink," I say, rubbing a strand of reddish hair between my fingers.

"Any colour you want," she promises, winding her arms around my shoulders.

"Don't say that. Taking that pitch to the head messed up my perception of colours. I'm technically colour-blind."

"Are you really?" she gasps. "What does—?"

I stop her with a kiss, fitting my lips over her still moving ones like they were meant to be there. "That works," I whisper when we break apart.

"Just for a minute. I still want to know—"

This time I kiss her for much longer, lifting her off her feet so she can wrap her legs around my waist, kissing her on and on, until we're joined by the wet nose of Hardy pushing against my leg. "Go away, dog," I mutter, shooing her away so I can go back to kissing Shae.

"Maybe your dad sent her." Shae giggles, her body wrapped around me like a monkey. I don't think I will ever get tired of having her in my arms. "Your dad is probably hungry."

I groan and set her gently on the ground. "You think they're all right together?" I ask.

"Of course. I think they'll be just fine together." She sets off down the hill at a run, tugging me after her, both of us laughing as we stumble over the uneven ground.

Something about her tone..."Are you planning something?" I demand as I chase after her.

She smiles mischievously over her shoulder.

Neely has had enough of being in love with Dawson.
Enter Grayson.
Ready for Neely and Grayson's story?

Don't Want to Be Friends

If you enjoyed Shae and Emmett, I'd love it if you joined my mailing list and find out more about my books and me!

When you sign up for my mailing list, you'll get a copy of the short story, **Cupcake Connections**!

In Pain au Chocolate patisserie, the cupcakes are becoming more popular than the pastries. Reuben, the big, burly Scotsman, is an expert on sugar and sweets, but his love life has fallen flat.

And when one of the customers catches Reuben's eye, Adam decides to help him win her over. While planning a makeover for Reuben, Adam digs into Reuben's past and discovers that Reuben is doing just fine on his own.

Packed full of character cameos from Beautifully Baked, Unexpectingly Happily Ever After and The Hidden Past of Pippa McGovern, Cupcake Connections is a sweet story about finding your own way.

Sign up now!

Acknowledgments

I came up with the idea for Don't Tell Me You Love Me pre-Covid, but it's the first book I've written during the pandemic. And thanks to the continual presence of my family, it was a challenge! So while I am grateful to all the front-line healthcare workers for their selfless dedication during this challenging time, I have a special place in my heart for all the teachers. You have no idea how much I appreciate you being back to work so my kids can go to school! And my kids are older—I have no idea what I would have done if they were still little! So thanks to all the teachers who allow me some quiet time to write.

But even though I jumped for joy the mornings they slept in, I have to thank my kids—for Kaitie for reading and re-reading my blurb until she was as sick of it as I was; to Sarah, for listening to all the weird questions I would ask her, about yoga poses and terminal illnesses and Instagram; and for Sam, who still thinks it's cool that his mom is an author.

Thanks to Regina for her eagle eyes, and Nita, for your coaching/critiquing help.

Thanks to E, for your endless support and encouragement, and for just listening to me talk about writing. You have no idea how much I appreciate it.

And finally, for Mom. For everything.

About Author

Holly Kerr is the author of over twenty-five chick-lit, romantic comedy, and women's fiction novels. She grew up a farm girl but now calls Toronto home, where she lives with her three very tall children (compared to her), following their sports exploits like any dutiful mother would.

She's a lover of Marvel movies, Star Wars movies...really, any movies, and has a surprising amount of worthless pop culture info stored in her head. She likes oceans over mountains, tea over coffee, and can mix a darn fine dirty martini. With extra olives, of course.

Visit her at www.facebook.com/HollyKerrAuthor and www.hollykerr.ca to sign up for her newsletter.

Suitor Science

Hating the Chemistry Teacher
Falling for The Suitor
Fraternizing with the Ex
Marrying the Billionaire Best Friend
Loving the Wrong Guy
Finding the One

Love & Alliteration

Perfectly Played
Beautifully Baked
Pleasantly Popped

Don't

Don't Tell Me You Love Me
Don't Want to Be Friends
Don't Stop Me Now
Don't They Know It's Christmas

Sisters in a Small Town

Coming Home
Hanging On
Stepping Up

Charlotte Dodd

The Secret Life of Charlotte Dodd
The Missing Files of Charlotte Dodd
The Best Worst First Date Ever
The Hidden Past of Pippa McGovern
The Last Stand of Charlotte Dodd

Unexpecting
Unexpectingly Happily Ever After

Absinthe Doesn't Make the Heart Grow Fonder

Oceanic Dreams - I Saw Him Standing There

Kid Lit

The Dragon Under the Mountain
The Dragon Under the Dome